THREE DROPS OF BLOOD

THREE DROPS OF BLOOD

GRETCHEN MCNEIL

HYPERION
Los Angeles   New York

First Edition, March 2023
10 9 8 7 6 5 4 3 2 1
FAC-004510-23034
Printed in the United States of America

This book is set in AGaramond, Melior/Monotype; Badhouse Light/House Industries
Designed by Marci Senders

Library of Congress Cataloging-in-Publication Data

Names: McNeil, Gretchen, author.
Title: Three drops of blood / by Gretchen McNeil.
Description: First edition. • Los Angeles ; New York : Hyperion, 2023. •
   Audience: Ages 14–18. • Audience: Grades 10–12. • Summary:
   Seventeen-year-old Kate Williams is willing to do whatever it takes to
   get her acting career back on track, even if that means getting a boring
   office job to support herself—but when she witnesses a double murder in
   the office across from hers, will she be able to get anyone to believe
   her before she becomes the next victim?
Identifiers: LCCN 2022021813 • ISBN 9781368072151 (hardcover)
   • ISBN 9781368094108 (ebook)
Subjects: CYAC: Murder—Fiction. • Actors and actresses—Fiction. •
   Overweight persons—Fiction. • LCGFT: Thrillers (Fiction) • Novels.
Classification: LCC PZ7.M4787952 Th 2023 • DDC [Fic]—dc23
LC record available at https://lccn.loc.gov/2022021813

Reinforced binding

Visit www.HyperionTeens.com

SUSTAINABLE FORESTRY INITIATIVE

Certified Sourcing
www.sfiprogram.org
SFI-01681

Logo Applies to Text Stock only

For my own Katie-Bear

"I'll prove this truth with my three drops of blood."
—Nestor, *Troilus and Cressida*

PROLOGUE

KATE SAT AS STILL AS SHE COULD IN THE FAUX-LEATHER ARM-chair, sweat pilling up on her forehead and chin beneath the intense heat of the two-thousand-watt open-face tungsten floodlights while Marielle, her makeup artist, stood at her shoulder, powder brush poised and ready.

Kate was used to these moments of forced stillness. After three months in production on the *Dirty Pretty Teens* series, she'd gone from acting novice to seasoned pro, and she'd learned to sit quietly between takes and let the professionals do their jobs.

At first, she'd wondered why they couldn't, like, turn off the damn lights so it wasn't as infernally hot while the actors held in place, but since the rest of the cast—all television veterans—were unfazed by the uncomfortable heat, Kate kept her thoughts to herself. Eventually, she realized that the grips frequently scuttled around resetting and rearranging the entire lighting apparatus during brief interruptions as the AD and cinematographer tweaked their setup. These pauses in the action were only a pause for the actors. Everyone else was still in motion.

But this hold was different. Instead of the usual flurry of movement, most of the crew was focused on a corner of the coffee shop set where the director and producers were huddled around a small playback screen.

Even blond teen sensation Belle Masterson, the star of *Dirty Pretty Teens*, who rarely paid attention to anything that wasn't directly related to Belle Masterson, was interested in this coterie. Sure she'd whipped out her phone the moment the director yelled "Cut!" and had pretended to swipe through screens to avoid human interaction, but though her chin was tucked down, her pale cheeks had flushed pink and her blue eyes were fixed on the production team.

Or on Dex Pratt's ass.

Which was essentially the same thing.

Kate was new to the entertainment industry, but she was pretty sure that seventeen-year-old actresses throwing themselves at their married, thirty-eight-year-old show runners was frowned upon. Not that it stopped Belle. She took every opportunity to touch Dex—a hand on his arm, a brush against his shoulder, a playful shove like prepubescent kids who were learning that even negative touching was still *touching*. When Belle wasn't eliciting skin-to-skin contact with Dex, she was flirting with him from afar with signals even Kate's cataract-ridden great-aunt could have spotted from fifty paces.

That girl was wild bananas.

Marielle made her finishing touches on Kate's nose, her eyes straying to the brain trust in the corner. "They'd better make a decision soon. You're going to pumpkin at the top of the hour."

Kate wasn't supposed to move when getting her face touched up, but she always smiled when someone on set used *pumpkin* as a verb. It meant she, as a minor, was about to hit the end of her workday when the director would lose her for the next twelve hours. She was the only official minor on the production—Belle Masterson had miraculously passed her California High School Proficiency Exam at sixteen, which meant she could work on set as "legal eighteen" without fear of pumpkining—and working around Kate's availability under California labor law was a huge concern for the production. Usually, everyone moved at lightning speed as Kate's pumpkin hour approached.

But not today.

Marielle swept her long jumbo box braids behind one shoulder and stepped back to check her work. "All set."

"Thank you!" Kate said, smiling. Marielle had been a huge help to her throughout the production, especially the first week on set when she'd offered gentle nudges and suggestions when Kate had no idea what she was supposed to be doing. Kate was pretty sure she'd have been fired if not for the kindness of her makeup artist.

The scene they'd just shot was a poignant reminder of Kate's bewildering first day on set. She and Belle—or rather their characters, Noelle and Piper—at a coffee shop, arguing over their romantic entanglements, a mirror image of the first scene they'd ever shot together. She and Belle had sat in those same sticky, slick chairs, morphing from near strangers to BFFs the second the cameras started to film. Kate recalled how desperately nervous she'd been sitting across the table from the former Disney Channel star in her formfitting body-con minidress while Kate's size-sixteen curves were camouflaged by an open plaid blazer that couldn't have buttoned over her ample chest without popping a seam.

Even with brand-new highlights in her reddish-brown hair and

Marielle's contouring skills, Kate had felt like a double-wide trailer parked beside a Ducati, and she was positive someone would realize she wasn't actually an actress, that chubby girls weren't supposed to star in Netflix series, and that casting her had been a horrific mistake.

Kate kept trying to remind herself of how awesome this opportunity was—the role of Noelle in the Dirty Pretty Teens books was certainly *not* written as a plus-size person, and how often did actresses who looked like Kate get to indulge in frothy, soapy roles like this? But instead of calming her down, this only increased her stress as Kate felt the pressure of representation, and the only thing that had saved her were her dad's parting words when he'd dropped her off that morning:

"All the world's a stage, Katie-Bear," he'd said in his deep, booming bass-baritone. "When in doubt, look to the Bard."

Usually, Kate rolled her eyes at her dad's insistence that every situation in the entire universe, from asking someone on a date to negotiating global disarmament treaties, could be solved with a simple "look to the Bard." As if Shakespeare was a soothsaying prophet like Nostradamus and his plays were merely blueprints for the centuries that followed. Mack Williams—Shakespearean scholar, former amateur actor, and adjunct professor of Jacobean literature—was biased, but that day, his advice had struck a chord with his daughter. As she'd sat nervously at her makeup station, frantically going through the upcoming scene in her head, she'd started to panic. She was dropping words, reciting her lines out of order, forgetting her blocking. What was her motivation? Why was her character doing any of this bullshit in the first place? None of it made sense.

When in doubt, look to the Bard.

Kate had focused on her character, Noelle Wagner, spunky best friend of Belle's Piper Payne. Noelle was trustworthy and brave, though she harbored a secret crush on Piper's on-again, off-again boy toy Sebastian, who had once asked Noelle out before falling for Piper. Meanwhile, Wyatt, the guy Piper *really* wanted, was pretending to be interested in Noelle in order to make Piper jealous, driving a wedge between the two friends that fueled most of the series's plot points. It was a ridiculous and convoluted soap opera, and Kate was thankful that she'd never read the young adult novels on which the series was based because there was no way she'd have been able to keep a straight face at the audition if she'd known what was coming.

Still, convoluted or not, the story lines were reminiscent of the four Athenian lovers in *A Midsummer Night's Dream*. Piper, Sebastian, Wyatt, and Noelle were easily superimposed onto Hermia, Demetrius, Lysander, and Helena.

Helena, whose boyfriend falls in love with her best friend.

Helena, who sees her best friend turn on her after the gods make both of the men lust after her.

> *Love looks not with the eyes, but with the mind,*
> *And therefore is winged Cupid painted blind.*

In an instant, years of Kate's dad drilling Shakespeare into her unexpectedly paid off as the entire role of Noelle had come into focus. What she wanted, why she wanted it. For the first time since Kate had been cast, it all made sense.

Maybe Shakespeare really was a prophet?

Bananas.

Time and again over the past few months, Kate had returned to Helena and *A Midsummer Night's Dream* when she felt lost. Even now, on the last day of shooting, in this final scene, a pivotal confrontation between best friends, Helena was a beacon.

> *Is all the counsel that we two have shared,*
> *The sisters' vows, the hours that we have spent*

When we have chid the hasty-footed time
For parting us? Oh, is all forgot?

"Act three, scene two," she said under her breath.

"What?" Belle turned to her sharply, eyes narrowed, as if she'd caught Kate talking shit behind her back.

"Oh, um, nothing."

"Did you say something about my acting?"

Not everything is about you. "I was quoting Shakespeare."

"Why?"

As someone who didn't care how the sausage was made, the word *why* never came out of Belle's mouth. Kate was momentarily thrown. Most of their interactions had been Belle monologuing about herself or giving unsolicited advice to her costar, neither of which required much of a response. Which was fine. When Kate wasn't sure about a social cue, she usually stayed quiet, and that seemed to be what Belle wanted most of the time anyway.

Now Belle was looking at her intently, eyes pinched with suspicion, waiting for an answer.

"I just . . . I use Helena in *A Midsummer Night's Dream* as inspiration for Noelle." She paused, wondering why she felt the need to explain herself, but couldn't stop talking. "My dad says you can solve almost any problem by looking to the Bard."

It sounded super corny when she said it out loud.

Belle was silent for a moment, eyes still locked on Kate. "Hot or not?"

"Shakespeare?"

"The chick. Helen."

Belle's priorities were so out of whack. "I guess Helena's hot?"

"You guess." Belle dropped her phone to her lap, suddenly interested. "And who am I?"

That was a loaded question, but Kate decided to stick with Shakespeare. "I suppose that makes you Hermia."

"Awful name," Belle said, wrinkling her upper lip. "Is *she* hot?"

Kate needed to extricate herself from this conversation before her brain exploded. "Well, she has two different guys in love with her at the beginning of the play."

Belle gasped. "That sounds just like me!" Then she picked up her phone and went back to watching Dex while pretending to swipe.

And I have to shoot a whole second season with her. . . .

Movement and raised voices from the corner of the coffee shop forced everyone to attention. Dex shook hands with the AD, then slapped the director on the back before turning around to address the entire room. He smiled broadly, an unfamiliar expression and one that made his overly tanned face seem more cheerful than shrewd. For half a second, Kate got what Belle saw in him. He was handsome—sure, like, whatever. This was LA. *Everyone* was hot. And Dex's brand of hot was "white frat boy" laced with "privileged douchebaggery," which negated the hotness. But his authoritarian power on the set was, at the very least, arresting, and paired as it was with a cheerful smile, Kate kinda sorta understood the appeal.

Except, no, ew. He was, like, almost as old as her dad.

"Well—" Dex began, then paused dramatically, stretching his arms wide, holding everyone's attention in his embrace. "That's a wrap on season one!"

Belle bolted to her feet, rapidly clapping her dainty hands like a mad pair of hummingbird wings, and let out a high-pitched cheer. It was the signal to celebrate, and the rest of the crew hugged and high-fived on a job well done.

Dex made his way through a shallow sea of assistants and technicians, shaking hands and slapping people on their backs as if they were all his close, personal friends. He caught Kate's eye and made a beeline for her.

"Excellent job, Kate," he said, flashing that Hollywood smile—dazzlingly white teeth against overly tanned skin.

"Thank you."

He opened his arms, inviting a hug. "Bring it in."

That's a first. Dex usually kept his cast at arm's length, which was fine because Kate wasn't exactly the touchy-feely type, and as he squeezed her shoulders, she felt her body tense.

"I, uh, can't believe it's over," she said awkwardly.

"Only season one!" Dex lingered, holding Kate in place long after she'd have been comfortable pulling away. "I get the pleasure of seeing you again in just a few months."

Out of the corner of her eye, she saw Belle snarl.

Dex tugged on her shoulders, pulling her body into his. A fatherly gesture, but Kate didn't love how her double Ds smushed into his abs. "I'm so glad your friend dragged you to that audition."

"Uh, me too."

"So. Glad." He tightened his embrace with each word, his arm dropping from her shoulders to her waist.

Kate tried to express "I'm stuck here against my will" with just her face, but Belle was all daggers as she rounded the small table that buffered Kate from her rage.

"Are you done?" Belle practically spit out the words.

Kate wasn't sure if they were meant for Dex or herself, but Dex took his time releasing Kate from the forced embrace, slowly letting his arm fall away. She scampered aside, smoothing down the lines of her shirt and blazer. "Thanks, Mr. Pratt," she said, intentionally formal. "I appreciate all of your guidance."

Belle stepped between them, honed in on Kate like a cheetah on a wildebeest. "I'm sure you do."

"You're very welcome," Dex said, ignoring the starlet's jealousy. "See you at the wrap party tomorrow, yes?"

"Of course." Suddenly, the *Dirty Pretty Teens* wrap party was the last place on the planet Kate wanted to be, but she couldn't no-show. She'd promised to take Rowan as her plus one, and her best friend would never forgive her if she backed out. "See you then."

Dex opened his mouth to respond, but Belle tugged on his arm, shutting him up. Kate headed for her trailer, her actor's high from shooting the final scene of the season dimming as she struggled with the weirdness of her encounter with Dex and Belle.

She ventured a glance back at them as she slipped through the door into the tepid February sunshine. Belle was still pouting, arms crossed over her chest like a toddler on the brink of a meltdown. Dex leaned down, whispering, his lips close to her ear. Then just as he was about to pull away, he paused.

And Kate thought she saw him plant a kiss on the arch of Belle's porcelain neck.

ONE

KATE KNEW SOMETHING WAS WRONG THE MOMENT HER PHONE buzzed.

Well, maybe not the *exact* moment. But, like, pretty soon after. Once her brain registered that the clock read six thirty.

In the morning.

During summer break.

And she'd already missed, like, five messages from Rowan.

Six thirty a.m. texts were never a good thing.

Kate grunted as she pushed herself to a sitting position, running her fingers through her tangled rat's nest of wavy auburn curls. She took a deep breath and steeled herself against Rowan's news.

Although, seriously, how much worse could it get?

It had been less than twenty-four hours since the bomb dropped, since the cops had shown up at Dex Pratt's Bel Air home and arrested him for sexually assaulting Belle Masterson.

A year ago, those names wouldn't have meant shit to Kate. The BelleDex scandal would merely have been an internet fiasco Rowan followed obsessively. A show she loved, an actress she loved to hate, sexy tidbits about people she didn't know but who lived not far from her Burbank home. Hell, Rowan's entertainment-attorney dad might even have represented one or more of the people involved. That, like, practically made it her business and by association, Kate's business, as Rowan would have shared every nuance, every post, every video snippet with her best friend.

But that was a year ago.

Now Dex Pratt and Belle Masterson *were* Kate's business. Like, literally. *Dirty Pretty Teens* wasn't just some Netflix show; it was *her* Netflix show. And Dex Pratt wasn't just some Hollywood douchebag; he was the Hollywood douchebag who had plucked Kate from a massive open-call audition and thrust her into the limelight, practically against her will. She'd only gone to that stupid audition to dutifully accompany her actress best friend who desperately wanted to land a role on the show adapted from her favorite books.

But it wasn't Rowan who had caught the show runner's attention.

Suddenly, Kate was famous, or "fame-adjacent" as she liked to joke, and she had Dex to thank for it.

Except he was, apparently, like, a total sleazoid.

Not exactly a surprise, is it?

Of course Kate knew that Belle had a crush on Dex. *Everyone* knew. Because Belle had all the subtlety of a contestant on *RuPaul's Drag Race*. Kate had been simultaneously repulsed and intrigued by Belle's audacity, especially since Dex kept her at arm's length. Except the last day on set five months ago, when Kate was kinda sorta almost sure she saw Dex plant an open-mouthed kiss on the nape of Belle's neck.

Not really arm's length.

Unless his arms were shorter than his penis.

Or his ego.

Yesterday, after the news broke about Dex and Belle, Netflix issued a statement halting production on season two, which was set to start filming in just a few weeks. Kate's social media accounts were flooded with messages from fans asking if she'd known about the affair, all of which Kate ignored, strictly following her agent Clementine's "no comment" order. Thank God it was summer vacation. If Kate had been at school when the news broke, she wouldn't have been able to hide.

And now, something new. Had to be. Kate's stomach fluttered as she unlocked her phone.

OMG!

BELLE.

VIDEO.

INTERNET.

OMG!!!!!

Rowan was so worked up, she couldn't even type full sentences.

"What did she do?" Kate said out loud.

As she was holding her phone, a new message popped up from her best friend.

You're still asleep, aren't you . . .

Calmer now. Able to think in linear sentences. Yay.

You need to wake up. NOW.

Calling in 10.

Most people swear that it's impossible to interpret tone through text messages, but after a hundred thousand or so texts over the last six years, Kate understood every nuance of her best friend's communications, from word choice to pacing to punctuation. Rowan had gone from giddy to somber in the blink of an ellipse. Whatever her costar had done, it had momentarily broken Rowan's brain, and Kate's fingertips tingled as she googled Belle Masterson.

The first hit was a video, Belle's perfect cheekbones and barrel-rolled blond hair were offset by uncharacteristically smudged mascara and puffy eyes.

Below that thumbnail was another identical one. Then another. Actually, the entire first page of hits was this video. Reposts, shares, even what looked to be an illegal download with armchair commentary. All in the four hours since Belle posted the original.

That had to be, like, the definition of viral. If this wasn't such a serious situation, Belle might have been delighted by her own popularity.

Kate's fingers hovered over the screen, as if they were hesitant to start the video. A dark, secret part of her hoped that Belle had done something so spectacularly awful that she'd be replaced on the show. She'd been a pain in the ass to work with, throwing around her three years' experience on some Disney Channel show Kate had never even watched like it had been a degree from the Actors Studio. Not that *Dirty Pretty Teens* was Shakespeare or anything, despite Kate's inspiration, but if Kate had expected a nurturing hand from her more experienced costar, what she got was a passive-aggressive bitch slap. Belle attempted to undermine Kate with snide, backhanded comments about everything from her size to her acting skills. It was difficult to feel sorry for her victimization.

Still, Belle *was* a victim. Dex had taken advantage of her. Belle might have been ruthlessly narcissistic, but she was a ruthlessly narcissistic *teen*. And Dex was more than twice her age.

Kate took another steadying breath. Belle deserved her pity, not her snark. And something in her bones told her that this video was going to be very pitiful indeed.

"Let me just say," Belle began, her blue eyes sharp and predatory, "no one asked me to post this video. I know some of you a-holes are going to assume that Dex put me up to this, but he didn't." Her lip quivered. "They won't even let me talk to him!"

Tears flowed down both of her pink cheeks, carrying a substantial portion of Belle's remaining eye makeup with them. Kate knew firsthand she wasn't that good of an actress. This mix of despair and indignation was real.

"I . . . I . . ." Belle covered her face with shaky hands. "I don't understand how any of this is wrong. What's so illegal about love?"

Oh, Belle.

Belle enjoyed a lot of freedom, had been given no boundaries, and was used to getting her own way. As "legal eighteen," she had no teacher or child welfare agent on set looking after her. Or even a parent. In their absence, Dex, freaking dickwad, had moved in. Kate hoped he got whatever was coming to him in prison.

"We didn't mean to fall in love," Belle pleaded, her voice cracking. "It just happened. I'm eighteen in two months. Like, if we'd waited, would that really be any different?"

Kate clenched her jaw in anger at Belle's myopic, self-centered white-privilege bullshit. How many girls had been taken advantage of by teachers, coaches, doctors—anyone with authority who used that position to at best manipulate a young girl into a shitty position, at worst force themselves on her? Especially girls of color, who were less likely to speak up, and less likely to be believed if they did. Defending Dex Pratt was defending every sexual assault since the dawn of time.

"No, it wouldn't have been," Belle continued. She spoke faster now, with a frantic edge to her voice that bordered on hysteria. "And listen, all you hypocrites out there judging us, calling Dex a monster and me a slut. You're all jealous of what we have. Yeah, *jealous*. Because *our* love is real and it's going to *win*. *We're* going to win.

"No matter what they say, everyone on *DPT* knew exactly what was going on and they were fine with it. Netflix? Producers and directors? The whole cast and crew? YOU ALL KNEW!"

They knew Belle was throwing herself at Dex, but no one thought he'd be sleazy enough to cross that line.

"AND I HAVE PROOF. That's right. Proof that everyone knew about Dex and me and no one cared."

Belle was silent for a moment as she fiddled with something on her phone; then, suddenly, the screen shifted from camera mode to screen share, and Kate was looking at a selfie from Belle's phone, one of the thousands she'd probably taken on set, showing her kissing Dex's cheek near the craft services table beside some bemused-looking crew dudes who were piling empanadas and salad onto their plates. It wasn't an overtly sexual pose, but it definitely bordered on inappropriate and hinted at their intimacy.

"See?" Belle cackled with glee. "These guys didn't give a shit."

A new photo wiped onto the screen. This time Belle was perched on Dex's lap while he sat in an overstuffed chair on a Christmas wonderland set. She was whispering in his ear like she was asking Santa for a naughty Christmas gift, one hand resting on his shoulder, the other on his inner thigh, disturbingly close to his junk.

Bananas.

Kate remembered that day—they were shooting a holiday episode at the Santa photo display at the Glendale Americana—but she hadn't seen this particular moment. She'd probably been in the school trailer taking a trig exam while Belle was studying anatomy.

"And let's not forget this," Belle said, swiping a video onto the screen.

This time, the breath caught in Kate's throat.

It was from the *DPT* wrap party, an event Kate remembered.

Mostly.

She remembered that she hadn't wanted to go but also didn't want to disappoint Rowan by bailing. Her best friend had an unholy crush on Dagney Malone, who played Asher on the show, her favorite character from the books. Rowan had also religiously watched the CBS drama *Vegas Nights*, on which Dagney had a recurring role. Kate had pulled out the dress meant for the junior-year winter formal she hadn't been able to attend due to filming, plastered on a smile, and headed to the party with Rowan.

Thirty minutes in, Rowan had followed Dagney to the bathroom line. They emerged chatting like best friends—that was Rowan's superpower—and Kate hadn't seen her again for hours.

She'd been alone at a party she didn't want to attend in the first place, so when a waiter came by offering her a glass of champagne on a serving tray, Kate thought, *What the hell?*

One glass turned into two. Then three. The champagne took the edge off and made Kate feel less awkward, but she was an inexperienced drinker, and after one too many glasses, parts of the night had become fuzzy.

Like the scene she was now staring at on her phone.

With house music thumping through tinny speakers, Dex danced with Belle, whose silver-sequined dress was hiked up enough to show a disturbing amount of her thighs as she straddled his leg. His tanned cheeks were flushed, hinting at his drunkenness, and he held a champagne bottle in one hand, which he used to fill both Belle's glass and that of another girl dancing with them.

As both girls downed their drinks, he ditched the bottle, then hooked one arm around Belle's back, pulling her close as he stared into her eyes. Without looking, Dex looped his other hand around the chest of the second girl, who was dancing with both arms in the air, eyes closed, oblivious to everything around her but the music. A freckled, plus-size white girl wearing the red baby-doll dress she'd bought, but never worn, for winter formal.

Though she didn't remember it at all, Kate couldn't deny that she was staring, horrified, at a video of herself.

TWO

KATE ONLY REALIZED SHE'D BEEN STARING AT THE PAUSED frame of Belle's video for slightly less than ten minutes when Rowan's call buzzed her phone.

Kate swiped open the FaceTime call, and Belle's video receded into the background. Out of sight but definitely not out of mind. "Hey."

"You saw." Rowan tucked a strand of thick black hair behind one ear, exposing a face that was pinched with worry. Her brows were crunched over her black-brown eyes, lips drawn flat against her teeth, and every muscle in her heart-shaped face seemed taut. She looked as if she was watching one of those *Red Asphalt* videos in Safety Ed, where they tried to scare teen drivers into not being assholes by showing them the bloody aftermaths of DUI accidents and improper seat-belt usage.

If the eternally rosy and optimistic Rowan Chen thought Kate's life was a gory, mangled *Red Asphalt* mess, then Kate was even more screwed than she realized.

"Yeah."

"Shit."

"That good, huh?" Kate tried to force some buoyancy into her voice, which came across as ghoulish.

Rowan's grimace deepened. "Don't joke."

"It's just a video."

"That went viral."

Why did Kate feel like she was on trial? "I didn't do anything wrong."

"I know, I know . . ." Rowan swallowed, her eyes darting away from the screen; then she dropped her voice. "Do you even remember that?"

"Nope."

"You were more wasted than I thought. How much did you drink?"

Rowan was the party girl, and Kate was usually tasked with keeping track of how many shots her best friend had done at parties. She'd never had to do it for herself. "I have no idea."

"I shouldn't have abandoned you for Dagney."

True.

Rowan's brows drew together over her nose. "This is all my fault."

"This is *not* your fault."

"But—"

"Ro, stop." Though her emotions turned on a dime, Rowan felt everything deeply. Every novel she loved was the best book ever. Every slight she endured was the greatest tragedy known to humanity. Kate didn't want her friend taking responsibility for Belle's video, even if her self-condemnation wouldn't have lasted long. "The only one to blame is Dex."

"I guess you're right." Rowan let out a long, slow breath and was back to her perky norm before she spoke again. "That guy is such a tool."

"Agreed."

"I hope his wife divorces him."

"I hope she's already filed."

Rowan paused, chewing at the inside of her lip near enough to one of her dimples that it made it look as if she was inhaling her entire cheek. "He's facing actual jail time."

"Good."

"Yeah, for, like, every girl on the planet. But it's not good for your show."

Kate hated the pang of fear that shot through her heart. She'd never wanted this gig on *Dirty Pretty Teens* in the first place—acting was Rowan's dream—but now that she'd had a taste of the addictive highs of performing, Kate wasn't sure she wanted to go back to her normal wallflower life.

It would be such a failure.

Kate wasn't particularly popular at Burbank High School, but she and Rowan had a core group of friends around them, which mostly consisted of Rowan's theater classmates. Kate was the quiet academic, Rowan the extroverted actress, and their personalities complemented each other: the actor who needed attention at all times and the non-actor who didn't mind giving it.

Until Kate stepped out of her lane.

Rowan had been nothing but excited for her best friend, but some of the theater kids resented that Kate had landed this dream role, stealing it from someone who had actually trained their whole lives for the chance. But though she hadn't acted before, Kate had been engulfed by her dad's Shakespeare obsession since before she could walk. She could dissect Hamlet's fourth soliloquy by preschool, and in kindergarten, she recited the St. Crispin's Day speech from *Henry V* for the school talent show. Kate vividly remembered the sea of glassy-eyed schoolmates, and their confused and horrified parents, as she brandished a wooden sword and lustily cried, "'And hold their manhoods cheap whiles any speaks / That fought with us upon Saint Crispin's Day!'"

Kate's childhood introduction to Shakespeare made her the perfect rehearsal partner. She'd been running lines and blocking with Rowan since her first lead role in sixth grade. Kate would play all the other characters in her friend's scenes, absorbing details about characterization, action, and motivation as Rowan learned her part.

Then Kate had gotten her shot, plucked from obscurity. And for the first time, she knew what she wanted to do with her life.

Kate's plan was to skip her senior year and graduate early, forgo college altogether, and throw herself into the audition process. Unbeknownst to her parents, she'd already taken the CHSPE and was only awaiting notification that she'd passed to let her agent know that she, like Belle Masterson, was now "legal eighteen." Kate would be an actual teen without the nuisance of the California child labor protections; plus she had Clementine DuBois, one of the hottest youth talent agents in the business, representing her; *plus* she'd have season two of *DPT* under her belt. Combined, it should be enough to get her in front of some top-tier casting agents, even if she wasn't TV-skinny like Belle or Rowan.

The idea that Belle's viral post might ruin things made Kate's stomach clench with a mix of fear and anger.

Which was actually pretty selfish of her.

She shouldn't be concerned with the fate of *Dirty Pretty Teens*. She should be worried about Belle and whether or not Dex had other victims. Kate's career aspiration needed to take a back seat.

But that video.

Whatever. So she'd been caught drinking. Her and, like, five bazillion other seventeen-year-olds. It wasn't *that* bad. Didn't Drew Barrymore snort coke at Studio 54 when she was, like, eight? She still had an acting career.

As much as Kate tried to marginalize its importance, she knew that video was going to bite her in the ass somehow.

"Hello!" Rowan snapped her fingers in front of her phone camera, and Kate realized she'd zoned out. "Did you hear me?"

"Yes. No."

Rowan chortled, the right side of her lips curling into a smile for the first time. "I asked if your parents have seen this yet."

"Judging by the lack of screaming from down the hall," Kate said, cupping her hand to her ear as if listening intently, "I doubt it."

"Never been so thankful that Mack and Andrea are clueless about technology."

They both knew that Kate's parents would find out about this eventually. A comment from the neighbors, or one of their students, or more likely, from Kate's aunt Emilia, who in addition to being an insatiable gossip, was also *Dirty Pretty Teens'* number one fan. She needed to get to Emilia first and ask her to keep this on the DL before her parents went absolutely ballistic and ruined all of her plans to—

"KATHERINE CRESSIDA WILLIAMS!"

A shriek from Kate's mom broke the silence. She used all three of Kate's names, an address that was reserved for only the most egregious transgressions. Like underage drinking facilitated by an adult male who also happened to be a statutory rapist. "Shit."

Even Rowan recognized the danger. "Dude, your mom is pissed."

Thundering steps echoed down the hallway, approaching Kate's door.

She was about to get hit with a category-five Hurricane Andrea, one of the most destructive forces in the universe.

"Gotta go." She smiled weakly at Rowan. "I'll update you."

"I'll be waiting with bated breath." Rowan kissed her index and middle fingers and turned them to face the camera before she ended the call. Then Kate dropped her phone, carefully turned it facedown on her nightstand so it didn't look as if she'd been glued to it for the last fifteen minutes, and lay back against her pillows just in time for her mom to barrel—without knocking—into her room.

Andrea Williams was a firecracker. She had a lightning-fast Irish temper that burned hotter than a million fiery suns, but like with Rowan, her anger flamed out quickly. The trick to dealing with her mom was diagnosing what DEFCON level her temper was at, weathering the initial onslaught, then going for sympathy once the ferocity had ebbed. Judging by the bright coral flush to her freckled cheeks, dilated nostrils, and buggy hazel eyes, her mom was at peak rage. Kate needed to get ahead of this one.

"I can explain," she said, holding both hands up in front of her for protection.

Her mom rolled her eyes, looking more like the high school students she taught. "Oh, really?"

"Yeah." *No.* "It's not what it looks like."

"That's funny." Her mom held up her hand, a piece of paper gripped between her palm and fingers. "Because it looks like you took the CHSPE exam in June, without permission."

Kate blinked. The paper—Kate's pass notice for her CHSPE—might have been the one thing that would have pissed off her mom more than a video of her daughter boozing it up at a Hollywood party while being groped by a sleazy old dude. *That* Kate was ready to combat. But this? Kate's mind was momentarily dulled by conflicting emotions of excitement and fear, which sent her mind racing to come up with some kind of coherent explanation.

"Um . . ."

"Does your father know about this?"

"Do I know about what?" Her dad's meaty bass-baritone drifted down the hall from the main bedroom, bouncing off the hardwood floors and stucco walls of their Spanish-style bungalow. His voice, equal parts Darth Vader and Santa Claus, had always been a source of comfort to Kate. Mack was the calmer parent, the more rational spirit. Even when he was upset, or "disappointed," as he liked to call it, he spoke in the same slow, metered pace with which he read Shakespeare aloud to his literature classes.

"I need you in here!" her mom called, the anger waning a touch. Kate's dad had a calming effect, even from the other room. "Family meeting."

"Coming, my love!"

Her mom shook her head, her sandy-brown ponytail whipping back and forth like the tail on an excited collie. "Are you going to break his heart, Kate, or shall I?"

Kate groaned as she threw her comforter aside and slid out of bed. "And you say *I'm* the dramatic one."

Kate's mom narrowed her eyes. "I'm glad you think this is funny. It'll make it so much easier to ground you until you're eighteen."

She was blowing this way out of proportion. Lots of teens started professional careers without going to college. Actors, athletes, Greta Thunberg. Yes, of course her dad's dream was to have her follow in his footsteps at Columbia, but if she was successful on her own terms, why would either of her parents begrudge her that?

Besides, they hadn't even heard her five-year plan. When she laid it all out for them, they'd come around, right?

Doubtful.

Kate's dad leaned against the doorway, his faded gray bathrobe drawn taut against his protruding belly. Half of his face was still lathered with shaving cream, the other half smooth, and Kate could already see a few tiny drops of blood beading up on his ruddy skin. Even half-shaved, his handsome face and buoyant energy lit up the room, defusing a teeny bit of the tension, and Kate smiled despite her mom's scowl.

"'Good morrow to you both,'" he proclaimed, sweeping his arm wide, a king addressing his subjects. "'What counterfeit did I give you?'" He smiled at his daughter, eyebrows high in expectation.

Kate sighed. This really wasn't the right time for their favorite game of Name that Shakespeare. *"Romeo and Juliet."*

Kate's mom clicked her tongue impatiently. "Not now, Mack."

He ignored her, cocking his head as he waited for his daughter to elaborate. "Yes? *And?*"

Crap. This was a deep cut. Wasn't nailing the play enough? "Act two, uh, scene two?"

Her dad made a loud buzzing sound in his throat, which reverberated through the walls. "Oh, sorry. So close. Act two, scene *four* is what we were going for. But I'm sure we'll have a nice consolation prize for—"

"MACK!" Her mom's temper spiked again, higher this time. At least her focus was now split between the two of them.

He instantly straightened up, saluting his wife. "Yes, ma'am! Reporting for duty, ma'am!"

And they wonder how I got the acting bug.

Kate's mom gritted her teeth. "This is serious." She held the results page up to his face. He squinted, his glasses probably abandoned on the bathroom counter, and leaned close. Kate could actually identify the exact moment the meaning struck him.

"A high school proficiency exam?" He laughed nervously. "But Columbia doesn't care if you graduate early. It's all about grades, test scores, and credits."

Of course he didn't get it. Of course she was going to have to spell it out. "Dad, I'm not applying to Columbia."

This time, his laughter was almost maniacal. "Ha-ha. Very funny. That's been your dream since fifth grade."

"*Your* dream," she half whispered, afraid to say the words out loud.

Kate's mom didn't give her husband time to process his daughter's betrayal. "And what is Kate's dream, huh? What exactly do you think you're going to accomplish by skipping college?"

Her dad gripped his heart like he was going into cardiac arrest. "Andrea, my love. Never say those words again. Our daughter is going to college. What else would she do?"

This was, like, way worse than explaining the video, which would only have *angered* her dad, not destroyed every dream he'd had for his only child since she was still inside the womb.

He'd been such a wonderful parent—both of them had been, actually—and she'd spent the better part of her life trying to make them proud. She got the grades they expected her to get, hung out with the types of college-bound kids she was supposed to hang out with, stayed away from parties and drinking and boys with too many tattoos. And she'd gotten so good at pleasing her parents that she'd forgotten to figure out what the hell *she* actually wanted from life.

Until that first day on set when the pilot director shouted "Action!" and suddenly Kate's soul blossomed.

Once, just once, she was doing something for herself. It sucked that it was the one thing her parents would never approve.

"Well?" her mom prompted. Patience was not one of her notable virtues. "Spill it."

Kate took a deep breath, attempting to ignore the rampaging buffalo that stampeded through her lower intestines, then finally voiced the words she'd been too afraid to share with anyone but Rowan.

"I'm not going to college because I'm going to pursue acting. Full-time." She swallowed. "I want to be a professional actress."

THREE

THE SILENCE IN THE WILLIAMS BUNGALOW HOME WAS LOUDER than an air horn on top of church bells with a volcano exploding in the background. It permeated Kate's bedroom with a murky emotional stew of anger, confusion, and indignation that spoke more than mere words.

She hadn't meant to tell them this way. Kate knew her parents a hell of a lot better than that. Despite her mom's temper and her dad's passion for the Bard, her parents were cool, rational people. Decisions were never made in the heat of the moment—they were always discussed and decided upon as a family, where each member was able to bring their own logical argument to the table for consideration. Even in the worst throes of puberty, when Kate's brain was a tangled, pulsating mass of hormones, she was able to have a levelheaded conversation with her parents about the benefits of using tampons over pads.

Like, who even did that?

The Williams family.

Dropping this no-college bomb on her Columbia- and UC Davis–educated parents wasn't something she planned to do at seven o'clock on a Tuesday morning right after her costar unleashed an insinuating video on the internet. Kate had drawn up a five-year business plan, like she was pitching to investors on *Shark Tank*, showing where she hoped to be by the time she would have graduated from college.

It was a modest career outline—no Oscar nominations or international press junkets. Those would come much, much later. Like when she was approaching thirty or something. Her teens and early twenties would be about building a brand, escaping the type-casting juggernaut of the fat funny girl from *Dirty Pretty Teens* by branching out into indie film. A risky lead role here or there, but nothing with a casting notice that used *plump, heavy,* or *dumpling-shaped* as a euphemism for *fat*.

Kate was more than her dress size and felt like she should be considered for the same roles as actresses like Rowan and Belle. In fact, some of the highest-profile reviews of the show mentioned how refreshing it was to see a character like Noelle indulge in the same romantic shenanigans her thinner counterparts had been enjoying for decades. Kate wanted to build on that, staying the hell away from cliché roles that portrayed fat girls as depressed, lonely, or who put up with a love interest who treated them like shit.

By twenty, she'd have at least three films under her belt. Five more by twenty-two, when she'd be in the seventh season of *DPT* and her contract option expired. Convenient timing because then she'd really bust out. Big-budget stuff. A superhero, maybe. Why the hell not? She'd look badass in spandex.

It had all sounded reasonable when she'd mapped out the presentation, especially now that she had her passing CHSPE grade. But as her parents gaped at her in horrified silence, no doubt wondering whether or not their sane and staid daughter had been kidnapped and replaced by a doppelgänger, all of Kate's well-thought-out arguments sounded like the half-assed daydreams of a six-year-old who thought "Disney Princess" was a viable career option.

"This isn't how I wanted you to find out," Kate began. Yeah, duh. Tell them something they don't know. "I love acting. I didn't know until I did it, but it's like I was born for this."

"You were born to do what your parents say," her mom cut in, rage simmering beneath the calm pace of her words.

Kate barreled on, undeterred. She needed to get everything on the table while she still had the nerve. "I feel like I'm finally good at something."

She paused, half waiting for her parents to jump in with "But you're good at so many things!"

They didn't.

"I've been thinking about this for a long time, and I—"

Her dad interrupted. Something he never did. "A long time? Kate, you've only been an actor for seven months. We've been targeting Columbia for seven years."

He's never going to let it go. "You've been targeting Columbia, Dad. Did I pick out an adorable Roar-ee bodysuit for myself when I was born? No. Then buy it in, like, every size from newborn to toddler? No again. Or sign me up for Ivy League sleepaway camp when I was eight so I'd be on Columbia's recruiting radar? Still no."

"But . . ." He faltered, glancing at his wife like she might offer some insight. "But I thought you liked Camp Ivy."

She did, but he was missing the point. For the first time in her life, Kate felt alive. Empowered. She wasn't tagging along with Rowan and her actor friends. She *was* the actor friend.

"Dad, Mom, I know this is a shock and it's disappointing and there's at least a decent chance that it will all implode on me and I'll end up going to college anyway. Just like when Dad took a year away from Columbia for that internship at the Public Theater."

Her parents frowned in unison. It was a risk to cite her dad's own history, but Kate wasn't pulling any punches. She needed to remind her parents that they hadn't always made the safest choices.

"Passing this exam will make me more desirable to studios," she continued, "and Clementine thinks—"

"Clementine!" The name practically exploded out of her mom's mouth. "Is *that* where this is coming from?"

Clementine and Kate's mom had never been on the best of terms, though Kate's mom had always kept her hostilities at a dull simmer, limiting herself to comments like "Easy when it's not your kid" that she'd mumble to herself. But now the gloves were off.

"Clementine only cares about what's right for Clementine's bank account. That's why she swooped in to sign you after you were cast." Her mom's upper lip curled in revulsion. "Low-hanging fruit is easy pickings."

Kate winced. *Low-hanging fruit* felt excessively cruel.

Sure, Clementine was Belle's agent, and when she heard that her client's costar was unrepresented, she stepped in, but so what? Clementine saw something in Kate and wanted to work with her. End of story.

Besides, Kate liked her agent. Her mile-a-minute enthusiasm about

Kate's career had been infectious from day one. If Kate was going to make this work, she had to trust her agent implicitly.

"She certainly doesn't have your best interests in mind," Kate's mom continued. "And I don't think you should be swayed by her argument."

"You sound like a lawyer," Kate said.

"No, just a mom."

"This isn't about Clementine," Kate said, sidestepping the argument. "It's about me. I need to try, and now is the one chance I'll have to—"

Before she could finish her sentence, a phone rang in the other room. Her parents' room.

All the warmth drained out of Kate's body.

"Who's calling at this hour?" Kate's dad said, turning toward the main bedroom. He might have been confused by the call, but Kate was not. She had a pretty good idea of who was on the other line.

Aunt Emilia.

"Wait!" Kate had never been so desperate for anything in her life as she was to prevent her dad from answering the phone. "Can you let it go to voice mail?"

Her dad waved her off as he hustled down the hall, bathrobe loose and fluttering open. Kate averted her eyes. Maybe she should go back to bed and stay there until tomorrow, when all of this might seem like—

Kate's phone buzzed with a text.

The phone was upside down, so she couldn't see a message preview, and before she could check it, her dad reappeared in the doorway, cell phone still in his hand, which hung limply at his side.

"Mack?" Kate's mom said, instantly alarmed. "What's wrong? Did somebody die?"

He shook his head, eyes staring out the window into the front yard. "That was Aunt Emilia."

Shit.

"*Dirty Pretty Teens* has been canceled."

* * *

You never wanted this.

You never wanted this.

You never really *wanted this.*

Kate repeated those words over and over in her head as she clicked on the thirtieth web article about the cancellation of her show in the wake of Belle Masterson's video. Terms like *shocking disregard for child safety* and *FCC investigation* swirled in her head as all of her dreams came crashing down in one giant champagne-fueled dumpster fire.

Try as she might to self-soothe, the mantra was hollow. Yeah, she'd never wanted this acting career before, but now? Now she'd never wanted anything so desperately in her life.

Her parents had spent the last half hour huddled in their room with the door closed. The only time the door to their bedroom was closed was when her parents were having sex or discussing their daughter. And since Kate could hear Belle's tirade drifting down the hall as her parents watched the video on her dad's phone, for the first time in her life she was disappointed that her parents weren't getting it on.

She just hoped that no one was googling *military school* or *convent admissions*. The CHSPE made her eighteen in the eyes of the entertainment industry, but not in the eyes of the law. Which meant her parents were still in control for eight more months.

Kate desperately wanted to debrief with Rowan, but she'd texted a dozen times with no response. Rowan's last message had been an echo of Aunt Emilia's phone call—*DPT canceled by Netflix!!!*—and unfortunately her radio silence was expected, if maddening. Rowan was in her second week of summer theater camp at school and was probably elbow-deep in warm-up exercises by now. Kate would have given a kidney to be there with her, studying Stanislavski technique instead of navigating the reputation minefield that was her professional life.

The internet was a vicious place.

Belle had somehow managed to upstage herself with the video footage of the wrap party. None of the articles Kate read even mentioned Belle's misguided justification of her affair with Dex. But all of them mentioned Kate, some even laying the blame for the entire fiasco at her doorstep, which blindsided her even though she really should have expected it. Why blame America's adorable little princess when the naughty fat girl with no self-restraint was clearly the bad influence? It was maddening, and Kate's fingers itched to write a defense on her behalf.

But each time she was about to unleash a biting comment, Kate remembered Clementine's text from yesterday.

DO NOT COMMENT ON ANYTHING!!!

Kate slammed her laptop shut, angry at her own impotence. Angry at her own stupidity.

And angry at Belle.

So angry, she didn't even hear her parents leave their room until they were filing into hers. They stood on either side of her door like sentries guarding a prisoner.

"Your mother and I have discussed your proposal," Kate's dad began, pushing his glasses up to the bridge of his nose. His professorial pose, though his half-shaved face undermined the authority. "And in light of recent events involving your behavior and the actions of certain people within your current environment, we are understandably concerned about allowing you to pursue acting in lieu of your education."

"Dad, I swear. That video was a fluke. I've never—"

He held up his hand, silencing her, and Kate noted that he wasn't looking her in the eyes as he spoke, as if doing so might crumble his resolve. Instead, he stared intently at the poster of Times Square above her bed.

"But you're practically an adult now, and once you turn eighteen, decisions about your future will be yours to make."

Kate bit her lower lip, cautiously optimistic. It sounded as if they were going to let her try, but knowing her parents, there would be strings attached.

"That said . . ." Her dad cleared his throat, and his eyes shifted to hers for the first time. Kate wasn't prepared for the depth of sadness she saw in them. "That said, we feel we need to address some of the issues with your plan."

"Issues," her mom said under her breath.

Kate's dad held up an index finger. "First, the issue of your *DPT* earnings. That money is currently held in a trust account, which you can't touch until you're twenty-one or until you start college."

"Oh." Shit. "Well, I can get a job."

"*Will* get a job," her mom said, correcting her. Ah, so this was the catch.

"Your mom and I think that if you're going to be an adult in the eyes of Hollywood, you need to act like an adult at home as well."

Kate tensed. She could hear the bomb being dropped, screaming down from above as it accelerated toward her. "Okay . . ."

"Which means," Kate's mom said with a smile, "as long as you're still planning to forgo college, you'll be paying for your room and board in this house, effective immediately."

FOUR

"DUDE." ROWAN PLOPPED DOWN ON HER BED BESIDE THE marked-up script she'd been studying when Kate arrived. "They're charging you *rent*?"

"Yep."

"Starting when?"

"When I give them my answer."

Kate's landlords, er, parents wanted their daughter to think about the terms. As long as she skipped senior year and didn't apply to any universities, she needed to pay three hundred dollars on the first of every month, a contribution toward her car insurance, utilities, and food consumption. Plus she still had to take the SATs in the fall no matter what. And find time to study for them.

It all seemed a little harsh. Like a punishment. It wasn't as if she was dropping out of school to smoke weed and play video games with "chill out" as her main life goal. She had, like, an actual career plan. It just wasn't the one her parents wanted.

She realized that Mack and Andrea were intentionally making this difficult in the hope that balancing auditions and some kind of part-time job would be too much. They hoped the harsh realities of "adulting" would cause Kate to choose the easier path: stay in school, give up acting, go to college, and then find a nice respectable career. Like they had done. Teachers. Noble and fulfilling and absolutely 100 percent not what Kate wanted.

"When do you have to decide?" Rowan asked.

"Before school starts."

"That's in, like, three weeks!" Rowan said, as if Kate wasn't keenly aware.

"Yep."

"So you haven't totally decided to drop out yet?"

"I—"

Rowan crossed fingers on both hands and held them up beside her face. "Please, please, pretty please tell me there's a chance you'll come back to school this fall?"

The Gordian knot that was Kate's small intestine tightened. Not only was she letting her parents down, but she was abandoning her best friend to endure senior year alone. Or as alone as an extrovert like Rowan ever was.

Which wasn't very.

"I'm not going off to war," Kate said, rolling her eyes. "We'll still see each other all the time."

Rowan pouted. "But not every day."

Kate ignored the dramatics. "You've got plenty of friends at school."

"Who are also going to miss you," Rowan said, twisting the knife. Kate's smile must have faltered, a look Rowan interpreted as doubt. She pounced on it. "Just promise me you'll think about it a little longer, okay?"

The words Kate wanted to say were *I've thought about it enough*, but Rowan's pleading eyes made them difficult to articulate. "Fine."

It was the encouragement Rowan needed. She sat up on her knees and grabbed Kate's hands, squeezing them tightly. She spoke so quickly her sentence sounded like one long word. "You know, I heard that Joseph Gordon-Levitt went to Van Nuys High *while* he was starring in a network sitcom, so, you know, it's totally doable. Plus, I read that even with a CHSPE pass you can still go to regular high school." She paused to take a quick breath. "If you want to."

"I . . . guess?"

"Then we could still go to prom together!" Rowan squealed, as if Kate's answer had been anything more than noncommittal. "You simply *can't* miss prom. We promised to be each other's dates if we were both single, remember?"

Kate remembered. She also remembered that the prom pact had been Rowan's idea—Kate would have been perfectly happy to skip that rite of passage altogether. "I mean, never say never, right?" She forced a grin, unwilling to crush Rowan's false hope.

But her friend wasn't buying it. "Which means never." Rowan flopped back against her bed pillows, arms wide in martyrdom. "I'm doomed to finish my last year of high school stag."

"Dex really should have cast you instead of me. Your sense of drama is so much more evolved."

"I know," Rowan said with a heavy sigh. "And I'd have had a much better time with those hot AF actors than you did."

"How many times do I have to tell you how boring they all were?"

Rowan gasped, sitting up. "Boring? What is wrong with you?"

"I have taste?" Kate said with a raised brow. Her friend was notorious for overlooking egregious personality flaws in pursuit of a hot guy.

"I talked to Dagney for, like, two hours at that party." Rowan flipped her long black hair out of her face with a toss of her head. "And he was utterly charming."

Kate winced at the mention of the wrap party. The scene from Belle's video flashed before her eyes, causing her physical pain. While Rowan had been flirting with Dagney—who was not only twenty-five years old but only dated models (runway, not print, as he liked to brag)—Kate had been humiliating herself.

"Have you heard from her?" Rowan asked. "Belle, I mean. Like, to apologize?"

Belle Masterson apologize? Not in this reality. "I didn't realize hell had frozen over."

"She owes you one. Getting thrown under a bus like that could cause serious injuries."

"Internal hemorrhaging," Kate said with a bitter laugh.

Rowan threw her arms around Kate from behind, hugging her tightly around the shoulders. "Don't worry. I'll be your tourniquet."

Though she knew Rowan couldn't actually fix this problem, it felt good to know she had someone in her corner.

Kate and Rowan had been inseparable ever since Rowan's first day as a transfer student into Kate's fifth-grade class. When their teacher asked Rowan why she looked like she was about to cry, she'd answered by quoting the opening line of *The Merchant of Venice*.

"'In sooth,'" Rowan had squeaked, "'I know not why I am so sad.'"

Kate was the only one in the classroom who knew what the hell she was talking about.

An unbreakable bond had been forged.

But lately, that bond had been stretched. Kate had been out of school for a big chunk of their junior year while filming *DPT*, an acting gig that had been Rowan's dream, and Kate was now threatening not to come back to school at all while she pursued a professional acting career, which was also Rowan's dream. Kate wasn't sure how many friendships would have survived that kind of strain.

Or how long theirs would continue to do so.

"I'm sorry," she said, reaching up to grab Rowan's hand, still draped around her shoulder. She squeezed it gently, a sisterly act that she hoped said more than the insipid, nonspecific apology that had come out of her mouth. "I really do wish you'd gotten cast instead."

"In addition to," Rowan corrected her.

"You'd have made a much better Piper."

Rowan sighed. "Making Piper Asian was not on their radar."

"Why not?" Kate asked with a shrug. "They made Noelle fat."

"You are *not* fat."

Which is something only skinny girls say. "According to the internet, I am."

Rowan rolled her eyes dramatically. "Marilyn Monroe was a size sixteen when she filmed *Some Like It Hot*, and no one thinks she was fat."

Which is something else only skinny girls say.

She knew Rowan meant well, but the myth of Marilyn Monroe's dress size during that production had done more harm to fat girls than almost any other fallacy about being "over" weight. While Marilyn was at her heaviest during that time, she was still only about a hundred and forty pounds, and the measurements of her dresses show she would have been a size twelve then, or an eight in modern dress sizes.

Not exactly plus.

Kate couldn't have fit an arm in any of Marilyn's clothes, even at the star's heaviest, but people who had never had to worry about the stigma of obesity loved to think that Marilyn Monroe, the foremost icon of female sexuality, was fat. It made their own deep-seated disparagement of fatness more palatable.

"I'm over it," Rowan said after a pause, though her taut smile hinted that was wishful thinking. "I mean, it's a miracle either of us made it on that show. Weren't there, like, ten thousand people at the audition?"

Thirteen thousand, six hundred eighty-two. "I don't remember."

"And out of all of them, Dex wanted you. I hope you realize what a huge deal that is."

"I guess."

"I'm sorry he turned out to be a perv."

"Me too."

Rowan shifted her body to face Kate. "Dex never, like, *did* anything to you, did he?"

"Other than groping me at the party?"

"Obviously."

Kate recalled the uncomfortably long and close hug from Dex on the last shooting day. "No."

"And you're not, like, sad about that or anything . . ."

"Oh, hell no." Sad about Dex not targeting her with his predatory vibes? Definitely not. "I'm not into arrogant white dudes old enough to be my father."

"Good. 'Cause if he did, I'd personally castrate that asshole."

41

Kate snorted. "I'm sure his wife is first in line for that job."

"Seriously."

"But thank you," Kate added quickly. "It means a lot to me that you care."

"I know."

"You're . . ." Kate felt herself getting weepy when she thought about their friendship and how much it had meant to her over the years. "You're, like, the thing I'll miss most about school and—"

"Knock, knock!" The voice outside Rowan's door was not accompanied by actual knuckles rapping against the wood, and even before her friend could respond, the door cracked open. "Ro?"

Kate's brain recognized the voice, but she was still processing what it meant when Rowan marched across the room and threw the door open. Standing in the hall, his hand poised as if it was still holding the doorknob that had been unceremoniously ripped from his grasp, was Rowan's older brother, Tyson.

Kate didn't know Ty was home from Shanghai, where he'd spent his gap year before starting at Stanford. If she'd known, she would have prepared herself to see him again, to make sure her stomach didn't open up like a giant, gaping pit at the memory of their last encounter, and to be able to smile at him calmly instead of immediately breaking out into a cold sweat of guilt and confusion. She scrambled to her feet, back to the door in an attempt to compose herself, before she turned to face him.

Ty remained in the doorway, smirking at his sister, and if it wasn't for his old habit of running his hand repeatedly through his hair when he was uncomfortable, Kate might not have recognized him.

Not that there had been any significant physical changes. His heart-shaped face—one of the few features Ty shared with his sister—was clean shaven as usual, and his wide-set eyes, heavy at the corners as if he'd just been reliving a sad memory, were exactly as Kate remembered. Ty hadn't grown six inches or lost sixty pounds or suddenly shed his casual geekiness for some kind of chic world traveler veneer in the last twelve months, but there was something markedly different about him.

The hair, for one thing. He'd let his sideburns grow out, which accentuated his sharp cheekbones, and the rest was longer than Kate had ever seen it in her life, shaggy and tinged with amber overtones, as if his black strands had been bleached ever so slightly by the sun. He'd even used product, something pre-travel Ty would never have owned let alone used, which gave his hair a tousled effect as it fell thick and long over his forehead.

He wore a professional button-down shirt and tailored slacks instead of his old uniform of cargo shorts, T-shirts, and flip-flops, and he exuded an aura that was more confident and definitely more grown up than the guy she'd known since she was eleven.

Ty's reserved personality had always been overshadowed by his emotionally exhibitionist little sister, but while Rowan had made old Ty fade into the wallpaper, the guy standing in the doorway wasn't decor. His confidence was almost cocky, his eyes boldly shifting from his sister to Kate, and instead of avoiding her gaze, he met it with an ease that belied the crush Kate knew he'd had on her for the better part of their high school years together.

A crush he'd admitted to her the day before he left for Shanghai.

A crush she'd *literally* crushed, turning him down with a flippancy she regretted as soon as the words had come out of her mouth.

A crush she only realized she'd missed after it was gone.

"Kate," he said, jutting out his chin as he said her name. Casual and indifferent.

"I didn't know you were back." Good, she sounded just as cool as Ty did.

"Came back Sunday," he said, his face unreadable. "A few weeks at home before I head to Stanford."

"Oh." Kate felt a little pang of sadness that Ty's feelings for her seemed to have been left behind in Shanghai. But she refused to let him see that. If he was over her, then she needed to make sure she was over him being over her.

Because she *was*.

She thought.

Maybe not.

Shit.

"He wasn't supposed to come home until next week," Rowan said, flouncing back to her bed. "But he bumped up his flight to help Dad out at the office."

"Really?" Seemed like a shitty way to spend your last weeks before college.

Ty shrugged. "There's a big case coming up, and Dad could use the help. Besides, I find it interesting."

"Oh." He sounded so cold and detached. Though painfully shy, the Ty she knew was just as emotional as his sister, though he hid that side of himself from most people.

But not from me.

"How are you?" Ty asked, somehow managing to sound entirely disinterested in both the question and its reply. They might as well have been two colleagues meeting at the water cooler, and while Kate felt that the expected reply was just a simple "Fine," she wasn't going to stand there and pretend that their years of friendship suddenly meant nothing.

"Well, I got fired from my job because my boss is a sexual predator and my parents are charging me rent, so yeah, doing great."

Ty smiled, unflustered. That was also new. "Why are they charging you rent?"

Rowan answered for her. "Because Kate is abandoning me, throwing me to the wolves of the American high school system while she goes off to be a famous actress."

"Oh." Ty didn't follow up with any questions, as if Kate dropping out of high school and skipping college to pursue an acting career was an everyday occurrence. "My dad's got a part-time position open at his office. If you need a job."

"Oh yeah?" Rowan replied, seemingly interested. "Doing what?"

"They need a file clerk to come in after hours."

"Ooo, the dungeon!" Rowan cooed.

"Dungeon?" Kate asked. She'd been to Kleiner, Abato & Chen, Rowan and Ty's dad's entertainment law firm, many times over the years, and she was pretty sure the office was located on the third floor of a mid-rise office complex in downtown Burbank, not a medieval castle.

"That's what Ro calls the file room," Ty replied with an arched eyebrow. "Due to security precautions for the firm's A-list clientele, the files are kept in a locked, fireproof room."

"It has steel-plated walls and no cell-phone reception except by the window," Rowan explained. "And then only sometimes. It's basically torture to work in there."

"Wow," Kate said, "you're really selling this."

"Pays better than Starbucks," Ty said coolly. "And it's in the evenings, so after school."

"After *auditions*," Kate corrected him.

"Sorry, auditions." Ty smiled without warmth. "Sounds perfect, then."

"Except she'd have to work with you." Rowan laughed. "About as much fun as hip-replacement surgery." She definitely wasn't picking up on the weird vibe between her brother and her best friend, which was just as well. Kate had never told her what had happened between them.

"Thanks." Kate forced a smile that was just as cold as Ty's. "But my plan is to use the acting gigs to pay rent. I won't need a side hustle."

Ty shrugged. "Okay, then. Good luck."

She hated the note of condescension in his tone, like he'd blossomed into a seasoned adult in Shanghai while she was just some immature high school girl he'd left behind. "I don't need luck," she said, grabbing her bag from Rowan's bed. "I've got talent. Talk later, Ro."

She kissed her index and middle fingers, then flashed them at Rowan before she brushed past Ty into the hallway.

She never looked back.

FIVE

FOR SOME REASON, KATE WAS DEPRESSED BY THE TIME SHE pulled her dad's car into the driveway. She'd gone to Rowan's to talk through her current life crisis, hoping for some cheerleading, and she'd returned disillusioned.

Rowan's plea for Kate to come back to school was expected but irritating. She'd set her mind on this five-year plan, steadfast in her belief that she was doing the right thing, but Rowan's comments gave her a pang of doubt.

It wasn't just Rowan that Kate was going to miss. Imogen, Luca, Gabby, Ernesto, even Jeremiah, the irritating class clown—they'd all be experiencing senior year together without her. In the few months she was in class for junior year, Kate had a ton of great memories with her friends:

helping Luca pass his algebra final, tutoring Gabby through an entire semester of chemistry in one weekend, rushing over to Ernesto's with a half gallon of white-chocolate raspberry ice cream when his boyfriend dumped him. The memories flooded back, reminding Kate of the camaraderie she'd be missing.

Dirty Pretty Teens had been work, not friendship, and Kate and Belle had nothing like the best-friend relationship they portrayed on-screen. They'd rarely exchanged more than a few words when the cameras weren't rolling, and even those were mostly monologues by Belle, who needed someone to talk *at* rather than confide *in*.

Which was why Kate practically screamed in surprise when she found Belle sitting on the porch swing in front of her house.

"Kate!" Belle shot to her feet and dashed toward her, arms wide and ready to receive a hug that wasn't willingly offered in return. She wore a hoodie pulled low over her forehead, which flew back as she ran, releasing her sunshine-yellow hair, and though her oversize sunglasses were still firmly in place, if anyone had actually been watching them—paparazzi, weird neighbors, Kate's parents—they'd have recognized Belle Masterson right away from her signature hair.

"Um, hey." Kate tensed as Belle flung her arms around Kate's neck, hugging her so tightly an unwitting bystander might have thought these two dear old friends hadn't seen each other in years.

"I've missed you."

"Oh." Kate was pretty sure that the only thing Belle Masterson ever missed was her own reflection. She felt her former costar's arms tighten ferociously around her shoulders. Kate's cue that Belle was waiting for a response. "I've, uh, missed you, too."

Belle broke away, dabbing beneath her eyes with the pad of her middle finger, an actor's move to signify tears that Kate didn't see. "I can't believe how awful this has all been. Would you believe the media is stalking my house right now?"

Since Belle lived in a gated community off Mulholland, Kate seriously doubted that photographers could get close enough to her actual house to classify their presence as stalking, but she still felt sorry for Belle. Dex had really done a number on her, and her recovery, both personally and professionally, would be a long journey. "I'm sorry."

"I know you are."

Wait, why should I *be sorry?*

"Plus, the death threats."

"Death threats?"

Belle pulled off her sunglasses, exposing the same puffy, bloodshot eyes Kate had seen in her social media video. "But the worst is that they won't even let me talk to Dex."

Kate wasn't sure that preventing contact between a minor and a sexual predator was worse than death threats. In fact, it sounded like a good thing for Belle, who was clearly still in love with her abuser.

"Canceling the show was ludicrous. Insulting. Do you know how much money Netflix has made off of me?" Belle had started crying, for real this time, her hysteria increasing with every syllable, as if the affront to her career was more painful than her boyfriend's incarceration. "They're just trying to punish us."

Us? "I don't—"

"And to treat *me* like this . . ." She paused, squeezing her eyes together as she took a deep, steadying breath. When she opened her eyes, she was calm. Almost like she was acting. "If they'd let us be together, they'd totally understand that our feelings are real. They can drop the charges and we can film season two and it will all be fine."

Kate doubted anything would be fine. Even if Dex somehow eluded conviction, she was pretty sure he'd never run another show ever again.

"I'm sick with stress," Belle continued. "I've lost, like, five pounds since yesterday."

Kate blinked. Belle was already so thin that losing five pounds might result in catastrophic organ failure.

Belle turned sideways, flattening one hand against her abdomen. "Can you tell?"

"Oh yeah," Kate said with a nod. She'd learned to just give Belle the answers she wanted to avoid prolonged conversation. "Totally."

Belle's lips thinned out with a hint of a frown. "I see you're still the same . . . person."

Kate clenched her jaw. She'd gotten used to Belle's backhanded remarks about her size, recognizing that it came from Belle's own insecurities, but flexing that muscle after Belle had gotten their show canceled was testing Kate's restraint. She needed to end this conversation.

"I'm so sorry you're going through this." It was a struggle to get the words out. "My, uh, parents need me inside, so I'll just—"

"Clementine won't even talk to me."

Belle had been with Clementine since she was a kid, so her agent's coldness probably hurt. "Oh."

"Are you meeting with her soon?" Belle asked. "Phone call? Zoom? In person?"

Can't this girl take a hint? Kate tried to edge around her. "Um, tomorrow."

"Can you do me a teensy favor?" Belle asked, darting to block Kate's path to the front door. Her cheeks were dry. "Like, so tiny. And not even really so much a favor as, like, a little professional back scratch."

Kate didn't want Belle to scratch her back with those fingernails. "I guess?"

"Can you put in a good word for me with Clementine?" She blinked her eyes rapidly and made a little cringey face with her lips like the grimacing emoji, a look that was supposed to come off as cute and disarming. Kate knew this because she'd seen Belle use it on set when she was asking someone to do her a favor, which, like this one, wasn't really a favor so much as a thing she could easily do herself but wanted someone else to do instead. Like fetch her a vanilla almond-milk latte that most definitely was not part of the craft services spread, or deliver paperwork to the line producer because Belle didn't feel like walking it over.

This was the first time Kate had been on the receiving end of that look, and she did not like the feelings it engendered: guilt for wanting to say no tinged with the tiniest hope that in doing this favor, Belle might do her a solid in return.

Ridiculous. If there was one thing Kate had learned over the last seven months, it was that Belle Masterson only cared about one person: Belle Masterson.

Kate's silence as she tried to process all of these feels must have made Belle nervous because she immediately jumped in to fill the void. "I know, I know, it sounds totally ridiculous. Why would I be worried about Clementine? She's been my agent since I was ten. She's, like, practically my mom! And besides, she works for me, not the other way around. So what if she's mad at me?"

Kate pictured their effervescent middle-aged agent with her bright yellow eyeglass frames and a rainbow assortment of scarves for every season of the year, and wondered if she had ever been mad at anyone in her life. Clementine DuBois was like the charming white aunt on that sitcom you remembered from childhood, the one you wished was part of your own family: all smiles, all wide eyes, all laughter and arm squeezes and elbow nudges, as if she wanted you to be in on some joke. Her vision for

Kate's career had been bold and exciting, the platform on which Kate had built her own five-year plan, and Clementine had never been anything but encouraging of her new client.

Which made it difficult to understand why Belle seemed to be afraid of her.

"I doubt she's mad at you," Kate said, noncommittal. "And she's probably eager to help both of us through this."

For a split second, Belle's eyes narrowed and her nostrils flared, an ugly look and one, like Belle's calculated grimace, that Kate had seen a billion times, whenever someone did or said something that bruised the starlet's ego. Most recently, the last day of shooting when Dex had given Kate a lingering, bordering-on-inappropriate hug, right in front of Belle.

The ragey look was there one moment, gone the next, and Belle was smiling again. "I'm sure you're right. But I'm soooooooo nervous. Could you just mention my name and let her know that I'm willing to do whatever it takes to make things good?"

Kate had no idea what "make things good" might entail, other than that it sounded like something a mobster would say. "Sure."

Belle kissed her own hand, then patted Kate on the cheek with it before racing down the pathway toward the black Benz CLS with heavily tinted windows parked in front of the neighbors' house. As she opened the driver's-side door, Belle wiggled her fingers goodbye.

"Promise you'll talk to her?"

Ugh. "I promise."

"You're *the best*!" Belle cooed, then slipped into her car and peeled away from the curb with an earsplitting screech, leaving Kate on her porch, wondering why she felt as if she'd just made a deal with the devil.

SIX

THOUGH THE CDB YOUTH TALENT AGENCY WAS WITHIN EASY walking distance of Kate's house, when she set out for her meeting with Clementine the next afternoon, it was the first time Kate had actually made the trek on foot. It was also the first time she'd be meeting with Clementine without her mom in attendance. She wanted Clementine to know that newly "legal eighteen" actress Kate Williams was taking her career seriously, and she didn't want her mom there to interject, roll her eyes, offer erudite arguments against her lack of college plans, or any other type of behavior that might infantilize Kate in her agent's eyes.

She'd even, like, dressed up. Sort of. No jeans. No retro tees with eighties ad slogans for soda and chewing gum that her parents assumed she didn't really understand because they had no idea that those commercials lived forever on YouTube. No favorite pair of rainbow checkerboard Vans. Instead, Kate had chosen a knee-length peasant skirt in a subdued beige and a white drawstring-waist linen tank top with a waist-cinching belt, all of which had been part of her wardrobe on *DPT* that she'd been allowed to take home. She'd paired those with yellow rounded-toe ballet flats and a single gold-toned wrist cuff bracelet that screamed "edgy but confident," hoping the combined effect would make her look less like a child playing dress-up in mom's clothes and more like an emerging adult ready to take her life—and her career—by the horns.

She wanted everything to be perfect when she presented her five-year plan to Clementine. Her future. Her dreams. And she needed Clementine's help to make them happen.

Kate's veneer of self-confidence slipped as she walked into the lobby of Clementine's office, occupying a Tudor revival storefront in a strip mall behind Nickelodeon Studios. Was she in the right place? The lobby looked completely different. It had been widened, possibly by taking down the entire north wall and installing floor-to-ceiling windows, making the lobby look twice as large. Her eyes darted to the signage on the wall beside the door, large raised letters that read CBD YOUTH TALENT AGENCY in a sleek Century Gothic font.

Yep, right place.

Business must have been booming because in addition to the structural changes, the furniture had been updated from standard metal-legged waiting-room chairs to long faux-leather sofas raised mere inches off the floor. The beige walls were now painted stark white except for one red accent wall behind the receptionist's desk, and the guy who sat there was not the same one from Kate's last visit.

The wall of client headshots had also grown. Kate's eyes scanned down past the polished, smiling clientele and found her own stiff, uncomfortable headshot from earlier that year. The only plus-size girl on Clementine's roster. In the photo, taken under duress, Kate's smile looked forced, her eyes tight with the strain of doing this new thing she wasn't entirely sure that she wanted to do, and her pronounced double chin highlighted the fact that she hadn't learned about best angles yet. Kate cringed when she saw it, tacked up beside the glossier, more poised, and more seasoned child actors that Clementine represented.

Whatever. New headshots were at the top of her to-do list. Besides, not many of those seasoned actors had booked a role in a major series like *DPT* on their very first audition. Kate wasn't a nobody anymore: She was a known commodity. *DPT* had been a huge success, garnering millions of viewers in just the first month of streaming, and critics had called "captivating newcomer Kate Williams" a "great revelation" and "a young Melissa McCarthy."

Kate knew she didn't look anything like Melissa McCarthy, nor was she as talented as the Oscar nominee, and probably the only thing they had in common was that they both wore double-digit dress sizes, but it was nice to be compared to an established star, and the comment gave Kate a firm weapon with which to combat her imposter syndrome. She tacked on a smile, pinned back her shoulder blades, and approached the desk.

The receptionist's eyes shifted in her direction—first to her face, then down to her body before returning to his flat screen. "Can I help you?"

"I have a three thirty with Clementine," she said, noting with a swell of pride that she sounded strong and confident, like she'd practiced in front of the mirror.

"Ms. DuBois," he corrected her.

Kate wouldn't be shaken. "She asked me to call her Clementine."

The receptionist arched a threaded eyebrow. He looked about the same age as Kate's parents—young enough not to show wrinkles but old enough for the salt and peppers to creep in around the hairline. Kate wondered what kind of life choices had landed a middle-aged white man in the receptionist's chair at a children's talent agency.

"Hmm." His tone and face were neutral. "And you are?"

"Kate Williams."

It was the first time she'd spoken her own name with such authority, relishing the power that name now wielded, and she loved the rush of anticipation that someone might recognize her, put the name to the face, and then gush for twenty minutes about how awesome she'd been on *DPT*.

Except that didn't happen.

The receptionist hardly blinked at her name, and his ruddy, stoic face betrayed no emotion whatsoever at hearing it.

"Current client or aspiring?"

Knife to the heart. "Current."

The eyebrow again. As if Kate was lying. Like, would Clementine actually forget who was on her roster from day to day and then send some stranger out on an audition? Kate was still new to the business, but she was relatively sure it didn't work that way.

Kate wanted to say all of that, but she didn't. It was never a good idea to piss off the receptionist. They literally held the key to their boss's kingdom in their hands. But Kate still wanted to stand her ground, so she extended her left arm and pointed directly at her awful headshot without breaking eye contact with the snooty receptionist, matching his eyebrow of mockery with one of her own.

That's what a confident adult would have done.

That's what Belle Masterson would have done.

No, Belle wouldn't have needed to. This guy would have recognized her right away.

Ugh.

The receptionist quickly glanced in the general vicinity of Kate's head-shot, then smiled at her. "I'm sorry. I don't recognize you."

Kate's bravado abandoned her, rushing back into its hole somewhere deep inside her soul like a scared kitten, tail between its legs, mewing for mama. No amount of mirror pep talks were going to coax it out again.

"I'm on, I mean, I *was* on . . ." She froze. Using past tense to describe *Dirty Pretty Teens* still felt like a shock to the system.

But the receptionist wasn't listening. He had his hand on his headset, speaking to someone on the other line. "I have a Kate Williams"—he sounded incredulous as he said her name—"here to see you." He paused, listening, his poker face well intact. The only hint of emotion was a flutter in his right eyelid as if he was having a teeny, tiny stroke. "Ms. DuBois will be right with you."

Kate wasn't sure if she felt victorious or defeated as she perched on the edge of one of the low sofas.

The new office decor was certainly well designed. In addition to the sofas and the expanding client roster, shiny new chrome orb lights hung from the ceiling, a Nespresso machine had been added beside the water cooler, and instead of the ragged, half-torn issues of *Entertainment Weekly* and *Teen Vogue* that used to be scattered across the white oval coffee table, an oversize art book entitled *The CDB Agency* sat squarely in the middle.

Kate leaned forward, opened the thick cover, and found a collection of black-and-white stills from various CDB client projects. The first spread she recognized right away—Lexis Montero's Oscar-nominated turn as J.Lo playing Selena in *Fly Girl* from a few years ago. The next was Emma Beverly and Jacinta Xian, who starred on some mega-hit network sitcom Kate had never watched, and then a spread of the four tween leads of Disney's *Better Off Med,* about a group of middle school geniuses in medical school, a series that had been a huge deal almost a decade ago. Like every other ten-year-old with basic cable and not-overly-strict parents, Kate had loved the show, watching every season at least twice. Clementine repped two of the four leads, and the success of that series had been a huge bump in her career.

Kate turned the page and winced. She recognized the next actress immediately, not only because the photos were from a production she'd been a part of for eighty-seven days, but because she'd just seen this face on her front porch yesterday.

There were two photos of Belle Masterson on facing pages, both from *Dirty Pretty Teens.* In one, she was flirting with her character's crush, Wyatt, played by the hot but self-obsessed Emery Black, in a scene that had been filmed during the first week of production. Kate remembered watching them from behind a small army of grips and makeup artists, all waiting for a break to rush in and tweak lights or lip color, thinking that she needed to pinch herself because things like this didn't happen to normal boring people like herself.

The second photo was one with which Kate was even more intimately acquainted. Belle sat at a table in a coffeehouse, steaming cup of tea nestled between her hands as she leaned toward the person sitting across from her. She was mid-conversation, eyes wide with excitement as she told a story about Sebastian and Asher both asking her to prom on the same day even though she didn't want to go with either of them, 'cause, duh, Wyatt. Kate knew every word of that monologue and vividly remembered the expression captured on Belle's face as she delivered it because Kate was the actress sitting on the other side of the table.

But all you could see of Noelle Wagner was the side of her arm, resting on the polished wood table.

Kate had been completely cropped out.

She tried to tell herself that this was to be expected. Belle had done literally a dozen films and a series with Clementine over the years. Of course she'd be right near the front of the portfolio. Kate was brand-new—to acting and to Clementine's roster—so it would make sense that she'd be farther back. She flipped a few pages, then a few more. Nothing. Then she hoisted the book into her lap and quickly fanned through it.

She'd reached the end of the portfolio, her heart pounding in her chest with a mix of anger and shame that she wasn't represented in Clementine's premiere piece of agency propaganda, when she heard the receptionist call her name.

"Kate!"

His tone was sharp, irritated, and when Kate looked up, she saw that he was waving his hand over his head as if she was a mile away instead of across the lobby.

Oof. How long had he been calling her name?

"You can go back," he said once he was sure that he had her attention.

As Kate rose to her feet, placing the portfolio back on the coffee table with more care than calm, she was pretty sure she saw him roll his eyes.

SEVEN

"DARLING!" CLEMENTINE COOED THE MOMENT KATE STEPPED into her office. Her wan but heavily rouged cheeks beamed like shiny pink beacons as she rounded her desk, arms flung wide. She placed a hand on each of Kate's shoulders and air-kissed her cheeks, European style, before holding Kate at arm's length and staring critically at her face. "How are you holding up?"

"Fine," Kate lied. The butterflies in her stomach threatened to surge up through her esophagus and explode from her mouth in a stream of winged insect vomit.

"I. Am. So. Glad." Like Dex had done, Clementine squeezed Kate's shoulders on each word, as if to emphasize how much she meant them.

Was that some kind of entertainment-industry ritual? "Sit, sit. We have lots to discuss."

Clementine's enthusiasm buoyed Kate's mood, and she smiled as she sat at her agent's glass desk, all memory of her omission from Clementine's look book forgotten. Though the room decor had changed, the smiling, wide-eyed woman who bounced lightly in her brand-new leather chair like an excited eight-year-old visiting mom's office on bring-your-kids-to-work day was exactly as Kate remembered. From her neon-blue scarf and magenta blouse to the bright yellow frames of her glasses, her retro cherry earrings, and the loose metal bracelets that clanked and dinged with every movement of her arm, Clementine DuBois radiated positive energy, a rainbow of fun and hope and joy.

Clementine's steel-gray curls scrunched up as she raised her shoulders to her ears. "I want to start by saying that you. Are. So. *Brave*."

"Brave?" That's what you said to someone battling a cancer diagnosis.

"Absolutely! I knew you weren't the type to go fetal in the face of some hideous press."

Kate wasn't sure if *hideous* was the right word. It sounded severe.

"Or to publicly melt down in a grade A diva fit," Clementine continued. "Like *some people* we know." She inclined her head and laughed lightly, as if to indicate that she and Kate were in on this little joke about Belle together, except that Kate was pretty sure she'd somehow *become* the joke in all of this and she certainly didn't find it funny.

Clementine cleared her throat. "You're just boldly going about your life. I love that."

Kate snagged the opportunity to get a word in. "I'm excited about the future."

"Aren't we all, darling? Aren't we all!" Clementine's smile never budged.

You can do this, Kate. Be the adult. Take control.

"That's actually what I'm here to talk about," Kate began slowly. Testing the water with her words. "I passed the CHSPE."

Clementine shook her head, casting off whatever thoughts had been running through her mind. "That's wonderful! Definitely a plus. I'm waiting for Emmy to call in, and we can discuss next steps."

"Emmy?" Who the hell was that?

"She is the best. The. Best. At what she does."

Which could have been anything from massage therapy to Kate's tax returns. The name Emmy meant absolutely nothing to her. "Um, okay."

"You're going to love her. I promise."

It took longer than it should have for Kate to muster up the courage to ask "Who is Emmy?"

Clementine reared back, surprised, but before she could answer, she was interrupted by a buzz from her phone. "Emmy on line one," the receptionist said, pronouncing each syllable of the name distinctly.

"Darling!" Clementine purred as she put the call on speakerphone. "How are you?"

"I'm in the car, Clem." The voice on the other end was tinny and marred with static. "Sorry about that. Stuck in traffic coming back from Sony."

Clementine cringed. "Dear God, you poor thing."

"But I'm fine to talk," Emmy continued. "Is she there?"

"She is!" Clementine motioned for Kate to lean in toward the phone. "Emmy, Kate. Kate, Emmy."

"Hi, Kate," Emmy said before Kate could respond. "I thought your performance in *Dirty Pretty Teens* was absolutely inspired. Especially episodes 105 and 107."

"Um, thank you," Kate said, suddenly embarrassed.

"Binged the whole series last night. That story arc with Noelle's biological mom was such a 'coupé' for your character. Really gave you the opportunity to shine."

Kate had no idea why she was on this call with Emmy, who had watched the entire ten-episode season in one sitting, but she didn't care. Emmy's voice—perky with a bit of a twang—and words made her smile.

"I took the liberty of pulling up some audience studies from Netflix. Did you get that email, Clem?"

Clementine angled her computer monitor so Kate could see it. "Got it up right now."

"Excellent. As you can see, Noelle was very popular with test audiences. Which could really help us."

"Test audiences?" Kate wasn't sure she wanted to know what those were. She pictured the scene in *A Clockwork Orange* where the killer is forced to watch a bunch of movies with his eyes held open.

Clementine pulled her glasses down her nose as she tromboned the graph on her screen, attempting to get it into focus. "Especially with women, eighteen to thirty-five, who found Noelle, and I quote, 'realistic and relatable.'"

"I'm telling you, Clem, casting a plus actress plays in Middle America."

Kate cringed as her weight was commodified. Maybe she was just a good actress and *that's* what test audiences responded to?

Clementine sighed. "I guess you're right."

"That will definitely factor in."

"But let's not get ahead of ourselves," Clementine continued. She leaned back, fingers pressed together in front of her stomach. "Give it to us straight, Emmy. How bad is it?"

Emmy paused. A horn blared angrily in the background of her call. "It is . . . not great."

Kate couldn't take the vagueness anymore. "Are you talking about the *DPT* cancellation?"

"Pfft!" Clementine waved a hand on front of her face as if shooing off an annoying gnat. "Nobody cares about *that*."

I do.

"This is about damage control over that video."

Kate winced. She'd been having fun, cutting loose at the wrap party. Literally doing what every single other person at that event was doing—drinking a little too much, getting flirty, feeling invincible. She'd watched Rowan do it a half dozen times, shepherding home her over-partied friend to make sure she didn't do anything stupid. Why was she the only one being punished?

Kate had spent her entire life on the straight and narrow. Her only experiences with alcohol prior to the wrap party had been at Thanksgiving, Christmas, and New Year's when her parents poured her, like, three sips' worth of champagne for toasts, and that one time at her cousin's wedding in Dallas when a groomsman had gotten her a glass of chardonnay while chatting her up until he realized she was only fifteen, at which point he practically pulled a muscle trying to get away from her.

Belle's video had made it look like she was partying at a Jenner-Kardashian level of club kid savviness. Which was not even close to her uncool self.

Maybe things would have been different if Rowan had watched out for Kate instead of disappearing with Dagney for hours.

"I've never done anything like that," Kate blurted out, keenly aware of the silence in the room. "I swear. I'm, like, the nerdiest nerd in Nerdtown."

"I wish that mattered right now," Emmy said, her voice sympathetic through the speaker. "But it doesn't."

She sounded serious, deathly so, and Kate's stomach dropped out from her body, leaving a void quickly filled with a rush of anxiety, fear, and insecurity.

"The internet trolls are blaming Belle's actions on you," Emmy continued. "Calling you the instigator."

As if she had that kind of power over Belle Masterson. "This is so unfair!" Kate fought back the sense of despair threatening to overwhelm her confidence.

"Life ain't fair, sugarplum," Emmy said. "We can't make a story like this go away, but we *can* make it less desirable to the media."

"How?"

"Think of it like turning the volume up on one speaker and down on another. We release another story—something that will grab everyone's attention. It doesn't even have to be salacious, as long as it isn't about you."

"Meanwhile," Clementine said, fanning her hands wide like she was a magician revealing the chosen card to her amazed audience, "you're not so quietly building up some goodwill. Volunteer work at the food bank, meal delivery for the elderly." She snapped her fingers and pointed at the phone. "Emmy, do you still have that contact at the teen girls' shelter?"

Emmy chuckled, impressed. "Good memory. Coco is still at Pink Hope, and they always need volunteers to sort through donations."

"Okay, yeah. Whatever you need me to do." These sounded like the kinds of things Kate should have been doing with her privilege anyway. Though she wasn't sure how Emmy was going to dig up a story as interesting as the BelleDex affair. Would she have to wait for something else to happen? Or did Emmy mean that she'd invent something?

"You're a reputation fixer?" Kate asked tentatively.

"Public image manager," Emmy said. "*Fixer* makes it sound like I'm a hit man."

Which wasn't out of the realm of possibility.

Clementine nodded her head in approval. "See, Emmy? I told you she was a smart kid."

"Very smart," Emmy added. "Now, if we're all in agreement, I'll send over an invoice and get to work."

Clementine made an A-OK signal with her fingers. "Perf."

"The usual monthly should cover this."

Clementine nodded. "Kate, you can make the check out to Emmy directly."

Check? Monthly? Kate hadn't considered that this was going to cost money. She'd kind of assumed it was part of Clementine's service. Isn't that why she got a commission?

"Um, how much?" she asked tentatively.

"Almost nothing," Clementine said, smiling. "Just five."

"Hundred?" Kate hoped more than assumed this was the case.

"Thousand." Emmy's voice cut in sharply through the speaker, as if the implication that her services were worth five hundred dollars a month was insulting. "It shouldn't take more than two or three months to resolve."

Ten to fifteen thousand dollars? Kate didn't have that kind of money. "I . . . I don't think I can—"

"Take it out of your *DPT* earnings," Clementine suggested. "That's, what, an episode and a half? Absolutely worth it to salvage your career."

"And salvage it *quickly*," Emmy added. "Which is key if you want to get out there for pilot season."

Emmy's words caused the knot of fear in Kate's stomach to tighten.

Her five-year plan was crumbling before her eyes. "What does this have to do with auditions?"

Clementine blinked, holding her eyes closed for a dramatic second before reopening. "Well, everything. I can't send you out right now."

"Can't send me out . . ." Kate repeated the words as if they were in a foreign language and she was attempting to decipher their meaning based on phonetics.

"You're tainted," Clementine said. "If not the whole *DPT* cast, then you and Belle at the very least. Without some immediate PR intervention, we're looking at an almost full hibernation for . . ." She leaned closer to the speaker. "What would you say—three months?"

"Four to six." Emmy didn't even hesitate. "But that depends on when Dex's trial begins. If this is still a page-one search result by then, it could be a year or more before people forget about it."

A year or more. All because of Belle.

Belle, who could probably afford to pay for this kind of help, while Kate definitely could not.

"Well?" Clementine prompted. "What do you think?"

"The money's in a trust," Kate blurted out, fighting back tears. "I can't touch it until I'm twenty-one."

"Your parents, then?"

Kate could only imagine the shitticane that would be unleashed if she asked her parents for fifteen thousand dollars while they were already charging her room and board. "No."

Clementine sucked in a breath between clenched teeth. "Oooo. Going to be difficult, then."

"Can't you send me out on anything?" Kate asked. She felt a knee-jerk reaction against begging, but the desperation was making her break out in a sweat and she could feel the back of her thighs sticking to the chair. "Commercials, even? I . . . Maybe I could earn the money that way?"

"Hmm, commercial breakdowns usually call for average-size actresses."

That was the second time in as many minutes that Kate's weight had been brought up. She wanted to scream that she *was* average size in literally anyplace that wasn't Los Angeles, but she knew that wasn't going to help her cause.

"I'm sorry I can't be of more use to you," Emmy said, though Kate wasn't sure if it was directed at her or at Clementine. "Keep me updated, okay?" Then the line went silent.

"Ms. DuBois?" The receptionist's voice crackled through the speaker almost as soon as the call ended. "Your four o'clock is here."

"Kate," Clementine said, standing up. She leaned forward across her desk. "Please reconsider. If there's any way you can afford Emmy's services, you need to do so."

"Um, okay." Sell a kidney, maybe? That was the only avenue that came to mind.

"Excellent." Clementine straightened up and blew Kate a kiss. "Let me know, darling! I await your email with bated breath."

And that was it. Dismissal. Kate hadn't shared even two days of her five-year plan, not that it mattered. Without audition prospects for four to six months, her plan was over before it began. All that hard work and preparation for nothing. Kate hadn't accomplished a single goal she'd set for this meeting.

Except . . .

Kate recalled her conversation with Belle. Though Belle was the last person in the entire world she wanted to help, she *had* promised. At least Kate still had her honor.

"Belle's really sorry," she said, hating herself a little. More than a little. "She's worried that you're mad at her."

"Furious."

You're not the only one. "I think . . . I think she's going through a lot right now and feels very isolated. But she wants to make it up to you."

"Did she ask you to put in a good word? Because that seems like Belle's MO."

"No!" Kate blurted a little too quickly.

"Riiiiight." Clementine lowered herself back into her leather high-backed chair, a queen on her throne. "Then I'm sure she'll have no problem telling me that herself. Have her call me."

EIGHT

KATE'S TREK HOME WAS SIGNIFICANTLY LESS TRIUMPHANT IN mood than her inbound trip, and the quick twenty-minute walk, which an hour ago had flown by in a heartbeat of excited anticipation, was now interminable. She felt every crack, divot, and slope of the decades-old pavement beneath her feet, wishing for at least the dozenth time that she'd worn her Vans instead of these flimsy pieces of crap, and the afternoon sun glared more intensely than it had been earlier, burning off the lingering afternoon clouds that had once sheltered Kate from its late-summer rays.

She felt beads of perspiration dotting her brow and upper lip, and the underwire of her bra slid over damp skin from her underboob sweat, but Kate didn't care. She almost welcomed the added misery in her sucktastic day. Everything that could have gone wrong did go wrong. From the moment Kate walked into Clementine's office, she was off her game. The receptionist saw to that. And once she was face-to-face with her agent, it was clear that Clementine was driving the bus, not Kate.

Was Kate totally out of her mind for thinking she could make it in this business? Her audition had been a lark, her casting either a fluke or a miracle, depending on who you asked, and due to one stupid mistake, her career longevity might be shorter than the lifespan of the common housefly. In the last forty-eight hours, she'd gone from the next Melissa McCarthy to industry pariah. That had to be, like, some kind of record for fastest fall from grace.

I'll see what I can do, Clementine had said. Did that mean some auditions but not all of them? And what would that even look like: One or two a week? One or two a month?

No pilot season. Kate had overheard several of her costars discussing the upcoming pilot season one day while they were in makeup. Their tones had been reverential, quiet voices brimming with excitement as if they were in on some fantastic secret. Liam's agent was planning to send him out on at least six different pilot auditions while Emery's had an inside connection to a big new show at FX. It sounded like some kind of fast lane for young actors, where careers could be made overnight. That's what Kate wanted, what Kate needed, and now Clementine thought she'd be blacklisted unless she came up with fifteen thousand dollars to fix her reputation.

Kate groaned as she turned onto her street. Fifteen grand? There was no way. Her parents were the only people she could ask, and they would laugh in her face, high-five over a couple of *I told you so*s, and then shove a dozen college brochures under her nose.

But maybe they'd give her a moratorium on paying rent? If she just explained the situation in a calm, adultlike manner, maybe she could convince them to give her a few months' reprieve?

It was worth a shot.

Though she was pretty sure it would never work.

Like 99 percent sure.

But she literally had no idea what else she could do. Instinctively, she pulled her phone from her purse and texted Rowan.

Clem wants me to hold off on auditions.

4-6 months! WTF!

Unless I hire this fixer. With money I don't have.

Stressed. Help.

She stared at her phone for three whole blocks before Rowan began typing a response. Not normal for her friend, who almost always responded within nanoseconds. It was after four, which meant she was done with theater camp, and Kate, like, desperately needed to talk to her friend right now. Rowan's energy would help her figure out this problem.

But the response that came wasn't what Kate was hoping for.

Sorry. Going over lines with Jer. Call later?

Jer.

Jer?

As in Jeremiah Nuñez?

As in the most annoying guy in theater class, a person Rowan had literally been complaining about nonstop since the dawn of time?

JER?

She was about to type back and ask Rowan to use her safe word because obviously there was no way in hell she was voluntarily spending time with Jeremiah Nuñez when Kate recalled all the times Rowan had mentioned him in the last couple of months. The downcast eyes when she said his name, even when she was bagging on him. The way Rowan would touch her hair repeatedly while complaining about how annoying he was. Exact actions Kate used as Noelle in episode 105 when she was trying to hide her crush on Sebastian.

Holy shit. Rowan had a thing for Jeremiah Nuñez!

She wanted to know deets but didn't want to fluster her friend, whose already highly strung energy would be denser than a neutron star if she was spending time with a guy she had feelings for, and Kate certainly didn't want to be that asshole friend who only added to the stress. She'd bring it up later. For now, act normal.

Thanks, wifey. Miss you.

Kate turned up her walkway.

Rowan never responded.

The terra-cotta Spanish-style bungalow that Kate had called home for her entire life loomed before her. Well, not physically loomed because the single-story, eleven-hundred-square-foot three-bedroom was by far the smallest house on the block, one of the few unmodified structures left in a neighborhood that had seen a marked increase in teardowns and additions over the last few years. More like psychologically loomed, as it represented a new stress in her life. A three-hundred-dollar-a-month stress.

In reality, the house was cheerful and cozy, an outlier on a street where it had once been the norm. Her mom's prized gladiolas were in the last bloom cycle of the summer, soon to shed their final leaves and wait until the temperatures cooled. Not that it ever really got *cold* cold in Burbank, but gladiolas were, apparently, a delicate flower despite their robust, stalk-like appearance, and her mom babied them through the blazing hot summers, always watering them after the sun had gone down to make sure the stalks achieved maximum absorption.

Those pampered gladiolas had always made Kate smile: They were a sign that she was home, that she was safe, that this little slice of suburban bliss could exist literally blocks from massive media campuses of entertainment industry giants, had always given her a little bit of swagger. The Williamses belonged here. This was Kate's world.

But today, even the yellow-and-white flowers couldn't coax a grin out of Kate. Today all she could think about was how many months of gardening chores it would take for her to pay her parents back fifteen thousand dollars.

As Kate trudged up the paving stones to her front door, her feet prickling with a million needles after her death march in those stupid shoes, she noted that her dad's blue Subaru Forester was parked in the driveway while her mom's RAV4 was gone. The first stroke of luck Kate had had all day. Her dad was certainly the less stubborn parent, and if she could win him over, it would be two against one with her mom.

It was now or never.

"Hey, I'm back!" Kate said as she stepped into the living room, summoning up her most cheerful voice, as if she didn't just come from the worst professional meeting of her short career. She paused, waiting for a response, but the house was silent.

Kate poked her head into the kitchen, which was empty and pristinely clean, no signs of dinner prep anywhere, then headed down the hall, where she knocked on her parents' closed bedroom door. "Dad?"

She waited in the silence, then edged the door open a crack in case her dad was napping. The bed and the room were empty.

Weird. Normally about now, her dad would be starting dinner and her mom grading papers or sorting laundry or organizing the living room, a favorite activity. Despite their small family, the house was always bustling with energy.

Kate wandered toward her bedroom, body tense. What if something was wrong? Belle had mentioned that she was getting death threats. What if some lunatic had shown up at Kate's house while her dad was home, alone, unsuspecting?

She pulled her phone from her bag to call her dad's cell when she spotted a white piece of computer paper taped to her bedroom door. A handwritten note. From her mom.

Katie-Bear,

Your dad and I are going out to eat. Then a movie. We'll be home late. You're on your own for dinner. Not sure what's in the fridge, but you're an adult now, so you'll manage.

And don't forget, rent is due on the first!

Love, Mom

Kate sprawled across her bed, defeated. Date night on a Wednesday? Her parents literally never did that, and when they did go out together on the weekends, a rare occurrence, they'd always leave a meal prepped for her in the fridge, clearly labeled with heating instructions. And then they'd check in on her thirty bazillion times during the course of the evening.

Now she was just getting a note on the door saying she needed to fend for herself. Like she was their roommate, not their daughter.

Maybe that was the point? Part of this new tough-love response to Kate's career plan. And if that was the case, there was no way in hell her parents were going to front her the fifteen grand for a reputation fixer. She'd been an idiot to think she could convince them to help.

The final kick in the teeth. She felt abandoned by everyone: her agent, her best friend, her parents.

I am so fucked.

No auditions, no gigs, no money. She was out of options. Maybe she should give up on this whole stupid dream, give on the first thing she'd ever really wanted, and do what her parents expected. It would be so much easier.

And you'd hate yourself for giving in.

Kate's subconscious was right. Besides, she's wasn't totally without options. There was one person who hadn't let her down today.

Yet.

She grabbed her phone and texted Ty.

That job you mentioned. Still avail?

She wasn't even sure she had the right number, since she hadn't used it in a year, but unlike his sister, Ty responded immediately.

If you can start Monday.

Kate pictured the raised eyebrow and arrogant smile of Ty's I-told-you-so look. As with her mom, it was almost enough for her to double down on her defiance, but when she weighed the two evils against each other—giving in to Ty versus giving in to her parents—this one seemed easier to stomach. She took a deep breath, gritted her teeth, and typed.

I'll take it.

NINE

KATE WAS JUMPY MONDAY AFTERNOON AS SHE DROVE HER dad's Subaru down Alameda Boulevard to the Burbank Garden Towers Business Park, the five-story, two-building commercial real estate compound that housed the offices of Kleiner, Abato & Chen.

Since childhood, long before Kate had a best friend whose dad leased an office there, the complex, which occupied an entire square block, had fascinated her. The curved lines of highly reflective glass windows—so bright in the setting sun that she had to squint against the glare, even while wearing sunglasses—had always looked out of place. Situated between a Mexican restaurant and a car wash, it marked the "almost home" point of most drives. After hours stuck in traffic, crawling home from Orange County to visit her grandparents, they'd pass the Burbank

Garden Towers Business Park, and Kate knew it was just one more stop-light and a left past the library before home.

She'd been to Rowan's dad's law firm plenty of times during their long friendship when Rowan's mom—their designated school carpool driver—was out of town and Kate's parents were still at work. Mr. Chen's assistant would zip over to campus and return with Ty, Rowan, and Kate in tow, and Kate, who hadn't spent as much time in corporate office settings with her academia parents, was always wowed by the U-shaped complex of two identical towers separated by a thin, grassy courtyard and connected at one end by a shared lobby.

An awe-inspiring shared lobby, with its floor-to-ceiling windows and high-tech security desk, always manned by a watchful guard who would smile and nod as they filed past. Rowan merely rolled her eyes, but Kate got a thrill from sitting in the office kitchen doing homework while fancy entertainment lawyers came and went, talking shop as they filled stainless-steel water canisters from the cooler and freshened up their afternoon cold brews.

But that was years ago. Middle school. She'd been a child. Now Kate was going to work like a real adult at a real adult job in order to do real adult things like pay rent and feed herself, and as she pulled into an empty parking spot in the far corner of the underground lot, some-how the Burbank Garden Towers Business Park seemed significantly less glamorous than it had when she was twelve.

She might also have felt, like, a teensy bit of shame. The last time she'd been in that garage, she'd come with her parents to have Mr. Chen's associate look over the contract for the CDB Youth Talent Agency. Kate had been a client then. An entertainment-industry professional. Now she was showing up as the "after-hours file clerk." The stigma of failure was one she couldn't quite shake.

Kate cut the engine but didn't get out of the Subaru. Her heart was beating way faster than it should have been, and her palms felt slick against the steering wheel.

Why are you so nervous?

Was it the job? Filing should be something a relatively well-educated seventeen-year-old like herself could handle.

No, it wasn't the *what*. It was the *who*.

Kate was anxious about seeing Ty again. Other than the awkward meeting in Rowan's bedroom and a quick, logistical text exchange about the job, she hadn't really seen or spoken to him since that summer afternoon over a year ago when he'd showed up at her house and told her that he was in love with her.

It had been easy to put the whole episode out of her mind when Ty wasn't physically there. While he was half a world away in Shanghai, Kate wasn't confronted with Ty's feelings on a daily basis. Rowan, who had no clue what had gone down between her brother and her best friend, would give Kate occasional updates—a photo Ty had taken while hiking, a video of him warbling through some ill-advised karaoke—but Kate never had to contemplate his feelings, or her own.

Occasionally, a pang of regret would bubble up. Ty had always been the voice of reason in her life, the one Kate would go to if she needed parental advice but didn't want to solicit actual parental advice. During those first few weeks on set for *Dirty Pretty Teens*, she'd wanted to text Ty a dozen times when she was feeling anxious or insecure, but she'd always stopped herself. How could she selfishly pretend nothing had happened? They couldn't go back to the way their friendship had been after Kate had literally stomped on his heart. And so she'd stayed quiet.

Time passed. She was busy filming a Netflix show, building her career, expanding her world. The past was the past—best to leave it there.

Which was easier said than done if they'd be working together.

Maybe he'd already be gone for the day? The job title was "after-hours file clerk," and judging by the flow of employees streaming out of the elevator bay and into the underground parking garage, it seemed like this was quitting time. With any luck, she and Ty wouldn't have to meet at all.

She took a shaky breath and slipped out of the car.

Two elevators serviced the parking garage, delivering employees and visitors directly to the shared lobby, and Kate waited for one to empty at the garage level, then rode up by herself. The glass-enclosed, marble-tiled lobby seemed smaller and less grand than she remembered as she stepped up to the security desk.

The guard, an older Latino man in a navy shirt and matching tie, appeared to be packing up for the day when he noticed her signing her name on the visitors' check-in sheet. He flashed her a cheerful smile beneath his bushy, graying mustache. "And who are you visiting today, miss?"

"Kleiner, Abato and Chen," she said, fighting the urge to explain that she was a new employee.

He nodded toward the elevator bay. "I'll scan you up."

Kate felt like a fish swimming upstream as she followed the security guard through the narrow space. They waited until an elevator emptied of employees; then he ushered her inside before flashing his badge in front of a scanner below the car operating panel. He waited for a faint beep, then pushed the button for the third floor.

"Lobby is directly opposite the elevator bay," he said. "Have a nice evening."

"Thank you!" Kate said as the doors closed, mustering up some fake cheer and hoping she didn't sound ungrateful.

She stepped out of the empty elevator onto the third floor and was immediately greeted by the gleaming metallic letters etched onto a glass wall that spelled out KLEINER, ABATO & CHEN. The law firm occupied half of the third floor of the north tower, a huge amount of space, it seemed as she pushed open a glass door and entered the reception area. She knew Rowan lived in a much fancier house, in a much fancier part of town, but for the first time, Kate realized that Rowan's dad must have been more successful in his practice than she'd ever imagined.

Too bad it wasn't Rowan who needed to hire a reputation fixer. Her dad could have easily afforded that fifteen grand.

Like Clementine's office remodel, the Kleiner, Abato & Chen lobby reflected a sleek, modern vibe. Luxe and expensive, and decorated more like a SoHo loft's living room than a law-firm reception area. Black wing-back chairs were arranged in clusters of two or three, each around a short glass table. There was no desk, but a petite white woman in cropped black pants and a fluffy short-sleeved pink sweater sat perched on a barstool by a kitchenette against the far wall. Her dark brown hair had a vintage flip at the ends, and her whole retro vibe was chic and put together, especially in comparison to Kate's faded jeans, Rainbow Brite T-shirt, and matching Vans.

The instant Kate entered, the greeter bounced out of her seat and strode forward, flashing a confident, inviting smile.

"Welcome to KAC," she said, displaying a set of pristinely white and emphatically straight teeth that reminded her of Dex Pratt's smile: too perfect to be real. "Can I offer you a sparkling water? Tea? Biscuit?" Her voice lilted with a refined English accent.

"No, thank you." Kate felt the heat creep into her cheeks as she realized this woman thought she was a client, not a coworker. She was about to explain why she was there when the greeter tilted her head to the side and pointed a casual forefinger at her.

"You look familiar."

Kate involuntarily straightened. A *Dirty Pretty Teens* fan? It was one of her secret little dreams to have someone recognize her on the street, but so far, no luck. "I get that a lot," she lied.

"You've been here before."

"Yes, but—"

"And who is representing you?"

"No one, I mean—"

"Oh, you *haven't* been here before?" the woman asked, clearly confused about why this familiar-looking person would be standing in her lobby.

"I have, but . . . I'm on a Netflix series," Kate said, realizing too late that she sounded apologetic. "That's probably why I look familiar."

The greeter tilted her dainty little head to one side. "Which one?"

"*Dirty Pretty Teens.*"

"I'm sorry, I don't think I've seen it."

Kate's cheeks flushed even hotter, less from embarrassment than shame. Could this day get any worse?

"So how can I help you today?"

"I'm here to see, er, Tyson Chen."

At the mention of Rowan's brother, the greeter's face lit up. "Ty! How delightful."

Ty? That seemed rather casual for the boss's son.

"Wait right here while I fetch him, yes?"

Kate nodded, but the greeter had already flitted over to a phone mounted on the wall beside the kitchenette. She leaned against the counter, crossing one slender ankle over the other as she spoke into the receiver. After a moment of silence, she giggled loudly.

Which sounded a lot like flirting.

"Ty will be right with you," the greeter said, returning the receiver to its cradle.

Kate debated taking a seat or remaining where she was. She was an employee here, not a client, and sitting at one of the glass tables felt like an imposition. But standing there, while the greeter busied herself tidying the kitchenette, was awkward as hell. Maybe she should move to the window and stand there? At least then she'd be able to look out onto the grassy courtyard and pretend to be intently occupied by something happening below.

She was still staring absently at the window when someone emerged through the double glass doors that separated the lobby from the back office and approached the greeter. She giggled again—louder than before—and this time a low male voice joined her. Out of the corner of her eyes, Kate could see that the newcomer was dressed in typical businessman attire—slacks and a button-down shirt with sleeves rolled to the elbow—and he had an air of authority that probably indicated a senior-level associate. She chanced a second look in his direction. His back was turned, and he bent forward slightly as he spoke with the greeter. Kate noted the broad back and strong shoulders beneath the powder-blue shirt. The thin fabric clung to his skin, delineating his muscular frame, like one of those Olympic swimmers whose upper bodies looked like chiseled masterworks of the classical age.

After a few moments of muted conversation with the greeter, which Kate tried to overhear without looking like she was trying to overhear, the man turned. Kate quickly looked away, hoping she hadn't gotten caught ogling, but the man walked right up to her. Kate stiffened, wondering what he wanted and why he was standing so familiarly close, and she was about to say something when he saved her the trouble.

"Are you ready to work, or do you need another minute in your daydream?"

Kate started, turning toward the stranger. "Ty?"

He flicked his sun-streaked hair out of his eyes with a toss of his head. "Who were you expecting?"

Kate desperately tried to suppress the heat that was rising up from her chest to her neck as she realized that the "lawyer" she'd been perving on was a guy she'd known since she was eleven.

Known and rejected. *I think of you like a brother*, she'd told him the night before he left the country, the night he'd finally confessed his feelings for her. As an only child, Kate had no idea what "like a brother" even meant, but it seemed like the thing to say, the thing that would let him down easy. She had feelings for Ty, sure, but he didn't rev her engine.

Except she'd just literally been scoping him out. Like, if he'd been anyone else on the planet and had walked across the lobby to ask her out, she'd have probably said yes in a heartbeat. Kate didn't understand siblings for shit, but she was pretty sure that the current mix of emotions causing her skin to flush was *not* sisterly.

She cleared her throat, forcing her brain to work. "I thought maybe the partners would welcome the lowly new file clerk personally, but oh well. I guess you'll do."

"Almost as good!" the greeter piped up. "Ty's literally the best, plus his father is a partner, so really you're getting red carpet service."

She said *literally* as if the word only had two syllables the way only Brits could but somehow it was the most charming thing Kate had ever heard, and she kind of wanted to shove the greeter out the window.

Ty smiled, dipping his head. "Thanks, Albie. That's very kind of you."

Albie. Even her name was charming.

"But Kate is Rowan's best friend," he continued, his eyes avoiding Kate's face. "And she's like a sister to me."

Ouch.

"That's why I recognized you!" Albie squealed, delighted by the realization. "You're the kid who used to come and do homework with Rowan."

The kid? Kate's eyes drifted from Ty's business attire to Albie's retro chic. She looked like a kid in comparison. Not like an adult coming to do adult things. Not like Ty who easily fit into this world. Kate was just an interloper.

"This way," Ty said, motioning toward the double glass doors that opened onto the rest of the law office. "Let's get you squared away with Human Resources; then I'll show you to the dungeon."

"Thanks." Shit.

Ty was quiet as he led her down an open hallway with window offices on one side and a bullpen of cubicles on the other. As it was after five o'clock, some of the stations were already empty but most of the staff was still at their desks, diligently working at various tasks.

But not *that* diligently. As they passed by, every single person looked up, recognized Ty, and said hello.

Ty stopped near the end of the hall and introduced Kate to a harried Latina with wildly curly brown hair and three-inch-long acrylic nails who was apparently Maria, the head of Human Resources. She had Kate fill out a few forms, checked her ID, and snapped a quick photo of her while Ty quietly waited in the doorway, typing on his phone. Maria seemed more irritated by the added work than interested in who Kate was, but as they left, she smiled warmly at Ty and thanked him for no apparent reason.

Ty was like a rock star in this place.

He moved quickly out of Maria's office, back around the bullpen, and then down a dark empty corridor. Ahead was a clearly marked emergency exit door with the green-lighted sign above it, which probably would have dumped her back near the elevator bay, and to the left was a windowless door with a card scanner mounted beside it on the wall, similar to the one in the elevator. Ty whipped his employee badge from his pocket and flashed it in front of the security pad. A little green light popped on, and then Kate heard a heavy clank, as if a massive piece of metal had slid into place.

Ty wrenched the handle and pulled the door open, smiling at her for the first time. "Welcome to the dungeon."

TEN

KATE HAD IMAGINED A COFFIN-SIZE CLOSET HARDLY BIG enough to house the filing cabinets it was purposed for, maybe with some spare cleaning supplies or discarded lobby decor squirreled into a corner. That would have fit the moniker of *the dungeon*.

She was not expecting SpaceX HQ.

A blast of cold air and roaring machinery hit her the moment Ty opened the door. Even before her brain registered the square footage, the vibrating wall of electronics, or the high-tech filing cabinets that felt more like set pieces out of an Avengers movie than the organizational system of a medium-size law firm, the aggressive air-conditioning and thunderous white noise from two dozen computer servers washed over her like angry ocean waves on a blustery day. Four decks of servers lined the wall to the left of the door, six feet tall, with cage-like front doors that were padlocked to the frame. An array of green, yellow, and red lights flashed from within each cabinet, and Kate wondered why an entertainment law firm would need the technological capacity of NASA.

Running parallel to the wall of servers were three rows of imposing black filing cabinets arranged like library stacks, with lettered stickers to signify which alphabetical range was housed within. She and Ty had to walk single file through the narrow gap between the servers and the first row of cabinets, and their movement triggered massive overhead fluorescent lights, which flooded the space with a stark-white glow, highlighting the enormous size of the dungeon. The cabinets were imposing, and as Kate followed Ty to the far end of the room, she wondered how she was supposed to file in the topmost drawers, which opened at forehead level.

She rounded the row of cabinets and discovered that a huge window spanned the back wall of the dungeon. Well, that was something, at least. She could see the courtyard below and the south tower beyond, its highly reflective glass panes glinting in the afternoon sun. A long table had been pushed up against the window, strewn with loose pages, stapled stacks, and unfiled manila folders, all piled haphazard upon one another as if someone had tossed them at the table from two feet away before racing out of the file room.

Not that Kate blamed them.

This place kinda sucked.

There were no personal details in the dungeon. No stock photographs paired with inspirational sayings hung thoughtfully on the wall. No personal effects or coffee-cup rings or any sign of humanity. Not even a freaking chair, just a step stool pushed under the table, probably to access those top file drawers. This wasn't a break room from which people came and went, or a research room where employees combed through old files, hunting for some long-buried nugget of information that could decide a case. This room was clinical and cold—like, literally cold from the aggressive air-conditioning. Despite its expansive size, she understood exactly why Rowan referred to it as *the dungeon*.

"This is it," Ty practically shouted, his voice muted by the dull roar of cooling fans.

Kate rubbed her bare arms, already puckered with gooseflesh. "Thanks for the heads-up on wardrobe," she grumbled too low for him to hear. She needed to bring a hoodie in the future. Or a parka.

Ty held his white office identification card up to her face. The photo printed on the front was from over a year ago and Ty's smile was small and apologetic. The Ty she remembered. "This room is locked at all times, accessed by your ID badge."

That seemed excessive. Like, whose hospitality rider was worth all this security? "Are you keeping government secrets in here or something?"

Ty looked at her with cold, disinterested eyes. "Kleiner, Abato and Chen has a very exclusive clientele. There are people who would kill to get their hands on some of these files."

"I'm risking my life at this job?" Kate couldn't help teasing him when he looked that serious.

"No."

Ty must have forgotten to pack his sense of humor when he returned from Shanghai.

"Ro said there's no cell service here. Is that true?" she asked.

"Yes."

"What happens if there's an emergency?"

Ty arched an eyebrow. "In the file room?"

"Sure." Kate shrugged. "Like, a fire or, like, if one of these things falls on me."

"They won't." Ty flicked his head toward the door. "But there's a phone on the wall. Direct line to the security desk after hours. That's usually Donald during your shift."

"Seems safe."

Ty ignored her, turning to face the rows of file cabinets. "The i-Line two thousand," he said, his tone reverential. "Gypsum-insulated walls and drawers reinforced with fourteen-gauge welded steel wire, high-security drill-and-pick-proof locks, these are impact-, explosion-, and waterproof, and fire resistant up to seventeen hundred degrees."

How would they even test that? "So they'd survive on the surface of the sun."

Ty wrinkled his lips, annoyed that she was unimpressed. *This* was the Ty she knew—a guy who could recite the specs for a filing cabinet as lovingly as if they were a Shakespearean sonnet but who had never actually read a Shakespearean sonnet. He was like the left-brained version of her dad, and it was too easy to push his buttons.

"No," he said, taking her joke at face value, "but you could fire a gun in here and not damage the files inside."

"Good to know." Kate tucked that fact nugget away under "shit she'd never have to worry about" but refrained from more snarky comments.

For now.

"Like the door, these cabinets are kept locked at all times." Ty fished a silver ring out of his pocket with a dozen little keys dangling from it, all neatly numbered. "This is my set. Each of the partners has one, and me. That's it."

"What are they going to do when you leave for Stanford?"

Again, he ignored her. It was as if he'd practiced a script to introduce her to the job and refused to deviate from it. "These live in the top right drawer in my desk. You need to return them there before you leave at night."

"Sure." Which also implied she'd need to pick them up from Ty's desk when she arrived. Kate made a mental note to get to work later tomorrow. After Ty had left.

"Maria will request your ID badge. Pick it up at the security desk on your way in tomorrow."

"Okay."

"You'll need it to access the elevator, the main office doors if they're closed, and the dungeon."

"You enjoy calling it that, don't you?"

Despite his all-business demeanor, Ty half smiled and suddenly looked more like the boy she remembered than this weird corporate proto-adult he'd become.

But the glimpse of old Ty was short-lived. His eyes met hers, and Kate saw a flash of something cross his face. Sadness? Regret? She wasn't sure. It only lasted an instant before he cleared his throat, assuming his impassive business persona once more.

"That's it," he said, turning toward the door. "I probably won't be around much when you're here. I usually leave by six."

"Um, Ty?"

He stopped mid-stride, his body tense. "No more jokes, Kate. I have work to do."

She was ashamed of how nice it felt to hear him say her name. "You haven't actually shown me what I'm supposed to do."

Ty sighed in annoyance, though Kate wasn't sure if it was at her or at himself, then jutted his thumb toward the window. "The table is the staging ground. People will leave files there throughout the day as they're done with them. By six o'clock, it's pretty imposing."

They were files. How bad could it be? "I'll take your word for it."

"Whole files you can slot back in, alphabetically by client name. Loose pages need to be added to their respective folder." He pointed to a two-hole punch and staple remover at one end of the table. "Unstaple, hole-punch, file on top. Think you can handle it?"

The question was insulting. A well-trained Labrador retriever could do this job. "Um, yeah."

"Great." He turned toward the door again, and this time, he kept his eyes downcast, clearly avoiding her. "I'll check back in an hour."

* * *

It was one long-ass hour. Like, maybe the longest of Kate's life? She wasn't sure. Time seemed to stop inside the dungeon, cut off from the rest of humanity and surrounded by nothing but whirring machines, oppressive lights, and thick, heavy file cabinets.

And paper cuts. So many paper cuts. She was pretty sure her blood was now permanently smeared across the profit-participation agreement between Seth Rogen and some production company called Chuckle Monkey Films.

Ty hadn't undersold the imposing chaos of her job. The sheer number of loose pages and the vastness of the filing system made for slow progress, and by six thirty, she'd only made a dent. The process of hole punching, opening brads, slotting the pages in, then refiling the whole thing was monotonous. Worse, there wasn't enough juicy information to make the monotony worth it. Instead of spicy divorce filings and outrageous contract perks, most of the files had to do with property holdings, corporate name changes, and loan-out formations.

Even the names of the clients were a disappointment. Ty bragged that Kleiner, Abato & Chen had A-list clientele, but aside from Seth Rogen, she didn't recognize anyone else. There were no folders for Charlize Theron or Michael B. Jordan. Just the anonymous names of loan-out companies. Winsome Losesome Inc., Four-Cornered Hat Productions, Purple Pineapple LLC. She probably could have googled them to find out the celebrity behind the corporation, but as Rowan had promised, there was almost no reception in the dungeon. She'd managed to find a fleeting bar by climbing up on the table and waving her phone around, but it hadn't remained long enough to fire off a single text.

While up there, searching for a signal, Kate noticed two domed security cameras affixed to the ceiling adjacent to the window. Turning, she found two more in the back of the room—one even mounted right above the door. More security for the most boring place on the planet. Sheesh.

She was going to need to find some way to make this job exciting or she'd lose her mind by the end of the week.

A few times, the cell signal must have been strong and unwavering because Kate's phone would vibrate on the table, over and over as several messages all came in at once. Rowan had checked in twice and included multiple references to Jeremiah. Kate had smiled, recognizing that special new-crush excitement in her friend's words, and texted back a glittery heart of encouragement that didn't get delivered before the signal fizzled out.

Kate's parents had also checked in. First her dad with a little rah-rah speech that he punctuated with a quote from *Henry V* and then her mom, who reminded her that rent was due soon.

"Thanks, Mom," she said out loud to nobody in particular. "Always so charming when I—"

"How's it going?"

Kate shrieked and jumped away from the table, crashing into the corner of a file cabinet. That reinforced fourteen-gauge welded steel wire hardly budged, but it did knock the wind out of her.

She doubled over, gasping. Ty's hand was on her back in an instant. "Kate! Kate, are you okay?"

"Yeah," she croaked, her voice barely a whisper.

"I thought you heard me when you made a joke about my charm."

She took a deep breath, happy to have full function of her lungs again, and straightened up. "I was talking . . . to myself."

"You're okay?" Ty repeated.

She looked up, catching his eyes. There was no challenge in them, only genuine concern. She liked this face so much better than the facade of indifference he'd had on display since she arrived.

"I missed you," she blurted out between ragged breaths. *Holy shit, did you just say that?*

Ty's poker face reappeared in a heartbeat. "I didn't get that impression, considering I never heard from you once while I was gone."

Kate cringed. "I'm sorry."

"Don't be." He jumped on her apology, interrupting before she'd even finished her last syllable, like he didn't want to hear it.

"But—"

Ty's face had tensed, his eyes dark and hard as he quickly turned his back on her. "I'll check your work tomorrow. Good night."

The door slammed shut behind him before she could say another word.

ELEVEN

"HOW'D IT GO?" ROWAN ASKED AS SOON AS SHE PICKED UP Kate's video call. It was a rarity for Kate to call her best friend—she was a texter; Rowan was the one who usually followed up with the face-to-face chat—but after a depressing first day of work, she needed to leech some of Rowan's cheerfulness before she went home and faced her parents.

Despite the late hour, Rowan was still in the theater at school, Kate could tell by the booming echo that accompanied her voice, and judging by the ropes and pulleys framing her face, she was sitting backstage.

"Fine," Kate lied. "The work is pretty easy, and it's nice to have some time alone."

"Are you still in the parking lot?"

"Yeah."

"Hiding from your parents?"

Kate sighed. If the not-particularly-observant Rowan could read her mood, her parents certainly wouldn't be fooled by a plastered-on smile and some bullshit words about "fulfilling work." She was about to change the subject and ask Rowan how camp was going, when her friend giggled, and Kate realized that Rowan wasn't alone in the theater.

"Hey, Jeremiah."

A head of curly black hair pushed into the camera field as Jeremiah pressed his cheek against Rowan's. He smiled, exposing cavernous dimples in his brown cheeks, and winked at the camera. "Hey, Kate."

Rowan giggled again. "We're working on a scene."

"Uh-huh." A make-out scene.

"Rowan's kinda busy right now," Jeremiah said. "Can she, uh, call you back later? *Much* later."

Ew.

"Jer!" Rowan said, her mouth agape with mock horror. Kate could tell by her smile that she was relishing his attention. "Hoes before bros."

"It's okay," Kate said quickly. A front-row seat for their flirtation was not going to help her mood. Besides, Rowan looked genuinely happy with Jeremiah, however weird their relationship seemed to Kate, and she didn't want to intrude. She pressed her index and middle finger to her lips, then quickly flashed them to the camera. "I'll talk to you later."

She ended the call before Rowan could protest.

Kate sighed. She was sitting alone in a parking lot, unwilling to go home and with no one to talk to while her best friend made out with a guy she used to loathe.

It was all a little depressing.

Kate wasn't sure why she was so saddened by the realization that

Rowan's relationship with Jeremiah Nuñez had progressed to the point where they were getting hot and heavy in the theater after rehearsals. It wasn't the first time Rowan had made out with a guy backstage. There had been Armand the French exchange student and Steve, both crew members in *Once on This Island* sophomore year; Trenton, the assistant stage manager for *Radium Girls* last fall; and then hot senior baseball star Christakis, who had been Rowan's scene partner in drama class the semester before he graduated. Kate was almost jealous of that one.

The difference between those guys and Jeremiah was that Rowan had shared her crushes with Kate beforehand and then painfully walked her through every detail of every encounter when they finally hooked up. With Jeremiah, Kate was deciphering Rowan's feelings after the fact, and she wondered if her friend's secrecy meant that they were drifting apart, or merely that Rowan's feelings were real this time.

Kate squeezed her phone like it was a bulging-eyed stress doll as her sadness morphed into annoyance. There was more to her mood than anxiety over the health of their friendship or the emptiness of potentially losing her friend to a guy. Kate was jealous.

Not over Jeremiah.

Um, no.

Kate was jealous that Rowan got to spend her time after camp fucking around in the theater, flirting with guys, not worrying about paying rent or her professional reputation or disappointing her agent. Meanwhile, Kate had all of those real, tangible stresses weighing her down. She could feel her shoulders tightening up at the mere thought of Clementine and Emmy, and she quickly checked her notifications, hoping she had something, anything, from her agent. A missed call, a text, a ping from Actors Access signaling an upcoming audition.

No such luck, of course. Especially not at half past eight on a Monday night. Only in movies did the heroine receive a glimmer of hope at her darkest hour. The real world didn't work that way.

Kate sighed, dropping her phone to her lap. The real world was bills and rent and work stress. But this is what she wanted, wasn't it? This is what she'd signed up for.

Senior year might not be so bad . . .

Kate's phone buzzed.

Her heart thumped in her chest. Maybe this actually was her dark-night-of-the-soul movie moment when the heroine thinks that all hope is lost and she only has herself to rely upon. Then, in her hour of need, a timely text from an ally! Clementine messaging about a new audition, the surprise role that would reestablish Kate's fledgling career.

Maybe real life was more like the movies after all?

Except, no.

Kate had a text all right. From Belle Masterson.

Did you talk to Clem?

Kate gritted her teeth. Belle was the last person she wanted to hear from right now. Though maybe she could shed some light on the situation with Emmy? Belle had been around the business since childhood. She might know something about public-image managers. Kate swallowed her distaste and typed.

Yep. She suggested I hold off on auditions for a few months and recommended a reputation fixer.

Someone named Emmy. Do you know her?

Belle's response was instantaneous.

What did Clem say about me?

Why for even one fraction of a second would Kate have believed that Belle was interested in anyone other than herself? She needed to stop falling into Belle's traps. The girl was a toxic energy vampire.

Kate fired off a response, more blunt than usual in her escalating irritation.

She asked if you put me up to it and when I said no she just said you should call her.

A pause. That wasn't the answer Belle was hoping for.

Oh. Okay.

Kate waited for something more—an explanation, opening up about what was going on with her and Dex, a thank-you. Instead, Kate's phone fell silent.

Belle was done with her.

"Good riddance." Kate started the engine and backed out of her parking spot. The only positive in the cancellation of *Dirty Pretty Teens* was that she'd never have to see Belle Masterson again.

* * *

It was ten o'clock the next morning before Kate wandered into the kitchen to scrounge up some breakfast. She'd been in a funk by the time she'd gotten home from work, and it had taken her a couple of hours to fall asleep. Even then, it had been a restless night with a lot of tossing and turning, and at least one nightmare where Kate was locked in a meat freezer with Darth Vader, whose mechanical breathing reverberated off the metal walls as he chased her among hanging pig carcasses.

She'd slept through her eight o'clock alarm, silencing it without ever fully waking up, as well as two calendar reminders to check in with Clementine about possible auditions. She saw the muted notifications when she finally peeled her eyes open, but instead of dashing off a quick email to her agent, she left her phone on the nightstand. She couldn't face her new adult life without some coffee in hand.

"Morning, Katie-Bear!" Her dad's chipper baritone boomed ten times louder than usual, as if he was working hard to present a cheerful facade. He sat at the breakfast table, empty coffee mug and a plate full of crumbs pushed to one side as he worked on the most recent *New York Times* crossword puzzle he'd printed out from the website. His morning ritual, even on his days off.

"Hey, Dad," she said, stifling a yawn. His energy was usually infectious, but Kate felt lethargic.

"How was work last night?"

"Fine." She shrugged. "It's not particularly challenging."

She half expected him to say something like "Certainly less interesting than Columbia!" or "Are you sure this is worth throwing your future away?" but he didn't. Instead, her dad nodded in sympathy.

"I've had those jobs."

She vividly remembered her dad's tales of delivering ice and peddling herbal supplements in a pyramid scheme as he tried to make it as an actor in New York after college. "So I've heard."

Kate opened the cupboard where the usual array of pod coffee was stashed, but instead of open boxes, stacked by coffee type, she found that all of the pod boxes had been taped shut. Across the tape, written in black Sharpie, were her parents' names: MACK/ANDREA.

Okay, weird. Were they trying to keep track of how much caffeine they were drinking? Seemed like the kind of health fad middle-aged people might be into. She didn't feel like asking, but regular drip coffee was fine with her. Kate opened the next cupboard, where the bags of ground coffee were kept, and noticed that they, too, had been taped shut and labeled with her parents' names.

Kate pushed the coffee bags aside. Behind them, the boxes of cereal, instant oatmeal packets, and granola bars had all been given the same treatment. And almost every item in the refrigerator, from the milk to Sunday night's leftover meat loaf to every single condiment bottle shoved into the bins on the inside of the door.

Her parents had claimed ownership of every piece of food in the house. Like roommates.

"Seriously?"

Her dad didn't look up from his crossword. "Your mom thought you should be responsible for feeding yourself."

"I haven't started paying rent yet!"

Her dad shrugged, abdicating control of the situation to his absent wife.

"When was I supposed to have time to go grocery shopping?" Kate said, hands on her hips. Not that she had any money, but that was beside the point.

Her dad sighed, then put down his pencil and turned to face her. "Just make some coffee and breakfast, and we'll deal with it later."

"Thanks, Dad." Kate smiled, but she was still pissed off. She understood that this was simply one more hurdle her mom was throwing in her path, hoping that Kate would take the easy road and give up on her career plans, but Andrea Williams hadn't accounted for her daughter's inherent stubbornness. Stubbornness she'd learned from her mother.

Kate wouldn't give up without a fight.

And she was ready for a pitched battle.

Right after she had some coffee.

"Soooo," her dad began as Kate waited for her sourdough toast to pop up. "How are you feeling about . . . stuff?"

She arched an eyebrow. "Stuff?"

"Yeah."

"Like my parents charging me rent and possessively labeling all the food in the house?"

He pushed his unfinished crossword puzzle away, which meant he was expecting a prolonged conversation. "No, like your show being canceled. And that video. Emilia said there are a lot of awful comments about you online. A lot of . . . comments about your appearance."

Of course Aunt Emilia was all over this fiasco. And of course she'd gossiped to Kate's parents about it. Sometimes, having a superfan in the family was a pain in the ass. "The fat-shamers can die slow painful deaths," she said, pursing her lips. She was used to them. Being blamed for the actions of a statutory rapist? Not so much. "But I think it's unfair to treat Belle or me as the villain."

As much as she had grown to resent Belle, the truth was undeniable. Belle wasn't the bad guy in this story. Dex was responsible for getting the show canceled and now a lot of people like Marielle, who thought she had a makeup gig lined up for the next few months, were suddenly out of work. All because another white privileged douchebag thought he could do whatever the hell he wanted with no consequences. Wasn't society supposed to be beyond that?

"And I feel for all the people on our show who lost their jobs."

"That's very noble of you," he said. "I hope they find something. Those that deserve it."

Those that deserve it? She thought of the hardworking crew, the grips and assistants and PAs whose names Kate had never even learned. They all lived gig to gig, and from what she could tell from the off-set chatter, lining up the next job was a constant source of stress for many of them. "They weren't all like Dex Pratt," she said. "There were a lot of good people."

"Good people who apparently knew Dex was having an inappropriate relationship with an underage girl," he argued, his volume rising. "Yet said nothing."

He was angry. Mack Williams rarely got angry.

"Belle didn't have a guardian on set," Kate said, feeling the need to defend her cast and crew. "She's legal eighteen, so it wasn't required."

"Maybe not required, but she clearly needed someone to look out for her."

"We all saw her flirting with him," Kate said, slowly buttering her sourdough. "We should have said something." She paused. "*I* should have said something."

Her dad passed a hand over his thinning hair and cleared his throat. "'The dram of evil/Doth all the noble substance of a doubt/To his own scandal.'"

"Easy." The dram-of-evil speech was one of her dad's favorites. "*Hamlet*, act one, scene four."

"Easy but fitting," her dad said. "Hamlet's saying that even a tiny bit of evil can ruin a person."

"So I'm ruined now?" Kate was irritated by this game. "Tainted by the industry? Morally suspect because I didn't tell Dex to keep it in his pants?"

"I'm saying that perhaps the other adults involved kept quiet because they were so used to this kind of behavior that it didn't seem wrong."

Kate remembered how Marielle and Belle's makeup artist, Bradley, would meet eyes in the mirror and smirk at each other when Belle was droning on about the wonderful Dex Pratt. It was a knowing look, one filled with history and subtext. Had they worked on one of his shows before and seen this exact pattern play out? And if so, how many times had they gossiped and rolled eyes and never said a single word?

"I'm not saying that you've been ruined by the dram of evil," her dad continued in a gentler tone. "I'm saying that the industry can be vile."

While she appreciated his point, Kate couldn't ignore the hypocrisy. "A vile industry that you desperately wanted to be a part of."

Her dad winced, visibly pained by the reminder. "That was different."

"How?" He'd been an amateur player at Columbia, taken a year away from school for his internship with the Public Theater, then after graduation, he'd stayed in New York to pursue acting lessons. He had headshots and went out on auditions, the whole nine yards. It seemed myopic of her dad not to recognize the same drive in his own daughter. "Because you wanted it, while I just fell into acting?"

"No, because I was an adult. With a college degree."

Kate threw back her head in frustration. "Which I don't need! I already have an agent and a résumé. Your Columbia degree didn't help you get either."

"My Columbia degree helped me get into grad school and find a decent career when acting didn't pan out," he said calmly. His voice was measured, tone even, but he was working hard to keep his emotions in check. Kate wasn't sure if those were feelings of anger or regret.

"I'm not going to need it, Dad." Kate grabbed her empty plate and coffee mug, and pushed her chair away from the table. "I've already got the career I want."

Kate's words hung in the air as her dad shrugged and silently returned to his crossword puzzle. She was working as a filing clerk and paying rent to live in her childhood bedroom. Was this really what she wanted?

And if not, then what the hell was she going to do with her life?

Kate trudged back to her bedroom, defeated. She'd finally found the one thing in the world that spoke to the kernel of her being. The one thing that brought joy and excitement and a satisfaction that for once she was actually good at something other than reading and regurgitating, yet it felt as if everyone in her world was actively working against her pursuit of happiness. And she wondered how long it would be before she gave up, climbed back into her cave of obscurity, and let the light inside her soul peter out.

TWELVE

KATE ARRIVED AT KLEINER, ABATO & CHEN AT A QUARTER past six that evening, fifteen minutes *after* Ty usually left for the day.

The shame Kate had felt when Ty called out her lack of communication over the last year had devolved into anger. How dare he act so superior after his time away, like he'd come back an actual adult, all of his high school insecurities forgotten? As if. People didn't shed their skins overnight like a rattlesnake and become a totally different person. It was easy to play grown-up when it was only going to last three more weeks.

For Ty, a month-long job at Daddy's law firm was just a speed bump on his return trip to being a student, and he had an entire network of people supporting his choices. For Kate, this part-time job was the beginning of her adult life, the launchpad for her career, and unlike Ty, she was doing it without the blessing—or financial support—of her parents. Which of them was more of an adult?

Between her anger at Ty and the confrontation with her dad, Kate was in a shitty mood when she reached the security desk in the lobby, and was met by an equally sour expression from the white twentysomething security guard with hollow brown eyes and scattered acne whose name tag read DONALD.

"Can I help you?" he barked, implying that help was the last thing he was offering.

"My name is Kate Williams, and I'm supposed to pick up a security badge for Kleiner, Abato and Chen."

He snorted, lips curved into a cruel half smile. "You know that's a law firm not a doughnut shop, right?"

Seriously? Kate had heard better fat jokes on the playground in fourth grade. She wanted to point out that, yes, it was a law firm at which she was employed in a job that required at least a modicum of education and intelligence, unlike, apparently, working the late-night security desk at a sleepy Burbank office building, but decided that pissing off the guy who would answer the phone if there was an emergency in the dungeon was probably not the smartest move.

"Yes," she said through gritted teeth.

His grin widened, clearly pleased that he'd scored one off an overweight teenage girl; then Donald grabbed her ID from an unseen drawer and tossed it on the desk in front of her. "Badge is only good for the third floor, north tower," he said, eyeing her closely. "No snack bar up there."

Fuck you. Kate silently palmed her ID badge and trudged to the elevator bay. Okay, Donald was a dickhead. Good to know.

Adding to her evening's frustration, Ty was lingering in the Kleiner, Abato & Chen lobby when Kate arrived on the third floor.

So much for leaving at six.

He leaned against the wall beside Albie, who was all packed up to leave. Ty's hands were shoved into the pockets of his gray slacks, his eyes fixed on the greeter's face as he spoke, and she was utterly transfixed by whatever story he was telling. Albie's dainty hands were clasped in front of her, pink lips parted with an inviting smile, and she leaned forward ever so slightly, as if willing her body to be closer to his.

Ty never looked in Kate's direction as she entered, and though his voice was too low for her to overhear, his story must have come to a climax because Albie's jingling laugh danced through the lobby, her head thrown back in abject delight.

"Ty, that's amazing!" she said, lightly touching his arm.

Ty smiled. "You're sweet."

A pang of something like regret tugged at Kate's stomach, which tightened as she crossed the lobby. There was a time when Ty and Kate would have chatted like that, a time when Kate's hearty guffaw would have replaced Albie's bell-like giggle, and though she was loath to admit it, Kate missed the comfort of their old friendship.

She slipped silently through the double glass doors into the office, casting off whatever weird feelings that lobby flirtation had ignited as she trotted toward Ty's cubicle to retrieve the file cabinet keys. The sooner she was locked away in the dungeon, the better.

How sad was that?

"Wait up!" Ty called, jogging up behind her.

Shit.

Kate desperately wanted to avoid a rehash of yesterday's argument. "I know where your keys are." She grabbed them from his desk drawer and turned away, heading down the hall.

"Can you stop for a minute?"

She pretended she didn't hear him, lengthening her stride as she rounded the corner toward the dungeon, but his heavy footsteps followed her to the security door.

"Kate!"

"What?"

"Why are you running away from me?"

Her cheeks burned. "I'm not running away from you."

"I need to talk to you." His breaths came quickly, and his face was flushed. Kate wasn't sure if that was the result of chasing her down the hallway or the lingering effect of his conversation with Albie.

"I have a lot of work to do."

Ty rolled his eyes. "You haven't even been inside yet."

Can't you take a hint? "If you're going to rehash yesterday—"

"I just want to apologize for what I said last night."

"Oh." That was unexpected.

"It was utterly unprofessional to have that conversation in the workplace, and I hope I didn't make you feel uncomfortable." He sounded like a lawyer already, his tone even and cool, and despite his apologetic message, his face was a mask of indifference. "I've already reported the incident to Maria in HR, so if you'd like to file a report, please feel free to contact her."

File a report? Had Ty been replaced by an android while he was in Shanghai? "Ty, you're, like, one of my oldest friends. I'm not going to file an HR complaint against you."

He twitched at the mention of their friendship, but his professional demeanor only slipped for that fraction of a second. "Regardless of our past relationship, it is your prerogative as an employee of Kleiner, Abato and Chen to feel secure in your work environment and—"

"Stop!" She wanted to take Ty by the shoulders and shake him until this robot vanished and her old friend reappeared. "Are you listening to yourself right now? Who even are you?"

"The same person I've always been."

"No, you're not. You're, like, some businessman android."

He stiffened, his formal attitude morphing into annoyance. "It's called professionalism."

"It's called douchebaggery."

"That's inappropriate language for the workplace."

This was too much. "Ty, I've heard you use that exact word, like, a billion times. What the hell happened to you in Shanghai?"

"I grew up!"

The words exploded out of him, his anger finally breaking through the carefully constructed business facade, and though Kate didn't appreciate the implication that she, a seasoned working actress, was *not* grown up, she had to smile at his outburst. Anger was a hell of a lot better than indifference.

"Sure you did." She grinned as she scanned her badge against the security pad.

"You're impossible!" he cried, exasperated. "'Kate the curst.'"

The light on the scanner pad switched to green, but Kate didn't open the door. She'd known Ty since he was thirteen years old and not once in that entire time had he ever quoted even a line of Shakespeare. He'd complained bitterly about reading the Bard in English classes and generally viewed Shakespeare as a cross he had to bear. Since when did he start reading *The Taming of the Shrew*, the play after which her parents took her first name, let alone quote it?

"'If I be waspish,'" she said, throwing a quote right back at him as she pressed her card to the security scanner again, "'best beware my sting.'"

Then she whipped the door open and escaped into the dungeon.

Ty didn't follow her.

Which was probably a good thing.

Kate wasn't sure what was going on in her head surrounding Ty. He'd been casual and charming while flirting with Albie in the lobby, a side of him that kind of intrigued her, but around Kate, he was either distant and overly formal, or just plain pissed off. Which made her sad.

Not that she blamed him for his anger—she'd not only broken his heart, but she'd been flippantly casual about it. Condescending, if she was being honest with herself. The truth was that Kate didn't have a lot of experience with guys who expressed romantic feelings for her, and she'd indulged in the power of the moment, like a queen with too many suitors who could wave them off without a thought to their feelings.

But Ty wasn't just some random guy who'd asked her out; he was a friend. A good friend. A *cherished* friend. Someone that Kate had come to rely upon, and she didn't realize how badly she missed that friend until he was gone.

Kate shook herself, physically casting Ty out of her mind. She needed a distraction from these confusing emotions, and thankfully, the sorting table offered it.

Folders were piled on top of each other, loose pages were strewn haphazardly as if someone had launched them like Frisbees in the general direction of the table. Several large stacks of pages, practically a ream's worth of paper all neatly collated with oversize binder clips, hadn't been hole-punched yet. That job alone would take an hour.

She got to work, starting with all the loose pages, which she sorted into alphabetical piles: more nebulously named companies like Harpy Hour Inc. and Awful Cyborg Productions, which sounded as if someone had come up with the corporate entity by googling synonyms for the two parts of J. J. Abrams's Bad Robot Productions.

Or maybe it was an offshoot of Bad Robot? Kate scanned through the documents, looking for any mention of the director's name. No luck. Awful Cyborg seemed to be an animation company focused on children's programming with a first-look deal at Warner Bros. It was kind of fun theorizing about who and what these companies were, and she felt like an entertainment industry sleuth as she thumbed through the Awful Cyborg file. Right at the bottom of the file was the very first document, a client services agreement for Kleiner, Abato & Chen, and she could read the counter-signature clear as day: *J. J. Abrams.*

Damn, I'm good. She smiled at her success and wondered who else had files in these drawers. Blumhouse? Monkeypaw? Hello Sunshine? Royal Ties?

Kate stiffened as names closer to home popped into her head—what about Dex Pratt or Belle Masterson?

She eyed the nearest security camera, wondering if anyone actually monitored the footage. Though she knew snooping around for details on Dex and Belle was ethically cloudy, she wasn't a lawyer, and who was going to find out?

The Ms and Ps were directly across from each other in the middle aisle of file cabinets, and Kate was simultaneously relieved and disappointed that neither name had a file at Kleiner, Abato & Chen. At least the firm wouldn't be dragged into the impending criminal trial, but Kate sighed as she pushed the Pl–Py drawer back into place.

What exactly had she been expecting to learn? Evidence that Dex had done this kind of thing before? Unlikely. Information that Belle's career was suffering as badly as Kate's? Too soon. Some rationale of how this happened in the first place?

Maybe.

Her dad was right. Belle's affair with Dex should never have happened.

Belle's mom or some other designated guardian should have been on set with her, legal eighteen or not. Kate remembered Belle returning to her Star Waggon alone between scenes, unlike Kate, who would be whisked away to the school trailer as soon as she had even the smallest break. Kate had her set teacher and the social welfare officer looking out for her, making sure no one took advantage of her, personally or professionally. Belle had no one.

Maybe that was when Dex first made his move. He wielded a powerful magnetism that even Kate couldn't ignore—someone like Belle, who was drawn to power because it made her feel more important, would be defenseless against him.

Would the same thing happen to Kate? If she ever got another audition and managed to book a role, would she also fall prey to men like Dex Pratt? Kate liked to think that she was savvy enough, and tough enough, to fend for herself, but deep down she wasn't sure she was either. She'd allowed Dex that uncomfortably long hug last spring. That wasn't the action of someone who felt strong enough to say no.

Maybe she wasn't ready to navigate this world. She could always start back at Burbank High in a few weeks and finish with her peers, go to college somewhere with an acting program, and then start her career later. It wouldn't be such a bad thing, would it?

As if in response to her thoughts of giving up, the edge of a file folder sliced into her index finger.

"Damn it!" she cried, pressing the edges of the cut together to keep it from gushing. The only thing worse than a paper cut was a manila folder cut. Deeper and wider, and the moment Kate let up the pressure, blood flooded through the gash. Three heavy drops cascaded down the side of her finger and onto the table.

Tapping her back pocket to make sure she had her precious ID badge,

Kate hurried out of the dungeon to the ladies' room. She winced as she washed her finger, the icy-cold water stinging her flesh like she was pouring salt into the wound. She didn't have a bandage, so after dabbing away reddish-orange droplets of blood mixed with water, she unrolled a long line of toilet paper. Coiling it around finger, she was able to tie off a makeshift bandage.

Her finger throbbed beneath the pressure of her dressing. It was going to slow down her filing, but at least she wouldn't get blood all over the files. Again.

It was going to be a long night.

Kate was beginning to feel like the entire universe was telling her to quit and go back to school, when her phone buzzed.

Rowan, Kate thought with a smile. Communication between the two of them had been sporadic of late, and Kate missed her friend's infectious energy.

But when she slipped the phone out of her pocket, Kate saw that the notification wasn't from a call or text, but an email.

From Clementine.

Audition Friday morning, Fox lot. Indie feature. Sides coming soon!

THIRTEEN

CLEMENTINE'S EMAIL REENERGIZED KATE—HER THROBBING finger all but forgotten—and she returned to the dungeon even more determined to clear off the sorting table before she went home for the night.

Unfortunately, by nine thirty, that goal felt unobtainable. It was so late that the cleaning crews were going through the offices, vacuuming and dumping trash. No one came into the dungeon, of course, but through her window, Kate had seen them working across the courtyard in the south tower.

That probably meant everyone else had gone home for the night, while she'd only cleared half the clutter off the table. Her ratty bandage made sorting pages much more challenging, but it was the stack of un-hole-punched pages that turned out to be her undoing, a series of trial transcriptions that were all for one client, so in addition to the tedious task of hole punching the entire stack in small batches, she had to start two more file folders to contain them all.

Ty hadn't gone over that particular task with her. If she'd been in a regular part of the office with regular cell coverage, she might have texted him to ask the protocol on adding folders to an existing client's file, but she was in a concrete-lined, fireproof, soundproof bomb shelter, without any connection to the outside world other than a landline that dialed straight down to the dickhead security guard and the window that afforded her a boring view of the empty offices next door. So instead of asking, Kate riffled through the giant file cabinets until she found another client with enough paperwork to cause a spillover.

Said file was right at the front of the Ms and was only labeled with the initials M.E., which sounded like code. A celebrity's name? A well-known production company? The title of a famous movie? Another little mystery that needed solving, and while Kate went through the tedious task of adding new folders to the other file, she played a game, trying to guess what M.E. might stand for.

Mike Epps? He definitely had a long enough career to warrant a huge file at Kleiner, Abato & Chen.

Max Ehrich? Barf. Since he broke up with Demi, no thank you.

M. C. Escher? Yeah, that made absolutely no sense. She was pretty sure the artist had been dead since before Mr. Chen was born and why would they need to obscure his identity with initials?

Missy Elliott?

Kate sucked in a sharp breath. Missy Elliott was like her chubby-girl alter ego, a woman who displayed the kind of confidence in her body shape and size Kate could only hope for. "Lose Control" was the song

Kate played when she needed a boost of confidence, and singing along always helped Kate hold her head a little higher. She'd probably die from excitement if freaking Misdemeanor walked out from an appointment while Kate was arriving for work.

Okay, now she had to know who it was before she exploded. Security cameras in mind, she tried to look casual as she perved through the M.E. folder, hoping to find a hint to their identity, but the files inside were as anonymous and nondescript as the client's name, just a series of invoices, first *to* Kleiner, Abato & Chen for "client services" and then later *from* the law firm, as if M.E. had switched from vendor to client.

Kate seriously doubted whether Mike Epps, Max Ehrlich, M. C. Escher, or Missy Elliott would have been vendors for a law firm. So much for her powers of deduction.

Time passed even more slowly, now that she had nothing else to think about. By a quarter past ten, she was hungry. And bored. But at least she'd made progress. Judging by the stack of transcripts left to hole-punch, she had maybe another half hour of work ahead of her. She'd set up a little assembly line of pages, hole puncher, and prepped folders for the new material, and discovered that she could sit cross-legged on the table and still have room to work.

Which was good because her back was killing her.

Adulting kinda sucked.

Sitting on the table also gave her a streamlined view out the window. Not that there was much to look at. The south tower was a mirror image of the north tower, and with the cleaning crews finished for the night, there was nothing but dark windows staring back at her. Except for the third floor directly across from her where the lights were on, highlighting an empty shell of an office. A few cubicles were in place, clustered together in the middle of the floor, but other than that, there were no individual offices partitioned off and the false ceiling, which hid all the lighting and pipes, had been completely removed, exposing the inner workings of the building's electrical and duct work.

The bright interior lights against the darkness of the floors directly above and below it allowed Kate to see every detail of the empty office. Two A-frame ladders were set up at opposite ends of the floor—one near the elevator and one beside the cluster of cubicle walls—and orange industrial extension cords hung down from the ceiling. It looked as if they were in the middle of an office renovation before new tenants moved in, and Kate wondered if there was more to look at during the day when the workmen were around.

The space was huge—probably half of the floor, much like the Kleiner, Abato & Chen office—and while Kate was contemplating what kind of business might lease the enormous suite, a light popped on in the office upstairs.

Unlike the gutted third floor, this small fourth-floor office was outfitted as a proper business space, with walls separating a reception area from a private office, and decorated with generic high-end leather-and-wood furniture, tasteful wall decor, and a large potted plant in the lobby. A white woman had just entered from the hallway. She strode through the office with purpose, moving neither quickly nor slowly, but with a clear focus and a comfort with her surroundings that hinted at familiarity.

She was tall, her long legs accentuated by crisp cream-colored pants, and incredibly thin, which wasn't unusual in Los Angeles. But her lithe-ness appeared less like emaciated frailty and more like 3 percent body fat, 97 percent kickass. The bare, tanned arms exposed by a sleeveless black silk top were toned and sinewy, like someone who did CrossFit three times a week and trained for marathons on the other four, and though Kate was too far away to see any signs of gray in the wavy dark brown hair cut to a chin-length bob, she got the impression that this woman was not young.

There was something powerful about the way she walked, opening the door on the far side of the lobby without breaking stride. The woman reminded her of Ripley, the main character from an old sci-fi horror movie called *Alien* that Ty had made her and Rowan watch one night when Kate stayed over at the Chen house. All large and in charge and tough as nails.

Even Ripley's executive suite was like something off a movie set, with bookcases behind a sturdy oak desk, a low-back sectional sofa, and wet bar. The woman opened a closet, hung her purse from a hook inside the door, and returned to the front of her desk. She leaned back against the wood and heaved herself onto it, crossing one infinite leg over the other.

It was then Kate realized she held a phone in one hand.

Ripley didn't appear to be speaking, but she held the phone flat in her palm, its screen pointing up at the ceiling, and she bobbed her crossed leg up and down impatiently. Suddenly, the leg stopped and the mouth opened. Ripley spoke quickly and evenly, and though Kate couldn't hear anything she said, she could imagine this was an executive giving instructions to a subordinate. She didn't speak for long—just fifteen seconds before she tossed the phone onto the sofa. Then she leaned back onto the desktop, supporting herself with her toned arms.

The leg began to bounce again.

Ripley was waiting for someone.

Kate was entranced, filing forgotten. The effect of the dark building and the brightly lit office made it feel like she was watching a movie projected onto the side of the south tower. Intimate and yet distant. She felt a pang of guilt, an intrinsic sense of modesty that told her that she should politely turn away and ignore the rest of this unexpected show. But she couldn't. There was something magnetic about Ripley. Powerful, yes, but that wasn't as interesting to Kate. Power could be bought. This woman held herself as if she owned the world, and Kate desperately wanted to know who she was.

Ripley waited.

And Kate waited.

Five, ten minutes.

Kate continued punching holes in the transcripts, looking down only briefly to line up the pages before she utilized her body weight to push through. She felt a delicious anticipation as she continued to punch through stacks of paper, one eye always on Ripley, who waited patiently, confidently. Like she knew whoever it was would show up. Her focus was powerful—Ripley stared intently at the door while she waited, distracted by nothing, and Kate wondered if she could see movement from the dungeon window out of the corner of her eye, or whether the muted lighting in the file room prevented her from being seen.

Finally, just as Kate had lined up the last batch, she caught movement in Ripley's office again. The door opened, and a blond young man poked his head through.

He was tentative, unsure. Like maybe he didn't want to be there and was unwilling to commit his entire body to it. He was dressed in an office uniform, like Ty—steel-blue button-down, tie, gray slacks—despite the late hour. Was this Ripley's assistant, working late?

Ripley said something, and the young guy stepped into the lobby, pulling the door closed behind him. He crossed toward Ripley with slow stutter steps, running his pale, nervous fingers through his hair and occasionally looking around as if convinced someone was watching.

Kate intrinsically crouched down on the table, though there was nowhere to really hide. But the guy's gaze never landed on the third floor of the north tower, which meant he probably couldn't see her.

Phew.

Meanwhile, Ripley merely sat, bouncing one leg over the other. A spider enticing a fly into its web.

His nervous energy increased by the time he stood before Ripley, fidgety. Neither spoke. Ripley seemed to relish his discomfort. Finally, she sat up, slowly crunching her body from its reclined position, uncrossed her legs, then reached forward and grabbed the guy by the tie.

Their bodies flew toward each other, slamming together with enough force that Kate actually caught her breath. Ripley inhaled him, her lips sucking at his like she wanted to devour him whole. She was clearly in charge, moving his hands to where she wanted them—one around her back, one on her ass—while she unbuttoned his shirt and loosened his tie.

They were half-naked before Kate realized that she needed to look away. She spun around on her butt so her back was to the pornscape playing out behind her, and quickly finished the last of her work.

Before she left for the night, Kate couldn't resist one last glance at the fourth floor of the south tower. The lights were still on, but the show was over. Ripley and her boy toy had disappeared from view.

FOURTEEN

KATE HAD A LITTLE PEP IN HER STEP AS SHE DROVE INTO THE Burbank Garden Towers Business Park underground parking lot the next evening. It wasn't because she'd talked to Rowan and reconnected: They'd only exchanged a few texts since the weekend. It wasn't due to a message from Clementine with sides for Friday's audition: still radio silence there. And it definitely wasn't the result of her parents easing up on their demand for rent: Her mom had reminded her just before Kate left for work.

Not much had changed in Kate's life, but for some reason, she walked a little brisker, held her head a little higher, and was able to brush off Donald's judgy smirk as she passed his desk. She wasn't even cognizant of the reason behind her buoyant mood until she opened the door to the dungeon, ignored the roar of server fans and the frigid temperature, and headed straight to the window with her eyes on the south tower.

The third floor was still lit up against the darkening evening, its emptiness accentuated by the brightness of the unadorned overhead lights, but it was the office on the fourth floor, also brightly lit at almost seven o'clock, that captured Kate's attention.

Ripley was still working. She sat upright in her executive chair, typing away at the laptop on her desk. Kate could only see her profile, but she looked focused and intent, not even pausing to tuck her hair back behind her ear after some errant curls tumbled down in front of her face. Whatever it was she did for a living, it required a great deal of focus.

Her assistant was still there as well, staring at his computer monitor at the reception desk. It was positioned at such an angle that Kate could get a good view of his face, illuminated by the blue-white glow from the screen. He looked even younger than she'd guessed, and his close-cropped blond hair, thick brows, and narrow eyes reminded her of Emery Black, who played Wyatt, one of Belle's love interests on *Dirty Pretty Teens*. Unlike Ripley, Real-Life Wyatt wasn't typing. He leaned on his desk with one arm while lazily clicking his mouse.

Whatever it had been last night, today's dynamic between Ripley and Real-Life Wyatt was all business.

Boring, boring business.

Ripley typed, her assistant stared at his computer, and Kate sighed as she dropped her bag on the dungeon table. So much for the night's entertainment.

Maybe she'd find something fun in the files.

She turned to the pile of work strewn across the table and began organizing the chaos. More from Awful Cyborg and Purple Pineapple, a mundane stack of invoices that appeared to be for office supplies and water cooler deliveries, and a bunch of new files that should have ignited a spark of interest but . . . didn't. Kate's eyes kept trailing up to the fourth floor of the south tower, where Ripley and her assistant continued to work in silence, as the clock crept past eight, the night sky darkening from indigo to dusty purple to black around them.

Finally, movement from across the courtyard caught Kate's eyes. Real-Life Wyatt had pushed his chair away from his desk and rolled himself in front of Ripley's office door. He must have said something, because Ripley nodded her head in reply, though she never looked up from her laptop. This seemed to rattle Real-Life Wyatt, who hesitated at the door. Was he debating whether to ask a follow-up question? Hoping for another answer? Wondering if his boss was feeling romantic again?

Anticipation! Kate felt like she needed a tub of movie popcorn and a forty-ounce diet soda.

She wasn't sure if Wyatt had actually spoken again, but Ripley suddenly noticed his lingering presence. Her head snapped up, and she said a single word, so clearly articulated in such a way by both her lips and her facial expression that Kate could practically hear it in her head from a building away.

Yes?

"Yes?" Kate heard herself repeat, trying to infuse the word with the same level of impatience and contempt hinted at by Ripley's body language. Boss Lady had no time for her little assistant tonight.

Real-Life Wyatt jumped at the single word as if he'd heard it come out of Kate's own mouth. Ripley's tone must have been enough to put the fear of God into him because he immediately grabbed his messenger bag from a drawer and slung it across his body. He said something else, wordy and nervous. Fidgeting again. Kate wondered if that was part of his own anxious personality or the effect of his boss's domineering one.

Ripley simply nodded to whatever monologue her assistant had word vomited. He hesitated for another moment, second-guessing himself perhaps, then turned and hurried out of the office.

Kate smiled as the scene ended. She freaking loved how Ripley reestablished dominance over the relationship with a single word. There must have been an incredible amount of power in her tone and delivery.

"Yes?" Kate repeated, unhappy with her first attempt. Her voice sounded too high, too indecisive. She needed the word to be framed as a question but have absolutely no questioning about it, and spoken in a tone that would send Wyatt scampering off.

Look to the Bard. Ripley's large-and-in-charge demeanor reminded Kate of Lady Macbeth's first appearance, when she formulates the plan to kill Duncan. Cool, calculating, utterly confident.

> *Come, you spirits*
> *That tend on mortal thoughts, unsex me here,*
> *And fill me from the crown to the toe top-full*
> *Of direst cruelty!*

What would *that* sound like in a single word?

She tried again, lowering her pitch. Close but not enough. Again. This time, she elongated the vowel, kept her tone calm and even, and tried to make the question mark feel more like a formality than a concession.

"Yes?"

Nailed it.

Kate grinned. That was a voice that could send a nervous boy or an ambitious thane running. Who needed expensive acting classes when she could watch what was playing out in the building next door?

Shakespeare plus voyeurism was better than Stanislavski any day.

She turned back to her filing, but kept one eye on Ripley, who continued to work at her desk, laser-focused on whatever she was typing until her office phone rang.

Though there was no one but Kate to see her, Ripley smiled at whoever was on the other end of the call, and Kate imagined how different Ripley must sound now than she had half an hour ago when dismissing her assistant. She was now Lady Macbeth buttering up Duncan while she plots his murder. The phone conversation was short, but it must not have been unpleasant because Ripley was laughing as she replaced the receiver. She stood up, smoothed down the lines of her outfit—another pantsuit, but this one in navy blue with a lavender three-quarter sleeve blouse that tied at the neck—then crossed to her office door, closing it. Next, she opened a drawer on the far side of her desk, moved a few items around in it, before positioning her laptop at the corner and resuming her typing pose. She was now angled toward the window, and Kate wondered why she would have repositioned herself so deliberately and why the short phone call would have elicited this staging of her office.

That question was at least partially answered when the door to Ripley's office flew open seconds later and a middle-aged man with light brown skin and wavy salt-and-pepper hair stormed through her lobby. Like Ripley, he was professionally dressed in a slate-gray business suit, but he didn't carry a briefcase or portfolio with him. Definitely not a business meeting. He never even paused at Ripley's door, throwing it open with such force that Kate could practically feel the reverberations as it slammed into the wall.

The man roared up to Ripley's desk, planted his hands on the polished wood, and leaned toward her. He was shouting, Kate was pretty sure. She could see the droplets of spit flying from his mouth as the words exploded from it. Thirty seconds. A minute. Kate had read that anger was a difficult emotion to sustain for an actor because outbursts in real life tended to be short and explosive, but this guy was putting that theory to shame as he ranted on and on.

Despite the wall of rage in front of her, Ripley sat serenely at her desk, eyes fixed on her screen. But now that she was facing the window, Kate could clearly see the smile of delight on her lips. Whatever rage this guy was spewing, Ripley loved every second of it.

He paused, catching his breath, and once again Kate could easily read Ripley's lips as she simply said, *"Are you done?"*

"Are you done?" Kate repeated, using the Lady Macbeth tone she'd perfected earlier.

The man didn't answer either of them.

Ripley turned her face away from the window, but Kate supplied the dialogue she thought most likely. "I'll take that as a yes" delivered in her signature calm, cool demeanor. Ripley rounded her desk and looked the man dead in the eyes while she spoke, hardly moving a muscle except for a slight nod at the open desk drawer behind her. The man's eyes followed her gesture; then they widened. He faltered a few steps back toward the office door. Flustered. Whatever he'd seen in the drawer was unexpected.

Ripley spread her hands, first one, then the other, as if she was giving the man a choice. *An ultimatum.* He paused, indecisive. Then a look of disgust and impotent rage twisted his features. "Fuck you!"

There was no misinterpreting that lip-read.

Kate thought of the passionate, consuming foreplay she'd witnessed between Ripley and her hot-bodied assistant last night. "You wish," Kate said out loud.

Then, as if he'd gotten the same exact response from Ripley, the older man clasped his hands together, wriggling as he pulled something from his finger.

A ring.

A wedding ring.

He slammed the ring onto the desk, turned, and stormed off.

Ripley waited until he was gone, then returned to her chair, kicked her legs up in the air, and spun herself around with gleeful abandon. As she turned, her mouth was open, a smile beaming from her face. She was laughing.

After a few seconds, the momentum of the chair slowed. Ripley composed herself. She closed the desk drawer, lowered the screen on her laptop, and slid it into her leather satchel; then, without even touching the ring on her desk, she switched off the lights and left.

Kate stared at the dark, empty corner office in awe.

Had she just watched Ripley's husband announce he was going to file for divorce?

FIFTEEN

IT FELT GOOD TO BE OUT ON A REAL AUDITION.

Finally.

The open call for *Dirty Pretty Teens* had hardly been a normal experience. With over thirteen thousand hopefuls and no idea what actual roles were being cast, it had basically been a publicity stunt for the upcoming show. Kate had only been there because of Rowan. Audition buddy system, she'd called it. They'd waited in the hot sun for hours, shielded beneath Rowan's umbrella, while they inched forward. Surrounding them was a mix of fan girls from the *DPT* novels and wannabe actors, the former of whom tried to outdo one another with deep cuts of trivia about the books, the author, and preproduction elements of the show, while the latter postured, aloof and annoyed, ensuring everyone around knew they were "above" this kind of thing.

Kate had found it all incredibly entertaining. Even four hours in, she and Rowan were still having fun, chatting and joking and gossiping via text about the people around them in line. Rowan, of course, had made friends with everyone. Her superpower. Kate was content to let her, smiling in the background like usual.

When they reached the front of the line, snaking inside the building and through a security checkpoint before finally getting in front of casting personnel, Kate had planned to explain that she was only there for moral support, and step aside. But things moved too quickly. They'd been separated by age and gender, photographed, and given a number, then paraded through a production warehouse in groups of twenty, where the gathered producers and casting directors quickly jotted down which numbers they wanted to see read. Kate and Rowan had made that cut and sat another three hours for the opportunity to perform a scene in front of the camera.

Kate had thought about that moment a lot over the last few months, when she and Rowan, paired together for the scene, were escorted back into the warehouse. A couple of lighting rigs had been set up on either side of the casting table, now littered with Starbucks cups and half-eaten protein bars, and a single camera had been set up beside them on a tripod. Two marks had been delineated on the floor with large Xs made from white tape. There were no spotlights, no blinding floods that would bring blessed anonymity to the four sets of eyes trained on them. Kate could see them, and they could see her.

"I don't think I can do this," she'd whispered to Rowan as they were introduced by number. She didn't want to torpedo her friend's audition.

Rowan was a great actress, with an onstage charisma that enchanted everyone lucky enough to see her perform. And Kate was about to sink her battleship with her nerves and utter lack of talent.

Rowan had squeezed her hand. "Just pretend you're running lines with me at school. It'll be fine."

They'd been instructed to each stand on an X and read the scene once through, then swap roles and read it again. Easy-peasy.

It had been that opening scene from day one of shooting, Piper and Noelle at the coffee shop. An earlier version, but basically the same. Kate had read Piper, Rowan had read Noelle; then they switched. Approaching it like the hundreds of rehearsals they had done together over the last six years, Kate had relaxed, opened up, and landed a callback.

Rowan wasn't as lucky.

What Kate learned later was that Belle Masterson had already been cast as Piper, and the only lead roles available for that open call were Noelle and Asher. That helped Rowan's disappointment at being cut so early: She wasn't "sidekick" material.

But Kate was. She'd always been Rowan's sidekick, even tagging along on that open call so her friend wouldn't have to do it alone. From Rowan's wing woman to Belle's plus one.

Today's audition wasn't about either of them. This was Kate's first big step toward her future. And she was nervous as fuck.

Part of that was logistical. Kate hadn't received the sides from Clementine yet, despite repeated attempts to get them over the last few days. Clementine had promised them twice and blamed first the casting director and then Clementine's assistant for not getting them out.

"They'll be at the audition," Clementine said on the phone before Kate left the house that morning. "Don't worry, it happens all. The. Time."

All the time. Okay. If other actresses could audition successfully without preparing their scenes in advance, so could Kate. That was part of being a professional.

But the other aspect of Kate's anxiety wasn't as easy to control. Her imposter syndrome was strong. The voice of doubt in her head berated her the entire drive from Burbank to Century City with a constant refrain of *You're not good enough*, *You just got lucky*, and *You're not a real actress*.

Bananas.

Kate's heart was beating like an out-of-control conga drum as she turned her dad's Subaru onto Pico Boulevard, the looming facade of Fox Studios towering over her with posters advertising their newest shows and movies. Iconic palm trees lined the main street inside the lot, visible above the wall as she drove around the perimeter, and she smiled, thinking of the secret little world that existed inside, a world of magic and glamour but also incredibly hard work. A world she desperately wanted to be a part of again.

The light changed, and Kate turned onto Avenue of the Stars, carefully following the directions Clementine's assistant had sent. Parking instructions but no sides. Seriously? Not being able to prepare for this audition in advance was only adding to her anxiety, but that was the gig, right? Sometimes, you had to improvise. She'd gotten pretty good at that while working with Belle, who routinely couldn't remember her lines and would "guesstimate" what they were supposed to be while filming. Sometimes the director cut, but sometimes they rolled with it and Kate had to ad-lib based on her knowledge of the story line.

If she could do that on the fly with Belle Masterson sucking up all the energy in the room, she could do it by herself in an audition. Even without preparation.

Maybe that was *her* superpower.

There was a line of cars at the Galaxy Gate, and Kate was thankful she'd padded her travel time. Even with the long spiral to the bottom of the parking structure to find a spot and an unintentional detour around the far side of the lot while she looked for the right building, she still had fifteen minutes to spare when she arrived. At least that was one less thing to worry about.

Sixth Street Bridge auditions were being held, ironically, on the sixth floor of a nondescript office building at the west end of the lot, and Kate was delighted to find a waiting room with only four or five other actresses, as opposed to a line of thousands the last time around. Kate had agonized over what to wear, considering she didn't even know what the role was, and was happy to find that she was dressed similarly to the other actresses in the room in a green sweater, jeans, and those yellow ballet flats she still wasn't sure if she loved or hated.

A smiling redhead with almost as many freckles as Kate's mom, greeted her from a desk just inside the waiting room door. "Good morning! You're here for the *Sixth Street Bridge* audition?"

"I am!" Kate said, trying to match the girl's perkiness.

"Excellent. I'll have you sign in here." She pushed a clipboard over, and Kate quickly filled out her name and her agent's name but paused at the line marked ROLE.

"I'm sorry," she said. "But I didn't get the sides." Apologizing for something that wasn't her fault felt weak, but she didn't know what else to say.

The redhead cocked her head to the side. "You didn't?"

"My agent kept promising to send them, but . . ." She shrugged, not committing the blame to anyone in particular.

"So weird," the redhead said, reaching for her messenger bag. "They were posted on Actors Access."

Kate's face must have reflected the horror she felt at realizing she was the only person in the room who hadn't been able to prepare because the redhead quickly smiled reassuringly as she pulled a stapled packet of pages from her bag. "Here you go. They're running a little behind, so you still have plenty of time to read through."

"Thank you." Kate let out a slow, measured breath as she accepted the script.

The redhead gestured toward the waiting-room chairs. "Good luck!"

The assistant's helpful, non-judgy attitude helped calm Kate's rampaging self-doubt, and as she sat down at a lone chair in the corner to read through the material, she once again felt as if she could do this.

The packet consisted of one four-page scene, a brief synopsis of the film, and the character breakdowns. *Sixth Street Bridge* was a female-driven indie thriller about a young rookie cop with the generic name of Jenny Rogers who tries to break up a South Los Angeles sex trafficking ring. The scene was between Jenny, who goes undercover to infiltrate the gang, and Queenie, a pregnant teen who has information to sell.

Despite her boring name, Jenny wasn't a bad part. She was tough but compassionate, able to think on her feet, but always cognizant that she was undercover. In the scene, she was trying to get Queenie to understand the stakes: helping girls like her get back to their families. Once again, Kate's mind flew to Shakespeare, the fourth act of *The Merchant of Venice,* where Portia disguises herself as a male lawyer and legally argues Antonio out of his pound-of-flesh debt. In the scene, Portia first appeals to Shylock's decency in her famous "The Quality of Mercy" speech, then foils the moneylender by using his own words against him. Shylock is entitled to his pound of flesh, but that is all—he can't spill any blood in the process or his own life and goods will be forfeited.

Jenny has a similar shift in her tactics with Queenie, though in reverse, first pointing out the legal ramifications for her connection with the trafficking ring, then appealing to her humanity. Portia would be the perfect inspiration for this character.

She read through the lines a dozen times before her name was called, and Kate felt like she had a good handle on Jenny Rogers when she stepped through the door into the audition room.

There were three people in the room—two women and a man, all white—clustered around a setup Kate remembered from the *Dirty Pretty Teens* audition: a table, some coffee cups, and a camera set up on a tripod. The older of the two women smiled at Kate as she entered, flicking her thick sandy-brown bangs out of her eyes as she introduced herself.

"Thank you so much for coming today," she began. "I'm Sara Rhodes, casting director for *SSB* and let me just say that I loved your work on *DPT*."

It was a lot of acronyms to process in one sentence, but Kate was delighted that Sara had seen her work. "That is so kind. Thank you."

Sara gestured to the man on her left. "This is Marcus Chapman, executive producer for *SSB*, and Charlie here will be reading the scene with you."

The other woman, young with sleepy hazel eyes and a messy topknot of light brown hair, smiled tightly and slowly rounded the table to join Kate in front of the camera. She held the crumpled and bent sides in her hand, an indication that she'd done a lot of these auditions today. Kate could only hope hers would stand out.

Sara stood up and checked the camera, then retook her seat and nodded. "Whenever you're ready!"

"Thank you!" Kate took a deep breath, then was about to say Jenny's line that opened the scene when Charlie read it first.

"Queenie, come on," she said flatly. "A big girl like you can only hide a pregnancy for so long."

Kate froze, her eyes flitting from the script to Charlie and then over to the table, where Sara and Marcus stared at her with forced smiles that were stiffening by the second. Suddenly Kate realized that all the other girls in the lobby, though racially mixed, were plus size.

Clementine had sent her out for a fat-girl role.

"Kate?" Sara said, tilting her head to the side. "Is everything okay?"

No. Everything is fucked up. "I thought I was reading for Jenny. I didn't get the sides in advance."

Sara and Marcus exchanged a glance. "Oh, I'm so sorry. Jenny has already been cast."

Of course she had.

"We're only running auditions for Queenie today."

Of course they were.

"Are . . . are you okay to continue?"

Kate had two choices: leave and look like an amateur or suck it up and read the role they were expecting. Storming out would have been a statement, but it also might totally and completely fuck up her career. Casting directors were an actor's entrée into the business—if one liked you, they'd have you in to read for other parts, maybe even refer you to colleagues. If one didn't like you, they'd make sure you never read for them again. While her self-righteousness was earned, Kate swallowed it back down.

"Can we start again?"

* * *

Kate walked back to her car in a daze. Her first real audition could not have gone any worse.

After realizing that she'd prepared the wrong character, Kate was totally unable to switch gears. She didn't understand Queenie, hadn't put any thought into her needs and wants, her backstory or her stakes. Her brain kept straying from the script, fixating on her agent. Something inside told Kate that Clementine had intentionally kept the sides from her, knowing that Queenie the pregnant fat girl was exactly the kind of cliché role Kate didn't want.

Kate had read through the scene twice, each time struggling with her anger. The first was a mess, with Kate stumbling over lines and fluctuating between characterizations she was trying on the fly. A total train wreck that should have resulted in a taut "thank you" dismissal, but Sara had suggested a second pass. This time Kate read the damn part as if Queenie *were* Portia in *The Merchant of Venice*, using her own arguments to combat Jenny's perceived superiority.

It actually worked way better than it should have, and Sara had thanked her warmly when she left, but Kate knew the truth of what happened: Sara Rhodes, independent film casting director, would never audition Kate Williams again.

SIXTEEN

KATE SAT IN HER DAD'S CAR, PARKED IN THE UNDERGROUND lot at the Burbank Garden Towers Business Park, for over an hour, trying to calm down. Anger, indignation, panic, and shame had all washed over her in equal measure, but as she rested her forehead against the steering wheel, long, slow breaths quieting her frantic thoughts, all that remained was hopelessness.

Clementine had apologized profusely for the mishap with sending the sides, but she had gotten a little snippy at Kate's indignation at being sent out for a fat-girl role. Kate wanted to be taken seriously, didn't she? To do serious parts? That would stretch her small résumé?

"That's what a Queenie can do," Clementine had explained tersely. "You're just going to have to suck. It. Up."

Kate had texted Rowan, asking if she had time to talk. Her friend had done so many auditions over the years; maybe she could share some wisdom that might make Kate feel better.

But Rowan never responded.

Probably too busy doing whatever with Jeremiah.

At least Rowan was happy, but Kate couldn't ignore the bitter sting of her collapsing support system. No Rowan, no Mom and Dad, and the only other person she'd ever turned to for advice was Ty.

That door was definitely closed.

Kate's loneliness was only amplified when she scanned her card and entered the Kleiner, Abato & Chen lobby. The lights were already off, Albie long departed, and as she unlocked the glass doors into the rest of the office, she saw that it was mostly deserted as well. There were lights on in a couple of offices at the far end of the hall. Partners, probably. Or associates hoping to make partner. Rowan said they worked insane hours. Seemed like a miserable career choice.

Unlike acting, which is so awesome?

Kate grimaced. Even her internal monologue was betraying her.

The only bright spot in her day was inside the dungeon, where the accumulation of paperwork on a Friday night seemed smaller than it had been the rest of the week. Good. She wanted to finish up, go home, climb into bed, pull the covers over her head, and forget this day had ever happened.

The construction lights on the third-floor office across the courtyard were on as usual, and the harsh glow inside the completely empty office felt more isolating than comforting. It reminded her that most people had a life on Friday nights, but as Kate set up her hole punch and staple remover, she was surprised to see the lights in Ripley's office were on as well. Both Ripley and her hunky assistant were still at work, Ripley typing at her computer while Real-Life Wyatt tidied the lobby, adjusting the chairs in the waiting room so they were even and straightening the magazines on the table next to the large potted plant. Then he retrieved two small bottles of sparkling water from a mini fridge beside his desk and set them on a tray as if they were expecting a client.

At eight o'clock on a Friday night?

Weird.

Someone must have knocked on the office door because Real-Life Wyatt's head turned sharply; then, tentatively, the door crept open, and for half a second, Kate thought a gun muzzle was going to peek out from behind it like in one of the old James Bond movies her dad loved. Instead, a hooded figure quickly slipped into the office and closed the door behind her, leaning against it dramatically.

The visitor was wearing black pants and a hooded leather jacket that she held tightly around her ears, presumably to keep the hood from slipping back and exposing any parts of her face that were not obscured by a pair of enormous sunglasses. Though Kate couldn't see any facial features, she knew from the overly dramatic pose who it was before she even saw the sun-bleached blond hair or the haughty smile.

What the hell was Belle Masterson doing at Ripley's office?

Her work forgotten, Kate climbed up onto the table, totally transfixed by Belle's presence across the courtyard. True to form, Belle was hamming up the drama. After pushing back her hood and shaking out her beach waves, she took a moment to crack the office door and peek outside into the hallway as if checking to see if she'd been followed.

Into a secure building.

At night.

Bananas.

Seemingly assured that she hadn't, Belle whipped off her sunglasses, one hand clutched to her chest as she spoke. Kate could practically hear the self-indulgent monologue coming out of her.

I'm a prisoner, trapped in my own home by these bloodsucking paparazzi. Don't they understand that Dex and I are in love? Why is love so wrong?

Wild bananas.

Real-Life Wyatt bobbed his head up and down in silent agreement, whether or not he understood any of what she said. Belle didn't care. She only wanted an audience, and Kate guessed that she was running out of willing participants. He waited for a break in her diatribe, then gestured toward the sparkling water on the table. She smiled at him, reaching out a hand to touch his arm. *Aren't you sweet*, Kate could practically hear her say.

Belle sat and helped herself to a bottle, crossing one leg over the other, while the assistant knocked at Ripley's door before entering. The instant he was gone, Belle peeled off her jacket, flinging it onto the chair beside her. She wore a simple white V-neck tee underneath, and with her eyes fixed on the door to make sure the assistant wasn't returning too soon, Belle reached into her bra through the neckline of her shirt and lifted her boobs up to ensure maximum cleavage. Then she pulled the shirt down, lowering the V-neck to adequately show it off.

So much for her undying love for Dex Pratt.

Meanwhile, Real-Life Wyatt had announced Belle's arrival. Ripley gave him a single nod. The order was clear—show her in.

The assistant held the door open for Belle, who looked somewhat disappointed that she wouldn't get to spend more alone time with him, but she strode into Ripley's office with as much swagger as she could muster.

Ripley rose to meet her but did not extend a hand, merely nodding to the chair opposite her desk as the assistant closed the door.

Belle Masterson was the kind of person who liked to dominate a conversation, and the instant she sat down opposite Ripley, she tried to do exactly that. She spoke swiftly, judging by the rapid hand movements, and with a tremendous amount of energy, but though Ripley listened with an intent stillness, she only let Belle go on for about thirty seconds before cutting the starlet off. Just a simple word while she held up her hand for silence.

For the first time since Kate had met Belle, she shut the hell up.

Ripley is so badass.

It was a master class in dominance as Ripley quickly asserted herself as the alpha dog, and if Kate hadn't been enamored of her office neighbor before, she certainly was now. She wanted to high-five the first person to ever put Belle Masterson in her place, but since she couldn't run over to the south tower without the appropriate ID badge, she settled for a photo to commemorate the moment. A quick pic on her camera, and though the image was far away, Kate smiled when she saw the cowed look on Belle's face.

She'd treasure that photo always.

Ripley continued to speak with calm superiority, and once again, Kate wondered what kind of business she was in. Small office—only her and the assistant—and generically decorated, but Ripley was always meticulously dressed, and if Kate were given a closer look, she was pretty sure that she'd find a variety of designer labels on everything from Ripley's shoes to her power suits to her handbag. For some reason, that air of authority and money had screamed *finance industry professional* to Kate, but then why would Belle Masterson be there?

An agent. That had to be it. A small, one-woman show. Which begged the question: Was Belle shopping for an agent because Clementine had dumped her or because she was thinking about leaving?

Though Kate would love to have been a fly on the wall, she needed to get her work done and begrudgingly climbed down from the table. Ripley's lecture continued as Kate unstapled and hole-punched until both women suddenly stood up and shook hands across Ripley's desk. Their grips looked firm, their eye contact direct. A deal had been struck.

Belle, looking almost giddy, broke away first and practically pirouetted to the door, her long blond waves whipping around her shoulders with choreographed precision. There was a bounce in her step as she pranced by the assistant, and she hardly broke stride as she offered him a wiggle of her fingers as a flirty goodbye. She was so preoccupied, she left her leather hooded jacket on the chair in the waiting room as she flounced out the door.

Kate rolled her eyes. Belle's dramatic safety precautions must not have been so dire after all if she forgot the most important part of her disguise.

Three seconds after Belle was gone, Ripley called in her assistant. She was on her feet, speaking rapidly as she paced around her desk. Real-Life Wyatt thumb-typed frantically on his phone, trying to keep up with her. Whatever she and Belle had discussed, it had launched Ripley into action on her new client's behalf. She had so much energy, Kate could practically feel the floorboards above her creak with each step.

Ripley stopped abruptly, right in front of her assistant. She was breathing heavily, excited and flushed. Real-Life Wyatt looked up, waiting for the next wave of instructions, but whatever he saw in her face, he knew there would be no more typing. He tossed his phone onto her desk a split second before Ripley pounced.

This encounter felt more equal than the first. Instead of a tentative recipient of Ripley's lust, her assistant was more proactive. He didn't need her guidance to know where to place his hands on her body—he gripped her firmly at the small of her back while he kissed her, and instead of waiting for her to undo his tie and shirt, he used his free hand to do the work, expertly stripping them off almost without breaking his and Ripley's embrace.

Like he'd been practicing.

There was something sexier about this encounter, the kind of sexy Kate wanted to be even though she had about as much experience with guys as a cloistered nun. But the way they moved together, as if they knew what the other wanted without words being exchanged, was fascinating, and without even realizing she was doing it, Kate picked up her phone and snapped another photo, just before Ripley unbuckled her assistant's belt and slid down to her knees, out of view.

Kate was so absorbed in the foreplay that she almost didn't notice Ripley's lobby door reopen.

Belle must have remembered her jacket. She sauntered into the lobby, clearly expecting the assistant to be there alone. Instead, her eyes quickly found the pair in Ripley's office through the still-open door.

Belle watched for a moment—longer than she should have, although who the hell was Kate to judge? Then Belle picked up her jacket and slowly backed out of the office, closing the door behind her.

SEVENTEEN

KATE WAS HOPING THAT SATURDAY WOULD BE A RESET.

On her mood.

On her outlook.

On her friendship with Rowan.

When her best friend had finally texted back Friday night, it was long after Kate had gone to bed. Profuse apologies and a half-assed excuse about scene study were followed by an invitation for Kate to meet her at school after theater camp rehearsal the next day. Finally, she and Rowan would get some hangout time.

She hadn't physically seen Rowan since the day Belle's video dropped almost two weeks ago, and Kate was itching not only to share the bull-shit of the Queenie audition but also to hear all about Rowan's new relationship. Not that she was dying to learn what a great kisser Jeremiah Nuñez was or whether or not they'd rounded the bases yet, but *not* being in the know on her friend's love life made Kate feel even more alienated and alone, and she desperately needed a touchstone to her old life. She even smiled at herself in the mirror—a rare occurrence—as she surveyed her body in a ruffle-hemmed sundress and wedge sandals.

Unfortunately, Kate's morning smile of optimism hadn't lasted long. Both of her parents needed their cars, and with the thermostat already north of eighty at ten o'clock in the morning, the two-mile walk to Burbank High School to meet Rowan would have left Kate a gross, sweaty mess. Though ten minutes of forced conversation in the car with her mom was the last thing she wanted after cobbling together breakfast from the only unlabeled food in the kitchen—leftover quinoa salad and a stale English muffin—it seemed like a good idea to hitch a ride with Mom to her old school.

Old school. That was the first time she'd thought of Burbank High in those terms. Old. Former. She was no longer a high school student. She was a working adult, visiting a friend.

Bananas.

"I'm glad you're hanging out with Rowan today," her mom said as she backed the car out of the driveway. Her voice sounded tense, her words forced. They'd barely spoken all week, partly due to conflicting schedules but partly, Kate guessed, because her mom was avoiding her. But this was a direct invitation to talk, and though Kate wasn't exactly sure what she should say, she actually felt her shoulders unclench at a potential thawing of the ice between them.

"Me too."

"I've missed seeing her around." Her mom paused, glancing in Kate's direction. "And Ty."

Kate stiffened. How did she know he was back?

"When does he leave for Stanford?" her mom continued.

"Week after next, I think," Kate said, knowing that silence would not be an acceptable response. Her mom required confirmation that each comment, question, or instruction was heard and processed. It reminded Kate of the stage managers for Rowan's performances. Starting an hour before showtime, they'd walk through the dressing rooms bellowing "Curtain in one hour!" and later "Curtain in thirty!" and so forth. The cast was supposed to respond with "One hour, thank you!" to acknowledge that they'd heard and understood the warning. If they didn't, the stage manager would repeat the notice, louder and with more attitude.

That was Kate's mom. The Williams family stage manager.

"Do you think Rowan's mom can drive you home? Your dad and I were thinking about another date night."

"I'm sure she can."

"Or Ty."

Again, Kate tensed at the mention of his name. Why was her mom bringing him up so much? Did she somehow know what had happened between them? Or was Ty just such the perfect embodiment of who Kate's parents wanted their daughter to date that she was hoping to nudge Kate in that direction?

Her mom stopped for the light at Victory Boulevard, her eyes again drifting toward her daughter. Then she cleared her throat like Kate's dad did when a big, important parental thought was imminent. They were such a matched pair.

"I . . . I know this week has been difficult for you."

"Difficult," Kate mouthed. Her parents didn't know the half of it.

"And I hate that there's this distance between us."

A lump rose in Kate throat. "Me too."

"I just want you to know that your dad and I . . . we're just trying to do what's best for you."

"By charging me rent?" The words sounded harsher than Kate had intended, a result of her strained week, but the change in her mom's demeanor was immediate.

"Yes," she snapped as she pulled into the Burbank High driveway. "By charging you rent. This world isn't an easy place, Katherine. The sooner you learn that, the better."

Kate mentally kicked herself for swatting away her mom's olive branch, and while part of her wanted to backpedal, to apologize for her tone and try to grab hold of her mom's peace offering before it completely disappeared, Kate's other side—the stubborn side that she'd inherited directly from her mom—balked.

"I'm a fat girl trying to make it in Hollywood, Mom," Kate said. It was the one argument her size six mom could neither counter nor fully understand. "Don't think for a second I don't know how hard the world is."

"That's why we want you to go to college." Her mom's voice was plaintive, almost begging her daughter to listen. "Then you'll always have your degree to fall back on."

Kate threw the door open and clambered out of the car. "This is *my* life, Mom. Not yours."

"Kate—"

"I'll be home late." Then she slammed the door and stomped up the front steps of her old high school.

* * *

Kate's heart was hammering so fiercely in her chest that as soon as she was out of view of her mom, she had to lean against a wall to catch her breath.

Her mom hadn't meant to pick a fight; she'd just been trying to explain where she and Kate's dad were coming from. Kate knew that, intellectually at least. But emotionally, she was raw, an open wound irritated by every gust of wind that brushed against it. She'd lashed out, fight or flight in full effect. Could this week get any worse?

Kate pressed her back against the stucco wall and took a deep breath. This place wasn't helping her anxiety. Burbank High School during summer break was deserted, a far cry from the chaos that would fill the quad in a few weeks once classes began, and the surrealness of a sparsely populated campus added to her growing sense of unease.

As if she didn't belong.

As if the school didn't want her.

As if *no one* wanted her.

"Stop it," Kate said out loud. She was letting the conversation with her mom cloud her judgment. Of course Kate was wanted. Rowan had invited her to hang out, no strings attached. Her best friend would always have her back.

As Kate crossed the quad toward the theater, the pounding keys of the rehearsal pianist drifted out of the open lobby doors of Wolfson Auditorium. His name was Bob, if Kate remembered correctly. She'd turned pages for him at a rehearsal sophomore year during the fast-tempoed "Getting Married Today" number from the spring musical production of Stephen Sondheim's *Company*.

Two voices rose over the piano accompaniment—a robust female belt that overpowered a warbling tenor—performing "As Long as You're Mine" from *Wicked*. Kate recognized Rowan's voice right away—a clear, confident alto infused with all of her best friend's bottomless energy and verve, a musical explosion of her extroversion. The tone may not have been the most beautiful, but Rowan's singing voice was imbued with her charisma, which pulled the audience in and held them captive. Listening to Rowan sing was like hearing the core of her best friend's being transformed into sound waves.

The male voice she couldn't place, and it wasn't until she walked through the lobby and into the theater that she realized it was Jeremiah. *Jer.* He and Rowan were standing at the edge of the proscenium, arms linked together, looking out into the house.

Rehearsals always felt rather unmagical at this stage of a production, whether it was for a full musical or a play, or a performance of scenes at the end of a four-week theater camp. The actors in their street clothes, the work lights on, minimal sets and props. But even then, Rowan was emoting character and drama at 110 percent, and Jeremiah was hanging on to her for dear life.

The song crescendoed to its final note, which hung in the air, Rowan gazing up to the balcony as if she was watching the last beats disappear into the darkness, her face rhapsodic, her chest heaving. A moment of magic amid the unmagical; then Rowan broke the spell. She turned, her nose practically touching Jer's. She laid a hand on his cheek, caressing it; then, with an arm around her waist, he pulled her close and kissed her.

Kate had seen a lot of stage kisses. She'd seen Rowan do plenty of them right there on that stage. She'd seen them on the set of *DPT.* Hell, she'd even had one with Liam in episode 106. That one had looked particularly passionate when she watched it later, but she knew from firsthand experience that there had been about as much sexual energy in her kiss with Liam as there was when she kissed her grandmother. Zilch, nada. Not even a hint.

But this kiss between Jer and Rowan was *not* a stage kiss. It lingered too long. The passion was real, and Kate fought the urge to look away, as if she was infringing on a personal moment between the two of them.

A hoot went up from the front row, followed by some raucous applause from the other camp actors gathered in the house to watch.

"Get it, girl!" someone shouted.

Ew.

Ms. Montoya, Burbank High's Latina drama teacher, in her late twenties, mounted the rickety temporary stairs placed beside the orchestra pit. Her long brown hair was twisted up into a tight bun, and large black glasses accentuated the size of her doe eyes. "Excellent job, you two. How did the tempo feel in the recap?"

Jer deferred to Rowan. "Maybe a little more bounce going into the last page?" she suggested.

"Can do," Bob said. Then he immediately broke into the passage she referenced, his gnarled white hands whipping through a few bars before abruptly stopping. "Like that?"

"Love you!" Rowan said, blowing a kiss.

Ms. Montoya nodded. "Excellent. I don't think we need to touch that one again until dress."

Kate was pretty sure she saw a look of disappointment cross Jeremiah's face.

"Let's set for 'Lay Your Hands on Me,'" Ms. Montoya continued. "I want to see it with the flippers this time, everyone, before we lose Bob for the . . . Oh, Kate! It's so good to see you!"

The sound of her own name startled Kate so violently that she actually jumped away from the chair she'd been leaning on.

"H-hi, Ms. Montoya," Kate managed, ashamed by how unconfident she sounded. Why was she embarrassed to be there? She'd watched literally dozens of rehearsals from the anonymity of that darkened theater; why was it any different this time?

"I was sorry not to see you in camp this summer," Ms. Montoya continued, hands on her narrow hips. "Thought I'd finally get you on this stage after your big Netflix debut."

"Oh . . . oh, I didn't think . . ." Kate stumbled, feeling the heat rise up from her chest. She'd never considered taking a theater class at school. That was Rowan's world.

"Kate's had too many auditions," Rowan said, coming to the rescue. "She was down at the Fox lot yesterday for a feature." Kate hadn't yet given Rowan the download on how that audition had actually gone, but she appreciated her friend's support anyway.

"Oh, that's fantastic!" Ms. Montoya's face lit up, and Kate wasn't sure if she was actually happy for Kate's recent success or just faking it.

Hard to tell with actors sometimes.

"Well, it's nice to see you, onstage or off." Ms. Montoya turned back to the stage, where Jeremiah and four other guys who made up the entire male contingent of theater camp were lined up in flippered feet. "Shall we take it from the top?"

* * *

Kate watched the rest of rehearsal in silence. The *Mamma Mia!* number was cute, even if watching Jer flop around the stage in swim trunks was an image she could have lived without, and then she got to see Rowan in "La Vie Bohème" from *Rent* and, again, her friend outshone the other performers with her showmanship and charisma.

She really should have been Noelle, Kate thought for the billionth time. She'd second-guessed every moment of those initial auditions for *Dirty Pretty Teens*, wondering if she'd accidentally done something that undermined her friend. Deep down, Kate knew there was nothing she could have done to influence Dex's casting decision one way or another.

But almost a year later, she still felt guilty.

After Bob packed up, rehearsal shifted to the non-musical scenes, none of which Rowan was in. But instead of joining Kate in the theater, Rowan seemed to have disappeared.

And so had Jeremiah.

No one wants you.

Maybe coming back to Burbank High had been a mistake.

When rehearsal finally wrapped, Kate slipped out of the theater to wait for Rowan in the quad. She didn't have the energy for a hundred catch-up questions from Imogen, Luca, Ernesto, and Gabby. She wanted to get out of there and enjoy time with her best friend. But as Rowan and Jer walked out of the theater hand in hand, Kate realized that was not going to happen.

"Alfredo's sound good?" Rowan asked before Kate could say a word. "I figured we can all take over the patio at this hour."

Kate felt her body tighten. "All?"

"Just the usuals," Rowan said with a dismissive flip of her hand. "Imogen and Luca, of course. Darla, who you'll love, I promise. Gabby, Ernesto, Hiroki."

"And Ty," Jeremiah added. "I texted him to stop by."

Kate blinked, unsure which realization rocked her the most: that Jeremiah was on texting terms with Rowan's brother or that he would be joining them for lunch.

"Maybe I should head home," Kate suggested.

"No!" Rowan lurched forward and grabbed Kate passionately by the hand. "You *have* to come. I haven't seen you in ages!"

"You've been busy." The words sounded as bitter as they tasted.

"So have you," Rowan said, wounded. Her scrunched-up face spoke a silent question of "what is wrong?" and the answer was more complicated than Kate could nonverbally express.

"Just come with," Rowan pleaded, flipping her thick black hair over one shoulder. "You'll have fun, I promise."

She squeezed Kate's hand as if to emphasize how much she really, really wanted Kate to be there. Though Kate realized this was mostly to appease Rowan's need to have everyone she cared about in one big place together, she relented. Because that's what best friends did.

"Fine," she said, squeezing back. "But you're buying the guacamole."

EIGHTEEN

ALFREDO'S WAS A POPULAR SPOT BOTH BECAUSE IT WAS located almost directly across the street from campus and because it was cheap and delicious. Kate and Rowan had eaten there so many times, they didn't even need to look at the menu to know what they wanted, yet Kate had trailed behind the rest of the group, pretending to scrutinize the menu displayed above the restaurant's outdoor window. She ordered last, hoping that by the time she got to the long communal table on the outdoor patio, she'd have gotten over her disappointment enough to at least pretend that she was having a good time.

That was the pitfall of being best friends with a hyper-social, emotional exhibitionist like Rowan: A big group meal fueled her soul, while for Kate, it would take every last ounce of her energy to keep from looking as if she wanted to be literally anyplace else on the planet.

Her appetite had mostly evaporated by the time Kate ordered, so she went with her old favorite—rolled tacos—and a soda. She hoped that Rowan would have saved her a seat, but when she arrived at the patio, her best friend was ensconced in the middle of one bench, Jer and Hiroki on one side, Gabby and a white girl she didn't recognize on the other. That must have been Darla. The opposite bench was full as well, and the only open seats were at one end, directly opposite each other. One for her, and one for Ty when he arrived.

Welcome to hell.

"Hey, Kate," Luca said, motioning at the open seats with a flick of his teal-blue hair. The last time Kate had seen him, it had been blood orange, which had accentuated his olive skin, and she wondered how many shades of hair dye she'd missed in between the two. "Take your pick."

"Thanks." Kate smiled tightly and dropped down beside Imogen.

"It's really good to see you," Imogen said, sweeping her thick mane of curly brown hair over one shoulder. She hadn't cut it since her quinceañera two years ago, and the curly tendrils were so long she could have tucked them into her belt. "I'm dying to hear about the *DPT* cancellation. Are you traumatized?"

Right for the jugular. Kate knew Imogen didn't have a mean bone in her body, but the question still felt like a knife to the heart.

"Disappointed," Kate began, treading carefully, "but I think Belle's experience was probably more traumatizing than mine."

Hiroki, less kind than his girlfriend, snorted. "Boning the boss or losing her series?"

"The one that resulted in statutory rape." She may have hated Belle, but she wasn't going to let anyone disregard the fact that she'd been sexually assaulted, especially not a dude.

Thankfully, Hiroki had the good sense to realize he'd overstepped. "Right. Of course. Sorry."

Kate sighed. Thirty seconds into lunch and she was already sniping at people. "No, *I'm* sorry. It's been a tough week."

"I bet," Imogen said, smiling tightly.

Luca leaned over her shoulder. "Is it true that they'd been having sex since the first day of rehearsals?"

"I don't know." Kate spent almost all of her downtime in the school trailer, and since she and Belle weren't exactly close, she rarely saw the *DPT* star except when they were filming scenes together. "We didn't really hang out."

He hardly seemed to register Kate's answer. "And that she showed up at Dex's house and told his wife that they were in love and then his *own wife* turned him in?"

That sounded like something Belle would do, but even if Kate had been in her confidence, these weren't questions she should be answering in public. Not with a criminal trial pending.

"Honestly, I don't know," she said. "Dex's wife isn't exactly my best friend."

"Especially not after that video of you dancing with her husband," Luca cracked.

Kate looked to Rowan, hoping her friend might jump in with a subject change, but her face was turned away as she whispered something in Jer's ear.

Fine. Kate could manage to deflect all on her own.

Maybe.

"Your scene looked fantastic, by the way," Kate said to Imogen. "I can't wait to see the whole showcase."

"Wait until you see Jer's big number," Rowan said, joining the conversation from out of the blue, as if she'd been listening the whole time. "The *Mamma Mia!* scene is amazing."

"Thanks, Toots." Jer shot a finger gun at Rowan, who pretended to take a bullet to the heart and flopped onto his arm, dead. It looked like a routine they'd practiced.

"'Lay All Your Love on Me'?" Kate said, less of a question and more as a setup. "I saw it."

Rowan tilted her head to the side. "When?"

"Um, today. Just now."

"Really?"

"I was in the house watching rehearsal," Kate said, her annoyance at her friend's self-centeredness growing. "But you disappeared after the *Rent* number, so maybe you didn't remember I was there."

Luca stifled a laugh. "Rowan and Jer were backstage, er, running lines."

Rowan dropped her eyes to the table, but she didn't blush. She wasn't embarrassed at all, merely feigning demureness to invite more attention. Which it did.

"You two could have learned an entire show by now," Gabby said, twirling her pink extensions between her fingers. "With all the 'line running' you do."

Rowan lightly smacked her arm. "Shut up."

Gabby laughed. If Rowan was trying to send her a message, she didn't get it. "Isn't that what you were doing last night when I dropped you off at Jer's house?"

Last night. When Kate was at work, waiting for a text back from Rowan about her disastrous audition.

A round of whistles and *oooooo*s went up from the table, but everyone else suddenly felt miles away. Kate met Rowan's eyes across the table, and she saw the wave of guilt wash over her friend's soft features. Was it the guilt of not responding to Kate until after midnight? The guilt of not explaining why she'd been unable to talk earlier, when Kate really needed her? Or was it the guilt of not *wanting* to respond and ghosting Kate because of it?

Their locked gaze only lingered for a few seconds before Rowan broke away, pursing her full lips at Gabby. "Remind me not to share any secrets with you. Ever."

Gabby pouted, feeling the rebuff. "I didn't know it was supposed to be a secret. Especially not from Kate."

"I don't keep secrets from Kate," Rowan said, laughing nervously, which was as good as an admission of guilt.

"Don't you?" Kate asked.

"No," Rowan said. "You just haven't been around as much."

At Rowan's words, it was as if the entire table went rigid. Even Darla, the new girl, sensed the change in mood. She clutched her soda so hard the plastic lid popped off.

"I was working." *On a show you made me audition for.*

"So were we." Rowan didn't look at Kate as she shrugged. "Life goes on."

Life goes on? What the hell was happening? She and Rowan had talked almost every single day all through the *DPT* production and after. Right up until Rowan had started this romance with Jeremiah. How could Rowan be so cold to her best friend? It wasn't fair.

Kate fought the tears that were welling up in her eyes. Crying wasn't going to help anything. She needed to stay calm.

Like Ripley.

"If you're trying to make me feel unwanted and replaced," Kate said quietly, attempting to channel some of Ripley's demeanor as she rose to her feet and stepped out from behind the bench seat, "congratulations."

Kate's icy tone snapped Rowan out of her mood. Her eyes softened, feeling the reproach, and she reached across the table toward Kate. "I . . ."

Before she could say anything, her eyes shifted away just as Kate felt a presence behind her.

"Seems like I arrived at the right time," Ty said with an easy laugh. "Are you leaving already, Kate?"

She didn't have the energy for Ty right after Rowan's very public sucker punch. It was too much.

"Excuse me," she said. Without looking back, Kate rounded the corner of the restaurant to the restrooms.

NINETEEN

KATE CROUCHED ON THE GROUND BEHIND ALBERTO'S AND closed her eyes, resting her forehead on clenched hands. She'd been hoping for some much-needed time with Rowan to discuss theater camp, Jeremiah, and Kate's anxieties about her own future, and instead she'd gotten ambushed by her best friend, who had apparently been harboring a secret resentment for months.

This day was falling apart.

Your life is falling apart.

She felt blindsided and betrayed. She'd asked Rowan a million times if she was angry that Kate had been cast instead of her, and a million times Rowan had assured her it was fine. That *they* were fine.

Apparently not so much.

Maybe she should bail. Walk home. Her parents were out. They'd never know that Rowan's mom didn't drop her off or that the once-inseparable best friends were slowly drifting apart.

Tears welled up in her eyes once more. Sure there had been some missed calls and backed-up texts from Rowan while Kate was on *DPT*, but she didn't always have the chance to respond on shooting days. For nine and a half hours, her time was monopolized; then, before her next call time, she had to fit in all her homework, plus memorize lines and blocking because at a moment's notice she could be pulled away from a European history exam to shoot an emotionally fraught scene, then shift back to World War I sociopolitical allegiances the moment she was done on set.

Rowan and her theater camp friends might have thought that a role on a high-profile Netflix show was like hitting the jackpot, but only if the jackpot required a shit ton more work than you'd ever done in your life that left you emotionally and physically drained every single day.

And now Kate was working a soulless job, forced to pay rent to live in her own bedroom while she was sent on insulting auditions by a patronizing agent, and she had literally no one to talk to about any of it. All Rowan had to worry about was the expensive theater camp her supportive parents had paid for and whether or not they'd catch her sneaking in after curfew from a hookup with Jer without Kate running interference for her as she'd done countless times over the years.

Who should be jealous of whom?

"You okay?"

Ty's voice was edgy, the same slightly pretentious, slightly aloof tone he'd been taking with her since his return. He sounded put out, as if Kate's despondent mood was a chore he was forced to deal with, and she just wasn't strong enough to deal with that now.

"I'm hiding from my friends on the backside of a Mexican restaurant while pretending to go to the bathroom." She looked him dead in the eyes. "There's nothing 'okay' about that."

"Wow."

"Were you expecting me to lie?"

For the first time, his gaze faltered. "I . . . I don't know."

Kate sighed, smoothing out the wrinkled midsection of her dress as she pushed herself to her feet. This is why she hated social niceties. They were the coward's way of feigning conversation without risk or substance. "If you didn't want to actually know how I was, you shouldn't have bothered to ask. I'm not going to let you feel better about yourself if your check-in was meaningless."

She brushed past him, not even really sure where she was going.

"Hey, wait!"

Ty's hand slipped into hers so suddenly, she didn't even realize he was holding on until her arm straightened out. She spun around, pissed off and ready to unleash a tirade of her pent-up frustration at his condescending smile, but the words dissolved on her tongue. Ty wasn't smiling. He wasn't laughing at her. There was no triumph on his face. His eyes were soft, his pouty lips pressed thin with worry. The superiority was gone, replaced by something more like kindness.

The old Ty.

Without the battle she'd teased herself up for, Kate didn't know what to say. The familiarity and camaraderie she'd enjoyed with Ty had vanished that day last year when he told her how he really felt and she'd broken his heart. Where did they go from here?

"I'm sorry," Ty said, his voice measured, as if he wanted to make sure each of his syllables was heard and understood. "I *do* want to know how you're doing. I'm not sure what I was expecting to hear."

"Oh."

"And I'm sorry that you're not okay."

"Me too."

He nodded his head toward the front of the restaurant. "But you had to expect this kind of reception after all that's happened."

All that's happened. She certainly hadn't been prepared for any of it. First, when she was cast on *Dirty Pretty Teens*, there'd been a wave of excitement among their group of friends. Once shooting began, the excitement morphed into kissing ass—everyone expected to be invited to the wrap party, and many were bent out of shape when Kate could only bring one guest. Now that the show had been canceled and Kate's star wasn't shining so brightly in the Hollywood sky, Kate sensed an ill wind blowing in her direction. Which really sucked.

"I thought it was just going to be Rowan and me today. Then she came out of rehearsal with Jeremiah . . ." Kate shook her head, letting her eyes drop to the ground. She wasn't ready to verbalize what she thought about their relationship.

"Jer's a good guy," Ty said with a shrug. "He makes my sister happy."

"But they were just friends!" Kate said, realizing with a cringe that she sounded like an obstinate child. "She didn't even like him."

Ty paused, his breaths measured. "Sometimes friendship gets in the way."

Kate's words from last year flew back at her, a slap in the face.

You're my best friend's brother. We can't ever be more than just friends.

Kate looked up, keenly aware of how close their bodies were. For years, Ty had been in orbit around Kate and Rowan. They'd hung out all the time—watching Netflix on the sectional sofa in the Chens' family room, where Ty would lean over and playfully punch Kate in the arm after one of her snarky tirades; or at the bookstore when they'd all walk over after school—Rowan would flirt with the barista while Kate and Ty browsed the aisles until one of their parents picked them up; at the movies, when Ty always sat on one side of Kate, Rowan on the other, so Kate could steal popcorn from her and candy from him because her mom didn't believe in spending money on concessions.

Ty had been there for years, practically the third wheel on their friendship tricycle. Until suddenly he'd changed everything.

Kate had been waiting in front of her house for Rowan, sitting on the same bench where Belle had ambushed her last week, when a car pulled up. She'd expected to see Mrs. Chen with Rowan riding shotgun, but instead, Ty was driving one of the family's Teslas and Rowan was nowhere in sight.

"Is everything okay?" Kate had asked. She must have sensed Ty's anxiety without even realizing it, and assumed that something was wrong.

"I need to talk to you." Ty's face was pale, his voice trembling as he approached. He looked less sure of himself than ever before. Kate's brain immediately went to the nuclear options.

"Is Rowan sick? Is she in the hospital?" She'd sucked in a breath. "Is she dead?"

"No!"

"Then why do you look like you're about to throw up?"

Ty had sat down next to her on the bench. "I'm leaving next week. I'll be gone—"

"A whole year," Kate had said. They'd talked about this, like, a million times. "It'll be great. You'll have a blast in Shanghai."

"Yeah." Ty had cleared his throat. "Before I go, I need to tell you . . . I mean, I need you to know. I *want* you to know . . ."

Kate hadn't seen what was coming.

But she should have.

"Spit it out," she had said with a laugh. Which seemed so cruel now. "You sound like your brain's rebooting."

"I love you!" The words had been more of an explosion than a declaration, a single three-syllable word that burst forth from Ty's mouth almost against his will.

"What?"

"For a long time. As long as I can remember," he'd said, without actually repeating the words *I love you*. "And . . . and I needed you to hear it before I left . . . in case."

In case you die? In case I feel the same way? He'd let the sentiment linger, hoping, she thought, that Kate would fill in the blanks or at least make doing so moot by kissing him while she ran her fingers through his soft black hair. . . .

Stop it!

What the fuck was wrong with her? This was Ty. Rowan's brother. Practically Kate's brother. He knew that she still slept on the Minnie Mouse sheets she'd gotten for her eighth birthday and that she kept a copy of *Jude the Obscure* by her bed because sometimes she woke up in the middle of the night and the novel was so freaking boring that reading a few pages helped her fall back to sleep. They were too close. Too intimate.

You're my best friend's brother. We can't ever be more than just friends.

The look on Ty's face as he stood up was still burned into her brain a year later. Sadness, yes. But also pity.

Kinda like the way he's looking at me now.

"What do you want?" Kate asked, exasperated. Every part of this day had felt like a reproach, and she was so over it.

"I don't want anything." He dropped her hand abruptly.

"Then why are you here?"

He took a breath, about to say something, then bit his lip, second-guessing himself. "I thought you could use a friend."

Before she could respond, he swung around the corner of the building and was gone.

TWENTY

KATE SPENT MOST OF THE NEXT FORTY-EIGHT HOURS IN HER room, feigning a cold. She didn't want to talk to anyone, and she didn't want to think about anything. She just wanted to sleep and read and sleep some more. Until it was time to go back to work Monday night. Even an email from Clementine that morning with a new audition didn't brighten her mood. After the last disaster, Kate wasn't excited at the thought of further audition humiliation. The only thing she had to look forward to was her job.

And the prospect of more drama from Ripley's office.

Kleiner, Abato & Chen was no longer a punishment but a refuge, a place she could go where she was hidden away from the real-world stresses that weighed her down. At home, where all the food was labeled, her parents were there with watchful eyes, waiting for some sign of capitulation from their daughter. She and Rowan had texted a little, but the vibe was more of a "let's pretend that didn't happen" than "let's work through this," though even if they *had* talked it out, she couldn't hang with Rowan anymore unless she wanted Jeremiah along for the ride. Or worse, Ty.

Wherever Kate looked, there was someone waiting to judge her. Except inside the file room dungeon at Kleiner, Abato & Chen.

Which was pretty sad.

On Monday, she pulled into the underground parking garage well after sundown. Later than usual, as evidenced by the sparsity of cars in the lot. She was able to park right near the elevators beside the reserved spots for fancy tenants. CEOs and presidents. Those parking spaces were almost always filled with expensive European luxury sedans or Tesla Model Xs like the one Mr. Chen drove. But at this hour, those spots were long abandoned. Apparently, the people who ran these companies worked shorter hours than the people who worked for them.

As if to prove her wrong, a Porsche zipped up behind her, screeching into one of the reserved spots next to the elevators. It was an old model, more vintage chic than outdated sad, in a sassy candy-apple red. Kate was still climbing out of her Subaru when the door of the Porsche flew open and Ripley stepped out.

She was in a hurry, and judging by the ferocity with which she slammed her car door, she was pissed off.

Ripley took nothing with her, other than a set of keys gripped in her hand. Actual keys that jangled as she marched to the elevator, instead of a key fob like every other car made during Kate's lifetime. The vintage car juxtaposed with Ripley's pristine, lady-boss style made her even more awe-inspiring.

She stormed into the elevator bay, red-soled Louboutins clicking against the cement floor, and stabbed frantically at the up button as if the machine that controlled the call would move faster based on her level of agitation. Kate had just pulled her backpack out of the car when the elevator's up light blinked on.

Kate had a split second to decide what to do: ride up with her idol or wait for the next car. As if there was a choice. Ripley had already stepped inside the elevator when Kate sprinted for the door. She thrust her arm into the closing gap, causing the sensors to freeze the movement and reopen the doors immediately. Panting, she took her place beside Ripley for the quick ride up one floor.

Kate sensed Ripley's body stiffen beside her, and though she was too terrified to make eye contact, she was pretty sure that if Ripley could have murdered her with a look, she would have. Ripley tsked her tongue in annoyance and pressed the lobby button a couple of times in futile annoyance, but there Kate was, in the elevator with this strong, powerful woman who had no fucks to give. She was cheating on her husband with a hot guy half her age, she ran a successful business, and her authority was undeniable. Ripley was everything Kate wished she could be, and she wasn't going to let the opportunity pass her by without at least making some small talk or she'd never forgive herself.

"Sorry about snagging the elevator," Kate said, grasping at the first conversation point she could think of. She couldn't exactly open with "How's the divorce going?" or "Damn, your assistant is hot."

Unfortunately, the apology received no reaction. Kate chanced a glance at her elevator mate. Ripley was even more imposing up close. Her square jaw bulged from the violence of her clench, and her eyes, which could both seduce and destroy, were fixed at a spot on the doors, willing them to open.

"I hope I didn't make you late," Kate added.

"Late, no." Ripley's voice was higher than what Kate had imagined. She thought it would be a low, seductive tone, and instead, Ripley's voice was delicately girl-like. Even with the added bite of sarcasm.

"Okay, cool." Cool? Seriously? Why did she sound so infantile?

Kate was still trying to think of a way to prolong the conversation when the light dinged and the doors opened. Ripley bolted through them without ever looking at Kate and marched up to the security desk. Donald snapped to attention as he saw her approach, a smile of delight transforming his perpetual scowl.

"Ms. Eldridge! Back so soon?"

Ms. Eldridge! Even her name sounded important.

"I forgot to mention when I left," she said, her voice a purr. Donald's fat smile indicated that her charm was working. "If anyone shows up when I'm not in the office, will you call my cell?"

"I'm not sure that I—"

"Let me give it to you."

Kate tried to eavesdrop on Ripley's cell phone number, lingering as she passed the security desk, but Ripley had dropped her voice as she huddled with Donald, and Kate trudged to the elevator bay with only Ripley's last name as a prize.

Tucked away from view of the security desk, Kate hesitated before pressing the call button. There was a directory on the far wall, a listing of all the businesses in both towers, separated by floor. Kleiner, Abato & Chen was there in all caps, proudly in suite 300 of the north tower, which was actually two-thirds of the entire third floor, with a small post-production marketing company taking up the rest of the square footage.

Across in the south tower, the space below THIRD FLOOR on the directory was empty, but the fourth floor of the south tower had more businesses, broken into smaller office configurations. Like Ripley's two-room suite. Though Kate's security badge only allowed her access to the third floor in her own building, she could at least try to figure out which business belonged to Ripley, and discover what, exactly, she did.

Six businesses were located on the fourth floor of the south tower, but none of them had the name Eldridge attached. Half of those she could dismiss since they had the businessperson's name in the company name—Rooney Brothers, the Tovmasyan Group, Masoumi & Masoumi were probably not Ripley Eldridge in disguise. That left three nondescript businesses which could be hers: Image Partners, LLC; SafeCheck Production Payroll; and QED.

Kate quickly took a photo of the entire directory, then shoved her phone back into her bag as she pressed the up button.

* * *

Ripley never returned to her office, despite Kate's vigil at the dungeon window, and her tedious slog through her work pile felt tedious-er and sloggier without entertainment. Around nine o'clock, Kate left the dungeon and sat down on the floor in the hallway beside the nearest cubicle with a peanut-butter-and-raspberry-jam sandwich in one hand and her phone in the other. It was time to do a little research.

Scanning the photo she'd taken of the directory, she decided to start with the least likely candidate for Ripley's business: SafeCheck Production Payroll in suite 440. Ripley didn't dress like any accountant Kate had ever met, plus production payroll companies would probably need more than two employees. And there was no discernible reason why Belle would meet with them. Kate pulled up their website and scanned the "About Us" page, but none of the employee photos were Ripley, and Kate mentally crossed that candidate off her list.

Image Partners, LLC in suite 450 sounded more promising, but the website was noticeably vague and the company description was a word salad of business doublespeak with terms like *synergistic workflow* and *upmarket quotient gradients* that literally made no sense. Thankfully, the company's mission statement was more to the point. Image Partners was a stock photo and video company run by two dudes who looked like they were right out of central casting's dot-com-start-up-guy lineup. She had no idea how a synergistic workflow would help people licensing an image of a smiling customer service representative for their website, but whatever. Once again, she crossed the name off her list.

Which left QED. According to Mr. Google, *QED* stood for "quod erat demonstrandum" in Latin, and translated roughly to "thus it has been shown." Popular term with mathematicians and theorists, so it took some digging to find a company with that name located in Burbank. But the internet is a magical place, and since she knew the company's address, she was able to find a nebulous web presence.

There were no employee names and headshots on the website, no person registered as an executive or board member anywhere on the internet. Nothing that pointed a direct finger at Ripley, though by process of elimination, QED was her company.

Definitely not an agency, though. The website was too secretive. A lawyer, perhaps? Maybe one that specialized in difficult cases, like, say, helping a man accused of sexual misconduct with a minor. Belle was in love with Dex, so as sick as it sounded, it made sense that she was trying to help him.

Kate thought of the Kleiner, Abato & Chen offices. A much bigger law firm, of course, but Ripley's office didn't look like any law firm she'd ever been to. No framed diplomas on the wall, no library of legal tomes all neatly arranged on the shelf. And a support staff of one. Not enough resources to take on the defense of Dex Pratt. But what other options were there?

Googling *Eldridge* and *QED* was a bust, as was using Ripley's business address, and Kate was about to give up when she decided to just use *QED* and *Burbank* as her search terms. She was three pages into her results when she finally caught a break. It was a local news article from five years ago, a puff piece about a Santa Monica High School valedictorian interning with a private investigation firm in Burbank. The company was called QED.

The late hours, the small staff, the secretive flavor of the website. Ripley was a private investigator.

Super-cool noirish vibes only added to Ripley's awesome lady-boss mystique, but it did leave one huge question:

Why the hell was Belle Masterson hiring a PI?

TWENTY-ONE

WHILE KATE WAS THANKFUL THAT CLEMENTINE HAD BEEN able to secure another audition for her within days of bombing one, she was dismayed at the part. She didn't even need to read the dialogue to know. The character's name was "Hungry Diner Patron" and the breakdown was awful: *Female, 16–24, heavyset, comedic.*

Kate understood that she was new to this business, but what the actual fuck? She'd seen the breakdowns for *Dirty Pretty Teens* in which none of the characters' sizes had been specified. She'd assumed that was the norm. Sure, her character was white and skinny by default due to lack of specificity in the novels, but no one on the production seemed to care that they'd cast a size-sixteen girl as Noelle.

Ugh. Kate had thought Clementine understood her desire to do parts that weren't written specifically for non-anorexically thin actresses, parts that wouldn't cement long-entrenched ideas about fat people and their societal worth. But clearly her agent was clueless.

Still, Kate was determined to have a good audition, if not for Clementine than for herself. She needed to prove that she could do this, that she could rise above the bullshit and give a performance that would elevate Hungry Diner Patron in the rom-com *Sunny's Side Up* to something not quite so horrible. She'd gone to the audition despite her kneejerk reaction to bail, and the second she walked into the audition room, she regretted that choice.

"Kate!"

Sara Rhodes, the casting director for *Sixth Street Bridge,* strode toward her, hand outstretched with a smile that radiated enthusiasm. "It's so good to see you again."

"You too!" Kate said, flustered by the warm reception. She was pretty sure that after last week's audition, Sara would never agree to see her again. "Thank you so much for having me back."

"Of course! I was so surprised when Clementine submitted you for this, especially since she said you weren't interested in the part I requested you for."

"Requested me?" Kate's chest tightened.

Sara tilted her head. "Well, yes. For the lead in this film. After your Queenie audition, I thought you'd be perfect for Sunny. I'm sorry if you didn't like the script I sent over."

Lead role. Script she sent over. Kate's face went cold, and she was pretty sure she'd instantly broken out in a full-body sweat. "I . . . I never saw it."

"Oh." Sara looked confused for a second, as if not understanding how Kate couldn't have seen the script she'd been specifically invited to audition for; then her eyes grew wide in understanding, which quickly morphed to sympathy. "Oh!"

Kate was having difficulty holding back the tears, but she managed to ask in a shaky voice, "Is it cast?"

"We did, yes. Just yesterday. But I'm sure the director would see you for another project."

"I understand."

"And *I* will definitely keep you in mind for the next one."

"Thank you." The next one. Only if Clementine told her about it.

Only if Clementine is still my agent.

"Who did you cast?" Kate asked, hoping at least it was another plus-size actress. "If you can tell me."

"Press release doesn't go out until next week, but between you, me, and the wall, I can share. Especially since you're friends."

Oh no.

"The part went to Belle Masterson."

* * *

Kate called Clementine's cell phone three times on her drive back to Burbank. Three times, it went straight to voice mail.

Of course, it was after six o'clock, which meant theoretically, the offices of the CDB Agency were closed for the day. But this was Clementine's personal cell phone. Kate had witnessed Belle call her agent at all hours of the day—weekends, too—and Clementine had always answered. Belle was having a fit about wardrobe at a five a.m. fitting? Clementine was there with a fix. A meltdown over a second-unit director at midnight on a Friday? Clementine was all over it. But she wasn't picking up Kate's calls at six o'clock on a Tuesday. That could only mean one thing:

Clementine was avoiding her.

Maybe Sara Rhodes had texted her already, tipping Clementine off. Getting caught after withholding an audition was a good reason to ghost your client.

Kate might have cried over her situation if she hadn't been so angry. She'd been railroaded, gaslit, hung out to dry while Belle Masterson—America's skinny little princess—practically got away with murder.

Angry or not, the tears were flowing now, blinding Kate with a stinging mix of salt and runny mascara and bitterness as she crested the hill on Barham Boulevard and descended into the Valley. She didn't want to go home. Her mom and dad would immediately know that something had happened, would want to be there to comfort and console their daughter, but the subtext of "we told you so" and "can we please give up on this actor plan for a while?" would simmer beneath every word and hug. Kate couldn't handle that kind of sympathy right now.

Instead, she called Rowan. Since she rarely called, her friend should recognize that it was an emergency and pick up, but after four rings, voice mail kicked in.

"Hey," Kate said, her voice shaky. "Can you please call me back? I really need to talk."

She half expected an incoming call from Rowan while she was still leaving a message, but her phone never rang.

Kate considered just driving over to Rowan's house, but then, what if she wasn't home? What if Rowan had told her parents she was with Kate while she was actually hooking up with Jer? Kate would blow everything.

I thought you could use a friend. Ty's words from Saturday came flooding back to her. She hadn't seen him since their conversation behind Alfredo's, and though their friendship was a hot mess at best, the idea of talking her rage through with him made her smile.

"What are you thinking?" Kate said out loud, stopping her runaway imagination. She couldn't run to Ty in her hour of need. She'd given up that privilege when she'd broken his heart, and considering how he'd conveniently been absent from his desk Monday night when she'd arrived for work, she suspected that he was avoiding her.

But Kate literally had nowhere else to go, so she drove to the Burbank Garden Towers Business Park. At least she could get a good cry alone in the dungeon, hidden away from the world.

Kate pulled into the first empty parking spot she found, flew out of the elevator from the parking garage, past the empty security desk, and into the north tower elevator with blinders on, only focused on a small space directly in front of her. It felt like an eternity as she waited for the doors to open at the third floor.

One hand clapped over her mouth as if trying to keep her puke in, Kate raced through the lobby, not even glancing in Albie's direction, then down the hallway toward the dungeon. She almost made it, before she barreled directly into someone coming out of the men's room.

Not just someone.

Ty.

They both went sprawling onto the industrial carpet from the force of impact, like a head-on train collision, a tangle of limbs. Kate's head bounced off Ty's chest before her momentum carried her forward and she rolled awkwardly onto her side.

"Kate!" Ty gasped. "What are you doing?"

"I . . ." What was she supposed to say? She wanted to tell him what had happened, to unburden herself of her rage and seek comfort in his soft brown eyes and tentative smile, but once again, she rejected that idea. Not only did she not deserve the intimacy with Ty, but she wasn't entirely sure he'd even offer it.

As she hesitated, Ty pushed himself to his feet. She saw his eyes register her tear-streaked cheeks and smudged makeup, and the look on his face transformed from surprise to concern in an instant.

"Are you okay?" He reached out a hand and helped her to her feet. "What's wrong? What happened?"

She couldn't have answered him without breaking into incoherent sobs, which wouldn't have done either of them any good. But she also couldn't look him in the eyes. Instead, she fumbled with her security badge and kept her face angled away in case she lost it.

"I, uh, thought I was late." That sounded plausible.

"Late to an after-hours job with no set start time?" His hand still rested on her arm, guiding her back toward his cubicle. "Why don't you sit down and I can get you some water or—"

"No!" she said more quickly than she'd intended. It sounded like desperation. "No, I'm fine."

Ty wasn't buying it. He knew her too well. "If you need to talk, I can cancel my dinner plans and stay—"

"Dinner plans?" Ty didn't have a huge group of friends, and she'd never known him to refer to hanging out with them as "dinner plans" in the entire time she'd known him. "With who?"

Kate only realized that she didn't really want to know the answer to that question when she saw a blush sweep up Ty's neck like a pink tidal wave. "Just a friend."

A girl*friend*. "Oh."

Kate felt her stomach drop out beneath her. She'd never invited Ty's love. Never asked for it, never worked for it, and pushed it aside when it was offered to her. So then why did the idea of Ty going on a date make her feel like vomiting all over Kleiner, Abato & Chen's beige carpet?

"I . . . I need to go." She dashed back to the dungeon.

"But, Kate—"

"I'm fine!"

She scanned her badge and disappeared inside before he could confirm that she wasn't.

TWENTY-TWO

KATE ONLY REALIZED SHE'D FALLEN ASLEEP BENEATH THE table in the dungeon when she shivered so violently it woke her up.

She'd crawled down there as soon as she escaped inside, away from the prying eyes of the Kleiner, Abato & Chen security cameras, to indulge in some ugly crying, and like an infant in the throes of a tantrum, the sobbing had exhausted her.

It had definitely been an indulgent cry, the kind born of raw emotion, though Kate wasn't exactly sure *which* emotions fueled the outburst. Shame? Anger? Emptiness? Self-pity? Probably a heady mix of all four, but whatever the fuel, the fire had burned through it quickly and violently, and she was left drawn and exhausted.

Her back was stiff, her hip aching as she pushed herself to her feet. Her arms puckered like gooseflesh from the freezing-cold temperature of the dungeon, and when she wiped her fingers beneath her eyes, the pads came out black with smeared makeup.

It was dark outside, almost ten, according to the clock on her phone, which meant she'd slept for hours. She hadn't even noticed the mass of filing that had been left for her to do, and as she stood there staring at it, a thundering headache already pounding at her temples, she wanted to cry again. As desperately as she'd been to get to the dungeon, now she wanted out. Filing wasn't something she could focus on tonight.

But she couldn't leave the work sitting there, untouched. This was her job. This is what being an adult meant—dealing with your personal problems and not letting them impinge on your professional life. She'd have to get used to that mentality.

And besides, the last thing she wanted was for Ty to come in tomorrow morning and see that though she'd been to the office, she'd gotten nothing done. How could she possibly explain?

With a sigh that felt more like a groan, Kate trudged out of the dungeon to retrieve the keys from Ty's desk. The office was dark and silent, motion sensor lights flickering to life as she navigated the hallways, and her mood was as dark as the south tower as she returned to her prison, grabbed a stack of papers, and began sorting them on the table. Maybe she'd just organize them tonight, then come in early tomorrow and file it all.

Kate was just reaching for a second handful of loose pages when the light popped on in Ripley's lobby.

Ripley and her assistant tumbled through the door, lips locked together as they raced toward Ripley's private office, attempting to undress each other en route. Real-Life Wyatt had managed to get Ripley's blouse off, exposing a black lace bra beneath, and Ripley was working on his belt buckle as she dragged him toward the desk. She kept her skirt on as she pushed herself up on the wooden desktop, knocking her phone and a framed photo onto the floor. She edged backward, beckoning her assistant with a finger. He climbed on top of her and buried his face in her cleavage.

Not again.

She couldn't take other people's happiness tonight. Kate was turning away from the window when something Ripley did caught her attention.

As the assistant was kissing his way down her stomach toward the waistband of her skirt, Ripley stretched an arm out behind her and opened one of the drawers, removing an item that she then set on the desk beside her. It was a slow movement, furtive, and Kate was instantly intrigued.

Had she grabbed a condom? That made sense. Kate's parents had been preaching safe sex to her since the day she got her first period, and though she was still very much a virgin, she carried a condom around in her backpack. Just in case. It made sense that two people who were about to get it on would be thinking about sexual health and safe practices.

But Ripley had moved as if she didn't want her assistant to notice what she was doing. A condom wouldn't have required that level of stealth, would it?

Kate didn't have time to answer her own question before another figure barged through the door of Ripley's office. Kate recognized him immediately. It was the man who had confronted Ripley a few days ago.

The man Kate assumed was Ripley's husband.

The assistant scrambled to his feet, struggling to button his pants. He pressed himself against the window as if he might be able to disappear through the glass, and as Ripley's husband turned to face him, Kate saw why. The man was holding a gun.

Ripley didn't show any fear. Or surprise. In fact, as she sat on the desk in her bra, she looked almost as if she'd been expecting this confrontation. A smile played at the corners of her mouth while she watched her husband, her hands fidgeting with something just out of Kate's view.

Her husband was yelling, face red, spit flying from his mouth, but instead of attempting an explanation or begging forgiveness, Ripley merely tilted her head back and yawned.

Her husband paused, momentarily thrown by his wife's reaction. He stood in the door, his gun hanging limp and forgotten in his hand as he gazed back and forth between Ripley and her assistant. Suddenly, he seemed to realize where he was and what he was doing, as if arriving at his wife's office while brandishing a firearm had all been done unconsciously, under the influence of anger or booze or both.

He dropped the gun, jumping away from it in horror, then turned to leave. In the window, Real-Life Wyatt's body visibly relaxed.

But if Ripley shared her assistant's sense of relief, she certainly didn't show it. Instead of relaxing, she threw her arms up in dismay, and Kate could almost hear the single word she mouthed. "Seriously?"

Ripley sighed and grabbed the item she'd prepped on her desk. She must have said something nasty because her departing husband swung around. At the same time, Ripley raised her hand.

Kate registered two things simultaneously. The first was that Ripley had managed to pull on a pair of blue surgical gloves while her husband had blustered in the doorway, and the second was that she held a black metal object in her hand, but Kate only realized it was a gun when Ripley pulled the trigger, shooting her husband in the chest.

"Oh my God!" Kate cried out, though no one could hear her from inside the dungeon.

Holy shit. She'd just watched Ripley murder her husband. No self-defense, no the-heat-of-the-moment excuse. She'd calmly and stoically murdered him while he was unarmed and attempting to leave.

Ripley walked into the lobby and bent down, over the body Kate assumed, though she couldn't see the floor from her angle. Her assistant crept up behind her. Then, in one fluid move, Ripley swung aside and held something out toward Real-Life Wyatt. Kate thought she heard a faint *pop* reverberate across the courtyard. The assistant's body twitched, then hung in the air for a moment before he, too, crumpled to the ground.

Kate was pretty sure Ripley had killed him using her husband's gun.

TWENTY-THREE

KATE MIGHT HAVE SCREAMED.

Must have screamed.

She honestly couldn't tell.

She thought she *heard* a scream, and since she was the only person in the dungeon, if her ears were working normally, then the throttled sound must have come out of her mouth. But considering how difficult it had instantly become to simply inhale air into her lungs, she wasn't sure how she could possibly have been the one to scream. . . .

Stop.

Who cares whether or not you screamed? You need to call the police.

Right. Emergency. Call 911. Rebooting her brain, Kate grabbed her phone and slowly scanned the area near the upper right corner of the window, the only place she'd ever been able to get a cell signal in the dungeon. She saw a blip on her phone, indicating some kind of reception; then two small bars crept into view. Good enough.

She held the phone as motionless as she could and dialed 911 before switching the phone to speaker. The ringing that crackled through the roar of server fans was broken and choppy as the signal fluctuated. Kate held her breath, hoping it would stabilize long enough to report two murders. The second ring was stronger, only interrupted by the male operator.

"Nine-one-one, please st—" His voice cut out.

"Hello?" Kate said, hoping he was still there. "Hello, I need to report a murder. Two actually. Two murders!"

She waited, praying for a response, but the phone was silent. Then it beeped, and the message NO SERVICE popped onto the screen. The call had ended.

"Fuck!" Who would have thought that all the safety measures at Kleiner, Abato & Chen would actually aid and abet a murderer?

Kate's eyes darted back to the window across the courtyard. Ripley had disappeared with the two bodies presumably still on the floor of her office, out of Kate's view. What was Ripley going to do now? Call the police and turn herself in? Yeah, right. Ripley had taken the gun out of her desk while she was making out with her assistant so it was nearby and ready if she needed it. *When* she needed it. Had Ripley known that her husband was going to walk in on them? She certainly didn't look surprised by his arrival. Or scared.

Kate gasped. If she had known he was coming, had the double murders been a setup?

Premeditated murder. Ripley was getting rid of both her husband and her lover at the same time. She'd even made sure her husband was facing her so he wouldn't be shot in the back, and used her husband's gun to kill her assistant, making it look as if the two men had shot each other in the heat of the moment.

If Ripley had mapped out her details that carefully, she probably had a plan for what would happen next. Kate needed to stop her before she erased all evidence of her crimes. Someone needed to get up into that office fast. Faster than the police.

Donald.

Kate leaped off the table and sprinted down the row of filing cabinets to the wall-mounted phone. It took four rings before Donald picked up.

"Burbank Garden Towers Security Desk. Can I help you?" Despite the words, Donald sounded annoyed by the interruption.

"This is Kate Williams. I work at Kleiner, Abato & Chen, and I need to report a—"

He interrupted her before she even got to the word *murder*.

"Is this a prank call?"

Holy hell. "No, I work in the filing room. My name is Kate, and I just witnessed a murder!"

She sounded hysterical, and her story was fantastic at best. *My name is Kate, and I just witnessed a murder?* Yeah, no surprise that cranky Donald didn't believe her.

"A murder. Really." She could practically see the sneer on his face.

"Yes," she pleaded, desperate for him to believe her. "In the south tower."

"Which suite?"

"Uh . . ." Shit. She thought QED was the best candidate, but what if she was wrong? If she sent Donald to the wrong place, then he'd never believe her.

Apparently, her hesitation was worse.

"That's what I thought," Donald growled, patience gone. "If you call me again, I'm reporting you to the police!" Then he promptly hung up.

"FUCK!" Kate screamed. He thought she was a prank call. How was she possibly going to get him to believe her? She couldn't even tell him where Ripley was when she killed those people.

Ripley.

Ms. Eldridge! What can I do for you this evening?

Kate took a steadying breath. She couldn't tell Donald *where*, but she could tell him *who*.

This time, Donald picked up before the first ring had even finished. He had definitely anticipated a second call.

"What?!" he barked.

"It's Ms. Eldridge," Kate blurted out before he could hang up on her again. "I saw something in her office, and—"

"Ms. Eldridge? Are you okay?"

Seriously? "No, I'm not Ms. Eldridge."

"Who is this?" he said. The conversation was beginning to sound like an old-timey comedy routine, which might have been entertaining under different circumstances.

"Donald, I work at Kleiner, Abato & Chen and I just saw something in Ms. Eldridge's window."

"Impossible. I saw her leave hours ago."

Was he for real?

"She's in her office," Kate said slowly, articulating each word as if speaking to a small child. "Right now. She had a gun, and she shot two people!"

"Is Ms. Eldridge in danger?" Wow, talk about selective hearing. "I'll be right there."

The line went dead.

The Burbank Garden Towers Business Park night security staff was really aces. No wonder Kleiner, Abato & Chen jumped through such hoops to make sure their suite was secure. The clown show in the building was useless.

Kate considered calling 911 from outside the dungeon but thought she'd check on Ripley first. Maybe Donald would find the bodies and call the murders in himself. The police would definitely be more inclined to believe him over some teenager. But as she approached the window, she saw that Ripley's office was dark.

Had she moved the bodies already?

Or would Donald walk in on a murder scene?

Maybe that was her plan all along. The jealous husband and the angry boyfriend kill each other, their bodies left in the office for someone else to find.

Someone like the cleaning crew.

Of course. They came through Ripley's office every evening around nine thirty. They'd find the bodies tomorrow night, call the police, and Ripley would conveniently be miles away. Donald already said that he had watched her leave for the day. She probably had an airtight alibi all lined up.

Holy shit, it was the perfect crime.

Except for me.

Now Donald would find the bodies sooner than Ripley expected, which meant, maybe, she didn't have time to establish her alibi, whatever it was. Plus, Kate was an eyewitness.

She smiled ruefully. *I can't believe I ever thought she was awesome.*

Kate waited for the lights to flip on in Ripley's office, for Donald to open the door, see the bodies, and start the wheels in motion. She waited. And waited some more. Five minutes. Ten.

It didn't take that long to get from the lobby to the fourth floor in either tower. What the hell was going on?

Kate rushed back to the phone and tapped her free hand against her leg impatiently while it rang the security desk. At a dozen rings she gave up. Where the hell was Donald?

A new thought hit her. What if Donald had interrupted Ripley's plan? What if he caught her leaving the office? Her alibi blown, would she have murdered him, too?

Oh no. She needed to call the police. Donald's death was on her hands.

She let the phone receiver drop and wrenched open the dungeon door, fishing her phone out of her pocket so she'd be ready to redial 911, when she stopped short outside the door. A squat figure stood in the hallway, arms folded over his chest.

"You!" Donald said, clamping a hand on her shoulder.

"You're alive!" Kate cried. Her relief was short-lived as Donald's scowl deepened.

"Do you think it's funny to call in false alarms?" he said, ignoring her. "I can file a report against you for that."

False alarms? File a report? Two people are dead! "Did you go into her office?" Kate asked even though she knew the answer. "Because if you had, it would be kinda hard to miss two dead bodies in the lobby."

Donald preened, straightening his back and slicking back his greasy hair. "I ran into Ms. Eldridge coming out of the elevator."

"And?" She doubted good old Ms. Eldridge had copped to murder, but she wanted to know how she'd prevented Donald from entering her office.

His eyebrows arched in that same patronizing way Ty's did when she first started working at Kleiner, Abato & Chen. Intolerable then and now.

"She'd come back to the office because she forgot her cell phone. She was late for a dinner and had to rush off."

Of course he bought that. Donald was useless. "She's lying."

Donald snorted. "Just because *you've* never been late to dinner in your life . . ."

Really? A fat joke? "I'm calling the police." Kate reached for her cell phone, but Donald grabbed her arm, squeezing it viciously.

"*I'm* the security officer for this building," he snarled. "Not you."

You sure about that?

"And *I* say there's nothing to report."

Kate yanked her arm away. "I know what I saw." All the cops had to do was open the door to Ripley's office. She just needed to get them there.

But before she even had her phone out of her pocket, she heard the scratchy static of a walkie-talkie.

"Base Camp, this is Iron Man," Donald barked into the receiver. "Over."

The static cut out as the person on the other end hit the talk button, sighing heavily before they replied. "Donald, just say your damn name. We don't need code words."

Donald swallowed nervously but continued undaunted. "Base Camp, we have a teen delinquent here at Burbank Garden making prank calls to nine-one-one. How should we proceed? Over."

"Seriously?" Kate said.

"Seriously?" asked the operator at Donald's base camp.

"Seriously. Over."

"It's not a prank call!" Kate tried, hoping the person on the other end of the line was more reasonable than Dickhead Donald. "I saw a double murder."

But Donald had already released the talk button. "Not on my watch."

Kate sighed. Of course she'd get the one security guard who took his job as seriously as a Secret Service agent.

"I'll notify Burbank PD of a potential prank caller," the base camp operator said wearily. "Anything else, Donald?"

"Negative," Donald said with a triumphant smile. "Iron Man out."

Then without another word, Donald lumbered past her, out the door.

TWENTY-FOUR

FOR THE SECOND TIME THAT DAY, KATE WANTED TO CRY.

Or punch something.

Or break some shit.

But that wouldn't do her any good. What she really needed to do was think.

She pressed her back into the wall and slid down to the floor, clutching her knees to her chest. Was she going to let Ripley get away with murder? Kate might be the only person who knew the truth, and so far, the one person she'd tried to tell not only didn't believe her but threatened to prosecute her if she contacted the police. Really not a great incentive to do the right thing.

Logically, Kate knew she should walk away. Yes, it was tragic that two people had died, but what if that number became three? And what if that third was her? She could see the online obituary now: *Former overweight child actress shot dead by unknown assailant and no one cared.*

But something inside her positively curdled at the idea of letting this go. Of letting Dickhead Donald intimidate her. Every time she'd walk past his desk from now on, he'd mutter something insulting, or glare at her until she scampered out of his sight, or worst of all, laugh. And every time a piece of Kate would die.

I am not *going to let that happen.*

Kate pushed herself to her feet, scanned her ID badge, and marched through the dungeon to the window. Maybe no one would believe this story based on her word alone, but what if she had proof?

There were four security cameras attached to the ceiling in the dungeon, one dome in each corner.

Kate climbed up on the table, trying to gauge the line of sight from the two closest cameras. It was difficult to predict their width of vision, but there was certainly a chance that one of them might pick up images from across the courtyard. Images of murder.

There was only one person she knew who could get access to the dungeon security-camera footage, and he was the last person on the planet that Kate wanted to text at that moment. While he was at dinner. On a date.

How awful would that look? Ex-crush begs you to cut your date short and come to her aid. Ouch, pathetic.

But maybe Rowan would know? She wasn't exactly involved in her dad's law practice the way Ty was, but Rowan was the only other person Kate could ask, and the only person who might unconditionally believe her story of witnessing a double homicide.

If she would only take Kate's call.

* * *

It was eleven o'clock when Kate pulled up in front of Rowan's Tudor revival house in Burbank Hills. Mr. and Mrs. Chen were early risers, dead asleep by nine most evenings, so it wasn't a surprise that most of the rooms were already dark. The porch light was still on, and the Tesla that Rowan and Ty shared wasn't parked in the driveway, which, duh, made sense since he was out on a date.

A date that must have been going pretty well if he still wasn't home.

Which annoyed Kate for some reason.

She shook her head, pushing off the jealousy she only partially understood, and pulled out her phone. She hadn't let Rowan know that she was coming, just in case she wasn't actually home, but the lights were on in Rowan's dormer windows upstairs, a good sign that she was not only home but alone. Because who made out with every light on in the room? Kate didn't exactly have experience in this field, but she was pretty sure the answer was no one.

She pulled out her phone and immediately dialed her friend's cell.

For the second time that night.

Kate never called, so this was practically a signal flare of "I need you!" in their friendship, and Rowan answered on the second ring, her voice breathless, as if she'd raced up a mountain to take Kate's call.

"Who are you and what have you done with my friend?"

"It's me, I promise!" Kate said, smiling for the first time in hours. "I really need to talk to you."

"Of course!" Rowan said. "I'm always here for you, babe."

Except when I called you earlier. "Can I come in?"

A pause. Then Kate saw the hurricane shutters inch open in Rowan's room. "What are you doing outside like a creeper?"

"It's a long story."

"I bet." Another pause. Was Jeremiah in there after all?

"Can I come in?"

"Yeah, yeah," Rowan said, sounding flustered. "I'll be right down."

Kate half expected to see Jeremiah lurking behind Rowan when she opened the front door, but other than her friend, the foyer was empty.

"Do your parents know you're out this late?" Rowan asked. Her brows were knitted together. Kate's appearance had her worried.

Kate wasn't sure she wanted to get into the whole Belle Masterson and Clementine drama right before she launched into a story about witnessing a double homicide, so she decided to leave that part out for now. "They think I'm at work."

"Till eleven?"

"There was a lot of filing." *Which I didn't do.*

"I should talk to Daddy about your hours," Rowan said, starting up the stairs to her room. "So not healthy to be at the office that late."

Kate followed. "You alone?"

"Yeah. I mean, Mom and Dad are zonked out per usge. Ty's on a date, if that's what you're worried about."

Had Ty told his sister what happened between them? "Why would I be worried about that?"

"After the fight you had at Alberto's," Rowan said, "Ty told everyone he'd pissed you off and that's why you left."

"Oh." Well, that was sweet of him. Sort of.

"I'm sorry he was a dick," Rowan said, sitting down on her bed. "He's been a pain in the ass since he got home. Can't wait for him to go to Stanford already."

Kate took the chair at Rowan's desk. She noticed that Rowan's laptop, though dark, was running hot. As if it had been in use right before Rowan told Kate to come inside. Maybe that was where she was getting dirty with Jeremiah tonight?

Rowan folded her hands in her lap and fidgeted with one of her rings. "So what's up?"

"Something happened at work," Kate blurted out. She needed to say it, to make it real. And she needed Rowan to hear her.

"Yeah?"

"I witnessed two murders."

Rowan blinked. "Was one of them your sanity?"

"I'm serious."

"You mean, like, actual murder."

Was there such a thing as non-actual murder? "There's this woman who works in the building across the courtyard, and at night when her office is lit up, you can see, like, everything that happens in there."

"Everything?" Rowan said, lifting a brow.

Kate thought of the hookups she'd partially witnessed, and probably watched too much of, and felt the heat rise up from her chest. "I've seen her hook up with her assistant."

"Is he hot?"

"No. Yes." Kate sighed. Of course this is what Rowan would care about. "He looks like Wyatt from *DPT*."

"Oh, so def hottie. Check."

"Not the point."

"Not *your* point."

This was not going how Kate had imagined. "Also I saw Ripley have a huge fight with her husband last week."

"You know her name?" Rowan sounded incredulous. Not a great sign.

"That's just what I call her. Like Sigourney Weaver in *Alien*."

Now it was Rowan's turn to sigh. "She is so badass in that movie. Like, fierce but still, like, *so* feminine in her tank top and tighty-whities."

They were getting sidetracked. "I'm pretty sure I saw Ripley shoot two people in her office tonight."

Rowan stared at Kate, her eyes awash in horror and confusion while her lips, for once, were silent.

"I'm not fucking with you," Kate said, reading her friend's mind.

"Good, because if you are, I'm going to murder you."

"Bad choice of words."

"Sorry."

"You believe me, right?"

Rowan squinted her eyes like she was trying to read the small print. "Like *murdered* them? Not an accident."

"Definitely not an accident." Kate recalled Ripley's calm, measured response to her husband's frantic arrival, the fact that she pulled on gloves after he arrived, then made sure he was facing her so she didn't shoot him in the back. Those details were not accidental.

"What did you do?"

"Tried calling nine-one-one, but I couldn't get a signal in the dungeon, so I called the security guard. Donald."

"Is he the squirrelly guy who always looks like he's about to burp?"

"I . . . guess?"

"He's a dick."

"Hundred percent," Kate agreed. "Not only did he *not* believe me, but he called in 'a teen making prank calls' to the police from that address."

"Shit." Rowan got it. "They'd never listen to you, then."

"I didn't know what to do, so I came here."

"Good. Smart." Rowan glanced at her phone lying faceup on her bed. Was she looking for a message or checking the time? "Though I'm not exactly sure how I can help. Are we going to break into her office and catch her with the bodies?"

"No," a voice said from the doorway. Ty leaned against the frame, one ankle crossed over the other all casual, like he hadn't been eavesdropping on their conversation. "We're going to pull the security feed from the dungeon."

TWENTY-FIVE

NEVER IN HER LIFE HAD KATE BEEN SO THANKFUL TO HAVE TY inside her head. He didn't question, didn't accuse her of lying or misinterpreting or being dramatic. Instead, he understood exactly why she'd shown up and simply nodded down the hall toward his room, an invitation to follow. "Come on."

Kate hurried after him, but Rowan hung back, reaching for her phone.

"You coming?" Kate asked.

"Yeah." Rowan smiled as she hunched over her screen, typing quickly. "Give me a sec."

She left Rowan to text Jeremiah, wondering if she'd accidentally ruined a planned hookup or if Rowan was merely saying good night.

She hoped it was the latter.

Kate had been in Ty's room before, so it wasn't a new experience, but she'd never been alone there with him, and though a year ago that wouldn't have made her feel any differently, now her heart rate kicked up a notch as she walked through the door and sat down on his sensible gray plaid duvet cover. Ty's room was a far cry from Rowan's princess extravaganza, left over from her childhood fairy-tale obsession. There was no ornamentation here, no trinkets or keepsakes. His bed was a simple black wood frame with drawers beneath for storage. Desk and bookshelves were tidy and well-arranged. No clothes were thrown carelessly over the backs of chairs or dropped in a disgusting pile. Ty's room, like his mind, was orderly and undramatic.

That lack of drama had always seemed rather boring to Kate, whose media-fueled ideals of romance involved moody bad boys and enemies-to-lovers scenarios dripping with misplaced emotions and sexy subtext, but with all the other *real* drama going on in her life, Ty's calmness felt like a lifeline.

"I can access the footage from here," he said, sitting down at his desk. "Maria showed me how to log in, in case . . ."

He let his voice trail off, and suddenly Kate knew exactly why Kleiner, Abato & Chen's HR director had showed Ty how to view footage from the file room: to check on Kate and make sure she wasn't messing around on the job.

"I suppose I should thank her," Kate said dryly.

Ty snort-laughed as he opened a web browser and began typing user names and passwords on a series of screens. "I'm not sure the camera angles will catch the windows of the south tower."

"Shit."

"But it's a really good idea and worth a shot." One final flourish on his keyboard, then he pushed his chair aside and angled the screen for her to see.

Kate had forgotten what happened in the dungeon before she witnessed the first murder, but as they watched the black-and-white footage roll on Ty's laptop, the memory came flooding back. The instant she'd closed the door behind her, after running into Ty before his date, Kate had bent forward at the waist, fists clenched at her side, and let out a primal scream. There was no sound on the video, which somehow made her subsequent breakdown seem even more horrifying. She stomped her feet, threw her head back, wept openly. Even in black and white, she could see the tears and snot pouring unheeded down her cheeks.

She wanted to look away, but she was afraid to move her eyes. Afraid to catch sight of Ty and see the revulsion on his face. She watched in silence until it was over and Kate-Who-Hadn't-Yet-Witnessed-a-Murder was curled up beneath the table in the fetal position, sobbing intermittently.

"What happened?" Ty asked softly, breaking the silence. His voice was low and calm, the way a zookeeper might talk to an erratic lioness on the verge of an attack, but Kate's entire day had been a continuous train of bullshit. Where was she supposed to begin?

"It's a long story."

"We've got time," Ty said.

"No more dates tonight?"

Ty's face tensed, eyebrows crinkled together above his nose, and the cold hand of shame smacked Kate in the face. He was trying to be a good friend, but for some reason, Kate's knee-jerk reaction was to interpret his kindness as charity. She needed to get over herself.

"I'm sorry," she said quickly. "I didn't mean it like that."

Ty arched an eyebrow. "Didn't you?"

"I mean, yes, but no."

"Yes, but no," he repeated slowly, the taut lines of his face uncoiling. "Kate, you made your feelings about me very clear last year. Why would you care that I went on a date with Albie?"

The perky, petite little office greeter? Albie was the polar opposite of Kate. Is that what Ty was into now?

Before Kate could answer or ask a follow-up, Rowan's voice cut them off from the doorway. "Is someone going to tell me what the fuck is going on between the two of you, or am I going to have to hack into one of your phones to find out?"

"Nothing," Kate said. Which wasn't a lie. But Ty felt the need to elaborate.

"I asked Kate out last year," he said simply. "And she turned me down."

That might have been a slight oversimplification—the truth was more like "I laid my unrequited heart bare and she ripped it in half"—but still the words stung.

Rowan turned on Kate, eyes widening in disbelief. "You were going to tell me this when?"

It wasn't any of your business, she wanted to say.

But Ty said it for her.

"It wasn't any of your business."

"You're my brother," Rowan said, jabbing her finger at his chest before she pulled it back and thumbed in Kate's direction. "And she's my best friend. If you two are hooking up, I should probably know."

"We didn't hook up!" Kate and Ty said in unison. Kate would have laughed at their sync if she wasn't afraid her maniacal outburst would devolve into tears.

"Like you would have told me if you did." Rowan crossed her arms over her chest, pouting. "We're supposed to be best friends."

Rowan's hypocrisy sparked Kate's temper. She usually rolled with her friend's emotional outbursts, but this one rubbed her the wrong way.

"Oh, like you've been so open about your relationship with *Jer*." It was the first time she'd used his nickname, and she really imbued the single syllable with all of her indignation at being left out of this new phase of Rowan's life.

"What are you talking about?"

"You never even told me you were dating."

"Of course I did," Rowan snapped.

"When?"

Rowan paused, trying to remember, but it was clear from her grimace of annoyance that she couldn't remember the exact conversation. Because it never happened.

"I had to put the pieces together on my own," Kate said. "Whereas everyone at theater camp seemed up-to-date on all aspects of your personal life."

"Well, maybe that's because they've been around my personal life for the last six months. Unlike you."

And there it was again. The pent-up resentment, rearing its ugly head. It was amazing that they'd made it all those months from the open-call audition to Kate's casting to the shoot, wrap party, and premiere without any eruptions of hurt feelings, but it suddenly occurred to Kate that Rowan had dealt with the shift in the friendship by pulling away. Unconsciously, maybe, but between her theater friends and Jeremiah, Rowan had built herself a crash pad if her relationship with Kate imploded.

Which was fine.

Except Kate didn't have a safety net.

Other than Rowan, she had no one.

"I'm sorry I haven't been around," Kate said. "And I'm sorry that I'm not coming back to school this fall. I've spent my whole life doing things for other people. Even going with you to that stupid audition. I didn't want to be there in the first place!"

"It's not your fault you got cast," Rowan said. The words were acquiescent, but Kate detected an edge of anger Rowan couldn't suppress. "And now you're doing auditions and castings and basically living my dream life."

"Dream life." Kate shook her head. "You wanna know why I was crying myself into a sniveling ball of snot in your dad's file room tonight?"

Rowan shrugged. "If you wanna tell me."

"My agent sent Belle on a huge, important audition for a lead in an indie film but never told me that the casting director had specifically asked her to send me out for the role. Even worse, Belle booked the part, Clementine sent me to audition for the fat-girl role of Hungry Diner Patron instead, and now my agent is ghosting me."

"Shit, Kate." Ty took a step toward her, and for a split second, Kate thought he might take her hand again or, even better, enfold her in his arms, but Rowan got there before him, flinging her hands around Kate's neck.

"Oh my God, I'm so sorry!" She squeezed Kate so hard it was painful to breathe. "I had no idea. I'm such an asshole."

Kate fought back the tears. She was tired of crying. "No, you're not."

"I've been so wrapped up in Jer." Rowan sniffled.

"Just like I was so wrapped up in the show."

Rowan released Kate from the hug. "Yeah."

"I'm sorry, too," Kate said. She felt like a hypocrite. Rowan had always been there for her—they'd been there for each other—and she needed to cut her friend a little slack. If her thing with Jeremiah really was love, then how could Kate fault Rowan for being distracted? "It's been a rough day."

"It's okay not to be fine," Ty said, hovering behind his sister.

It was. She knew it was. She appreciated that Ty was trying to help her process Clementine's betrayal, but it was easier to focus on something else, something bigger. She just needed his help to do it. She took a deep breath and pushed her career drama aside.

"Clementine sucks, but she's not important right now."

Ty nodded his head, whether in approval or agreement, Kate wasn't sure.

"We need to catch a killer." Kate grinned. For the first time in over a week, she felt like she wasn't alone. "Then I'll fire my agent."

TWENTY-SIX

"KEEP GOING."

Kate leaned over Ty's shoulder. They'd been watching fast-forwarded footage of a seemingly empty file room for several minutes, Kate's sleeping figure barely visible beneath the table. She was embarrassed at how long this part went on.

Ty nodded, then sped up the forwarding. Video-Footage Kate didn't move for what felt like an eternity, then finally, in creepy double speed, like some horror movie demon girl, she crawled out from underneath the table, stared blankly at the papers strewn on top of it, then disappeared and returned two minutes later to begin her sorting.

Ty slowed the video to normal speed. Almost immediately, Video-Footage Kate's head snapped up and she climbed onto the table.

"There!" She tapped the screen. "Ripley and her assistant just came in."

The camera caught Kate's full body as she knelt with her forehead resting against the window. But that was as far as the camera reached. The south tower was out of frame.

Even without the ability to see those events playing out, the images from earlier that night were burned into Kate's brain like a movie reel, and she was able to narrate them in real time as they watched her on the screen. "I saw the lights come on in her office. She barged in with her assistant. They were undressing each other as they climbed up on the desk. Ripley leaned back, opened her drawer. She took something out, placed it on top of the desk, then went back to sucking face."

"How much of this did you watch?" Rowan asked.

Ty shushed her. "What happened next?"

"The husband came in. At least, I think he's her husband." She paused, swallowing as she realized she needed to correct her verb tense. "*Was* her husband. They had a huge fight last week."

"Again," Rowan said, "how much of this did you watch?"

Kate ignored her, focusing on the sequence of events. "He had a gun, but he didn't fire it. Just threatened them. Ripley laughed, and then he dropped the gun on the ground. Defeated. He turned and started to leave, which is when Ripley pulled on a pair of gloves and grabbed another gun from her desk. She must have said something to him because he turned back around and then . . . then . . ."

Almost exactly on cue, Kate watched her image on the screen jump back from the window. Her hand flew to her mouth.

"Then she shot him?" Ty prompted.

Kate nodded. "In the chest."

"And the assistant?"

"He stood by the window in shock. Ripley dropped her gun, walked over to the body, crouched beside it. I couldn't see what she was doing, but when she stood up, she was holding her husband's gun, which she aimed at her assistant."

She remembered how she could almost hear the pop of the gun, feel the thud of the body as it hit the floor. She was practically there, living the events with Ripley. In the security footage, Kate saw her body twist away from the window, her mouth open in a silent scream. It was surreal to watch, especially since she didn't actually remember screaming, just the vague sensation that she heard something far away, barely cutting through the pounding of blood that echoed in her ears.

As traumatic as it was to relive those moments, there was something satisfying about seeing her reactions on the security footage. They were exactly in line with what she remembered. It wasn't proof of what she saw, at least not the kind that would hold up in court, but it was confirmation that what she had witnessed had actually happened. In case anyone tried to convince her otherwise.

"Why are you waving at the window?" Rowan asked, jarring Kate from her thoughts.

"She's trying to get a cell signal," Ty said. Once again, she was thankful that they were so in tune. "To call nine-one-one?"

Kate nodded. "I managed to get two bars and dial. An operator answered, but it cut out before I could report the incident."

"That's good," Ty said, exhaling quickly with the words, signaling his relief. "There will be a record of the call from your number to establish the time of death. What did you do next?"

Kate quickly recounted her calls to Donald, his non-appearance in Ripley's office, and their confrontation outside the dungeon, all while the security footage continued to roll, showing an empty file room.

When she finished, she was afraid to look at either Rowan or Ty, afraid that without the video proof she'd been hoping for, they wouldn't buy her story. Silence stifled the room. On Ty's laptop, the door to the file room opened again and Kate entered unhurriedly, gazed out the window for a full minute, then grabbed her bag and marched back out. Considering everything that had gone down in those twenty minutes, she was impressed by her own calmness.

"Then I got in the car and drove here." Kate let her aching body unclench.

"Did anyone see you leave?" Ty asked.

Kate shook her head. "Donald wasn't at his desk." *Thankfully.*

"And you haven't told anyone else?"

"No."

"Why don't we just call the police now?" Rowan said, lifting her cell phone from beside her on the bed. "Use my phone, in case Donald reported your name."

"That's not a bad idea," Ty said. "Once they find the bodies, we can explain."

Kate didn't love the idea of admitting to the police that she witnessed a double murder and then fled the scene. Without video footage of what occurred in Ripley's office, she was worried that the police—like Donald—wouldn't believe her, or worse, think that she was somehow involved, especially since Kate's reputation was already in tatters after Belle's video. But Ty was right—once they found the bodies, she could explain what happened. The sooner the police were on the scene, the better.

"Okay," she said, taking Rowan's phone. Her fingers trembled as she dialed 911 on speakerphone.

"Nine-one-one, please state your emergency."

"H-hi." Kate stumbled over her own words, unprepared with what to say. "I'd like to report a double murder."

Ty gave her a thumbs-up of encouragement.

"Ma'am, can I get your name?"

"Piper Payne," Rowan said before Kate could even open her mouth. She looked up at her friend in confusion.

"What the fuck?" Ty mouthed.

Rowan shrugged. "Can't use her real name!"

"Piper?" the dispatcher asked. "Is there someone there with you?"

Kate could already detect the incredulity in the dispatcher's tone. "No, sorry. I . . . I think I'm in shock."

"Okay. Can you tell me what's happening?"

"I just witnessed a woman shoot her husband and her assistant," Kate said, speaking slowly, "at the Burbank Garden Towers Business Park. Fourth Floor, south tower."

"Piper, are you at the location now?"

"Uh . . ." She was pretty sure they could triangulate her location from her cell signal, so there was no point in lying. "No."

Kate clearly heard a low sigh on the other end of the line. "How long ago did this shooting take place?"

Kate wasn't even sure how much time had passed, but Ty was on it. "An hour and twenty minutes," he whispered.

"An hour and twenty minutes."

"I see." She heard clacking through the call, as if the dispatcher was typing quickly on a keyboard. "And you're sure you actually witnessed this shooting?"

"Yes, of course!"

"Because we've had no reports of a shooting incident at that location. But we *have* had reports of prank calls. . . ."

This was a bad idea. "I know what I saw."

"I'm sure you *thought* you saw a crime committed, *Piper Payne*." The dispatcher wasn't even hiding her skepticism, and the steely tone she used when repeating Kate's alias indicated the words had probably been accompanied by an eye roll. "But this isn't a television program. You and Noelle and Sebastian need to stop pretending this is real life. Hang up the phone and keep this line open for actual emergencies."

What were the odds that they'd get the one emergency operator in all of Southern California who was a *Dirty Pretty Teens* fan? Kate was about to explain when the dispatcher ended the call.

"Shit."

"That went well," Rowan said with a grimace.

Ty shook his head. "Nice one, Ro."

"Me? What did I do?"

"Gee, I don't know." Kate stared at her blankly. "Maybe you shouldn't have picked an alias from a hit Netflix show."

"At least I answered." Rowan pouted. "You two just sat there staring at the phone."

"We were thinking, Ro," Ty said. He sounded exasperated with his sister, a mood Kate rarely saw. He was always patient with her, almost to a fault. "You didn't even give us time to speak."

Rowan folded her arms across her chest. "Stop ganging up on me."

"Oh my God, Ro!" Kate blurted out. "Two people have been murdered. Don't you think we have bigger problems right now?"

"Yeah, but . . ." Rowan bit her lower lip, her eyes flitting away from Kate's face. "If you're sure that's what you saw."

The statement landed like a sucker punch. Had they been watching the same footage?

"I'm one hundred percent sure I watched that woman murder two people."

"I mean, you'd had a shitty day and an epic meltdown. . . ." Rowan didn't finish her thought, allowing her voice to trail off in indecision. Or cowardice. Either way, it felt like a betrayal.

"Ro, you've known me for, what, like six years?"

"Yes."

"You know me better than almost anyone else."

"No *almost* about it."

Kate thought of Ty. "Have you ever known me to lie?"

"No."

"Make shit up to get attention?"

"Never."

"Enhance details to make a better story?"

"Nope."

"Demand the spotlight in any way."

"Not once."

Kate wondered if her friend realized that she was listing things Rowan did on the reg. "Hallucinate that I saw a woman kill two people?"

"Well, duh. No." Rowan stood up, hands on her hips. "But I've also never seen you under the kind of pressure you've got right now."

Rowan seemed determined to delegitimize Kate's story. "You're not hearing me."

"*You're* not hearing *me*." Typical Rowan. She loved using your own words against you. "You show up here in the middle of the night and tell me you witnessed a murder."

"Two murders."

"Not the point."

Kate was pretty sure a double homicide was the only point right now, but whatever.

Rowan turned away. "Why didn't you text first?"

Whether or not she texted Rowan seemed like an inconsequential detail. "I had to get out of there," Kate lied. Well, mostly lied.

"So you parked out front and called from your car like a creeper." It was a rarity that anything actually bothered Rowan deeper than surface level, so Kate was surprised by the degree of hurt she saw in her friend's taut features. "You *never* call."

I called you this afternoon after my audition. "I needed you to respond."

"When do I not respond, like, immediately?"

"All the time!" Kate shouted. The hurt in her voice surprised her.

"That's not true."

"You sure about that?" Kate asked. "If you'd come up for air with Jeremiah, maybe you'd notice all the ghosted texts. I called you this afternoon after the audition. *I even left a message.* And you couldn't be bothered to call me back."

Rowan's face tightened. "I was busy."

"I was hurting."

"Time-out!" Ty said, holding up his hands to form a T. "You two clearly have a lot to talk about, but right now, we should focus on the fact that two people were murdered and Kate is the only witness."

Kate forgot her anger in a heartbeat. "You believe me?"

"Of course."

It wasn't an automatic response. Without a discovery of the bodies, a missing person report, or actual footage of Ripley's office from the Kleiner, Abato & Chen security cameras, Kate could have been making it all up. Rowan clearly wasn't sure. But Ty didn't hesitate to give his support. She wanted to hug him.

"What do we do now?" Kate asked.

Ty closed his laptop with a satisfying click. "We wait."

Rowan snorted. "That was underwhelming."

"If Kate's right, and Ripley staged these murders to look like her boyfriend and husband shot each other, then she did it for a reason. Probably wants to make sure that the bodies are found . . ." He paused, thinking.

"By the cleaning crew," Kate said, completing his sentence. "That was my first thought."

Ty grinned. "They'll come through between nine and ten tomorrow night."

"Nine thirty," Kate said, matching his smile. "From what I've seen."

"I'm sure she has an alibi all lined up."

"Way out of town."

Rowan huffed. "I'm confused. What are we doing?"

"We're going to wait until tomorrow night when the cleaning crew finds the bodies," Ty explained. Slowly.

"And then I can come forward!" Kate cried. They'd have to believe her with two corpses on their hands.

Ty stood up. "We'll wait with you, Ro and me. In the dungeon. So you're not alone."

Kate and Ty were inches apart as they smiled at each other, so close Kate was pretty sure Ty could feel how violently her heart was beating.

"Can't," Rowan said quickly. Too quickly.

"Date with Jeremiah?" Kate couldn't believe Rowan would prioritize a make-out session over catching a murderer.

Or maybe she could.

"No." Rowan's jaw tightened. "Just scene study."

"Can't you reschedule?"

"Kate . . ."

"Ro, this is important."

Rowan sucked her bottom lip into her mouth, then slowly drew it across her teeth. Kate was bent out of shape that Rowan even had to think about canceling a make-out session with Jeremiah in order to support her best friend at a traumatic moment. Like she and Jeremiah didn't do the same thing every other night of the week. Kate had literally spent an entire day with Rowan at the *Dirty Pretty Teens* open call audition because Rowan didn't want to go alone. Kate was only asking for an hour or two on a Wednesday night. It was ridiculous Rowan's decision was taking this long.

"Fine!" Rowan grrrrr'd like a tiger, then stormed out of the room without looking back. "Tell me what time, and I'll be there."

Kate figured it was a fifty-fifty shot that she'd have Jeremiah in tow.

TWENTY-SEVEN

KATE SPENT THE NEXT MORNING TRYING NOT TO THINK ABOUT what had happened in Ripley's office.

Ty's plan to wait until the bodies were discovered had seemed like a good idea at the time—voluntarily marching into a police station wasn't something she was excited to cross off her bucket list, especially after her failed attempts with both Donald and the 911 dispatcher—but in the sober light of day, Kate worried that the delay would give Ripley time to cover her tracks. If it came down to her word against Ripley's, who would the cops, a judge, or a jury be more likely to believe: an upstanding local businesswoman or a D-list teen Netflix star who'd recently been slut-shamed all over the internet?

The anxiety was overwhelming, making focus impossible. She tried to read a book, but her mind drifted to that fourth-floor suite and its two dead bodies. How they must still be lying where they'd died. Alone, cold, forgotten.

What about Ripley? Had she gone about her Wednesday as if nothing had happened? Was she smugly congratulating herself on a well-planned crime, oblivious to the fact that there had been a witness?

And if she knew about Kate, would Ripley be willing to add a third murder to her rap sheet?

Probably.

Waiting was painful. Every hour felt like a lifetime. She'd picked up the phone a dozen times to text Ty and ask if he was sure they were doing the right thing, but each time she'd stopped herself.

We can't ever be more than just friends.

Kate and Ty had grown up practically side by side while she was inseparable from his sister. Of course she had feelings for him, strong ones, but they were platonic, weren't they? It was almost like having a sibling, or how she imagined having a sibling would be.

Then why were you so upset that Ty went on a date with adorable little Albie?

Kate shook her head. Maybe it wasn't the date so much as it was realizing that Ty, like Rowan, had a support system while Kate felt like a stranger in her own home. Worse, they had a support system that didn't involve her. Ty and Rowan had moved on.

Acting on *Dirty Pretty Teens* had given Kate the opportunity to reinvent herself, and in doing so, she'd pulled away from her friends. Excuses aside, she *hadn't* been there for Rowan, physically or emotionally. At least not in the way their friendship had been before. In fairness, being friends with someone like Rowan required a lot of output: attention, approbation, physical presence. But Kate got a lot in return. Rowan's energy was infectious, her positivity inspiring, and in the end, it had been Rowan's belief in Kate that helped her land the role of Noelle.

Maybe Kate had been a shitty friend to both of the Chens.

She was about to text those exact words to Rowan when someone tapped on her bedroom door.

"Kate?"

It had been years since Kate had heard her mom say her name that way. It was either *Katherine* when her mom wanted to be formal, *Katherine Cressida* when Kate was in deep shit, or her childhood nickname *Katie-Bear* for every day. Hearing *Kate* come out of her mom's mouth felt odd and distant, like her roommate was standing in the hallway instead of her mom.

"I'm here."

The door crept open. Kate's mom must have just gotten home from teaching summer school; her teacher-appropriate "summer casual" wardrobe of a flowy floral skirt, fitted tee, and cardigan had yet to be exchanged for her usual loungewear. She hadn't even put down her messenger bag, which she clutched to her body as if it held vital government secrets or the cure for cancer. It was clear that Kate's mom had come straight to her room after getting home, which meant whatever she had to say, it had been weighing on her for most of the day, and Kate girded her loins for another lecture on adulting.

"Can we talk?"

Kate was momentarily thrown. A question rather than an order. "Um, yeah. Of course."

Her mom let out a heavy sigh, dropping her bag to the floor as she exhaled, then trudged across the room to Kate's desk and pulled out the chair. "I . . . I want to apologize."

Kate blinked. Andrea Williams did not apologize. "I'm sorry, what now?"

Her mom smiled, freckles stretching across her pale cheeks, but instead of lightening up her face, the taut smile just made her look sad. "I know, I know. Not my MO. But the last couple of weeks have been tough on you and that's my fault."

"It's not." *Entirely.*

"I just don't want you to think your dad and I are doing this out of spite. We respect your right to make life choices but . . ."

She sighed again, but this time it was out of frustration, in place of feelings she couldn't articulate or words she didn't want to say.

"But you're worried about me," Kate said, filling in the blanks.

Her mom nodded. "Not because we don't think you can do this. You'll succeed at whatever you put your mind to. You always have. But this world can be an ugly place for women." Kate's mom rose and moved slowly toward the bed, sitting gently beside her daughter. "Going to college isn't about ditching your dreams. You *can* have both, Katie-Bear."

Kate's nickname had never sounded so sweet. And her mom's argument made sense. The entertainment industry wasn't a meritocracy, and the people she'd trusted weren't always looking out for her best interests. There would always be Clementines and Belles—not to mention Donalds and Dexes—who might have more sway in Kate's career than they deserved. Talent and ambition weren't enough, and maybe it wouldn't be such a bad idea to have an actual college degree on her side.

Besides, she'd had enough adulting in the last twenty-four hours to last her a lifetime.

"Maybe you're—"

Right was the word she was about to utter, but her mom cut her off.

"Don't answer now. Think about it." She squeezed Kate's hand. "And remember that no matter what, we love you."

"I know."

She wrapped an arm around Kate's shoulders and pulled her close, resting her face against the top of Kate's head. They sat that way for a few seconds before her mom kissed Kate on the temple and stood up.

"'You ne'er oppress'd me with a mother's groan, / Yet I express to you a mother's care.'"

Kate's eyes grew wide. *All's Well That Ends Well.* She'd never heard her mom quote Shakespeare before—math formulas were her poetry.

"Act one, scene three," her mom added with a wink as she whisked her bag off the floor and headed down the hallway. "You and your dad aren't the only fans in this family."

* * *

It was six o'clock exactly as Kate walked from her car to the parking elevators, her eyes locked on to the spot where Ripley had left her Porsche last week. The stall was empty.

Donald wasn't at the security desk when she strode past, and Kate breathed a small sigh of relief. She didn't need a repeat of his threats. Or watch his hawkish eyes follow her through the lobby. No, thanks.

Ty was typing at his computer when she rounded the side of his cubicle, and his face lit up as he saw her approach.

"Any news?" Kate asked, meeting his smile with one of her own. Despite the seriousness of the situation, she felt lighter the moment she saw him.

"Radio silence."

"Means no one's been into her office." Kate dropped her voice. "And the bodies are still up there."

"What time is Rowan coming?" he asked, handing Kate the keys.

"I told her eight thirty. So she can still get some make-out time with Jer if she wants."

Ty rolled his eyes. "I wish it was just that."

"Oh."

Had Rowan lost her virginity without telling Kate? It was a subject they'd discussed ad nauseam over the years. Rowan had a high sex drive, but she was a romantic at heart, and her fantasies about her first time were always histrionic. They'd sworn to tell each other when it finally happened, yet Rowan hadn't even shared that she was dating Jeremiah, let alone getting sexual with him.

Was their friendship already past the point of no return?

"I'm sorry you two fought," Ty said, watching her closely.

"Not your fault."

He shrugged in disagreement. "I should have told her what happened that day. She's right; it put her in an awkward spot."

Kate was pretty sure the only awkwardness that day had been between her and Ty, but she appreciated that he considered his sister's feelings. Without siblings, Kate didn't quite understand the bond but found herself envious that Rowan had someone like Ty looking out for her.

"Ro's lucky to have you."

Ty sighed, leaning back in his chair. Purple skin marred the inside corners of his eyes, as if he hadn't slept well. "I just hope Jer doesn't break her heart. It'd be a drag to have to come back down from Stanford to kick his ass."

"Don't worry," Kate said, laughing at the idea of Ty kicking anyone's ass. "I'll do it for you."

"Thanks." He paused again, this time stifling a heavy yawn with the back of his hand. "Are you okay going in there alone?"

"I'll be fine." Kate hadn't even considered that she'd be afraid of going into the dungeon. The murders had felt removed, away across the courtyard, almost like she was watching a movie projected on the side of the south tower.

"I'll bring Ro when she arrives," he said.

"Got it."

"And, Kate?"

"Yeah?"

"Come get me if you need anything."

"Okay."

"Anything."

The tips of Kate's fingers tingled with electricity. "I will."

* * *

"I hate this place," Rowan said for the millionth time. She leaned back against the nearest file cabinet and rolled her eyes up toward her forehead where a Post-it note with a picture of a sailboat clung to her skin. "Is it a tree?"

"Nope," Ty said, gleeful that she still hadn't guessed the subject of the picture he'd stuck to her head almost an hour ago. He turned to Kate. "My turn. Is it . . . a shark?"

"Yep!" Kate said, impressed. He'd been through six of the images while Rowan was still on her first. His deductive reasoning powers were impressive. No wonder he was planning on going to law school after Stanford.

"You're up." Ty nudged Kate with his foot.

She'd asked four questions already and had surmised that the picture Rowan had drawn was a flying animal but not a bird. Which left few options. "Is it a bat?"

"Ding, ding, ding," Rowan said with all the enthusiasm of a dead fish.

"Right again. I hate this game." She pulled out her phone, climbing up onto the table to try to locate a signal.

Kate met Ty's eyes and together they silently mouthed the same word: "Jer."

Kate had been waiting for an opportunity to voice her apologies to both Rowan and Ty, but it hadn't materialized. Ty had shown up with his sister at eight thirty, armed with Post-it notes and a Sharpie for their time-wasting game, and immediately took control of the stakeout by setting a tone of lighthearted fun. Rowan had allowed his mood to influence her own, and if she'd shown up with a chip on her shoulder, she'd quickly shaken it off.

But as the game continued, Rowan's mood had soured. Every time Kate or Ty laughed at something the other said, Rowan lost a little bit of her good humor, and after almost an hour, she looked as pissy as she had the last time Kate saw her, storming out of Ty's room.

Which probably wasn't the best time to approach her with an apology, and so Kate had kept her mouth shut.

Unable to find a cell signal, Rowan flopped down on the table, arms splayed wide. A martyr waiting for death. "How much longer?"

"Until the cleaning crew arrives," Ty said. Same thing he'd told her the other four times she'd asked. "It's almost nine thirty."

Kate's eyes drifted to the office across the courtyard. Ripley's windows were painfully dark. Not a single light shined through, not even the security light from the exit sign above the main door or the ambient glow of an open laptop left running since yesterday. The windows seemed particularly dark in contrast to the bright fluorescents blinding her from the floor below. Those lights hadn't been out once since Kate had started working in the dungeon, and she wondered who was footing the electricity bill if no one was actually renting the space.

While Kate could feel her anticipation building, pangs of guilt stabbed at her. Someone was about to stumble onto a grotesque scene, one that would forever be burned into their brains. As awful as it had been for her to witness the murders from afar, how much more traumatic would it be to actually see the cold, stiff corpses splayed out on the carpet? That wasn't something you'd get over quickly. Or ever.

"Maybe we should call the police," Kate said. "Let them find the bodies."

"You're worried about the cleaning crew," Ty said, nodding in understanding.

"I wish they'd hurry up!" Rowan whined.

Kate shook her head. "They didn't sign on for this. At least the cops have seen dead bodies before."

"I should have thought of that." Ty's eyes shifted to the window. "But it's too late now."

As he spoke, a light pierced the darkness of Ripley's office. The door had opened, flooding the space with an ambient glow from the hallway. A second later, the lights flickered to life and a young dark-haired woman wheeled a cart into the reception area.

Kate held her breath. This was it. Ripley's husband should be lying there beside the reception desk, the assistant's body behind him in the doorway to Ripley's private office. There was no way this woman couldn't see them. She was crouched down beside the cart, arranging some items; then she straightened up, turned around, and . . .

Nothing.

No shrieks.

No panic.

No running from the office in terror.

The cleaning lady went about her business as usual.

It was as if the murders had never even happened.

TWENTY-EIGHT

KATE COULDN'T MOVE, HER ARMS AND LEGS SEEMINGLY DIS-
connected from her brain. Everything in the dungeon disappeared—Ty,
Rowan, even the incessant hum of the server engines—as she leaned
against the table, staring vacantly out the window. "I don't understand."

"I knew it," Rowan grumbled under her breath.

Her best friend's dismissal cut to the bone, and the pain jolted her
body into action. She turned, looking directly at Rowan. "I know what
I saw."

"Clearly not." Rowan waved her hand at the window dismissively.
"Unless that nice cleaning lady just dusted around two dead bodies."

Kate knew her friend well enough to recognize that Rowan was
indulging in her sour mood, but the contempt in her voice still pissed

Kate off. She gritted her teeth and tried to stay calm. "Are you accusing me of telling lies or having delusions?"

Rowan clicked her tongue in annoyance. She didn't like being called out. "I'm just saying that your memory isn't always so great."

"Since when?" Even if the accusation was true, how would Kate's memory play into this? Like, was she supposed to have forgotten that she *didn't* see a murder? Rowan's argument made no sense.

"You don't remember dancing with Dex."

"Ro!" Ty snapped, then dropped his voice. "Not cool."

Kate had never been angry at her friend, not truly, but she couldn't believe Rowan was throwing the *DPT* party in her face. Rowan had done so many stupid things over the years—drunken cast parties, sneaking out to see boys, lying to her parents—and Kate always had her back. Meanwhile, Kate had done exactly one stupid, reckless thing in her entire life and it had immediately blown up in her face and now Rowan was weaponizing that mistake because she was pissy about losing two hours of Jer Time?

Fuck that.

"And where were you, huh?" Kate said, pushing herself off the table. "While Dex was pouring me champagne and getting free with his hands. Where were you?"

Rowan flinched. She was unused to Kate flighting back. "I . . ."

"It was a rhetorical question, Ro. I know exactly where you were. Flirting with Dagney Malone."

"I *wasn't* flirting."

Kate threw up her hands. "You followed him into the bathroom!"

"Wait, what?" Ty said.

"Yeah, she did." Kate was tired of keeping Rowan's secrets. "She'd been stalking him all night, since the minute we arrived, and as soon as he got into the bathroom line, she ditched me to stand behind him. I didn't see her again until it was time to leave."

"It . . . it was a long line." Rowan faltered.

"The one time we were at an event *for me*, when you should have been looking out *for me*, all you could think about was yourself."

"How was I supposed to know you needed babysitting?"

"Oh, I don't know. Maybe because I've done it for you, like, a million times?"

Rowan planted her hands on her hips, defiant. The Post-it with the sailboat fluttered from her forehead. "Like when?"

Was she joking? Kate tapped her fingers to count off. "Let's see. . . . When you were dating Armand and you wanted to go to that French Consulate party with him, but your parents said no, so I covered for you and pretended we were having a sleepover at my house. And then there was the *Radium Girls* cast party when you were trying to make Trenton jealous by grinding on that crew guy Julio, who was so drunk he puked all over you."

"I barely had any puke on me," Rowan said, her nose wrinkling at the forced memory.

Yeah, like *that* was the point to argue. "Or how about the time I needed my dad to pick us up at Gabe's house after you drank so many tequila shots you couldn't even stand up?"

"Wow." Ty looked stunned.

"I had to beg my dad not to tell your parents," Kate continued. "Or my mom. And he tells her everything. It was torture."

Instead of backing down, admitting that maybe she'd been wrong by not keeping an eye on Kate at that wrap party, Rowan doubled down, relishing the role of victim.

"Gee, I'm *so sorry* I've been such a shitty friend. I'm *so sorry* you've been forced to hang out with me every single day. Oh, until you abandoned me for that show."

"That show was my job!"

Rowan merely shrugged. "And it took all your time."

"Ro, that's kind of how jobs work," Ty said.

"Not that she'd know," Kate added.

Rowan turned on her brother. "Of course you'd take her side. Choosing love over your own sister."

"I'm not taking sides." Ty's cheeks flushed bright fuchsia. "But you're being deliberately cruel."

Rowan smiled. She thrust out her chin and pushed one hand against the small of her back, jutting out her shoulders. It was a pose, one Rowan frequently used onstage, and Kate guessed what was coming next.

"'Deliberate cruelty is unforgivable,'" Rowan said, using a hint of a southern accent as she morphed into character. "'And the one thing of which I have never, ever been guilty of.'"

Kate rolled her eyes. "*A Streetcar Named Desire.* Scene ten." She'd read Stanley to Rowan's Blanche when they rehearsed that scene freshman year, and remembered her friend's delivery of the line clearly.

Rowan dropped her act. "Oh, right. You're a big-time actress now. You know all the classic rep."

Cue the jealousy. "Only because I helped you rehearse it. All of it. Every scene, every show. For years."

"Apparently, I've been a horrible friend," Rowan repeated, tearing up. She paused, waiting for Kate to contradict her, but Kate kept her mouth shut, which merely escalated Rowan's shame. "And you clearly don't need me anymore."

"I needed you that night!" Kate shouted. She wasn't going to let Rowan make this about herself.

Rowan's chin quivered; then she turned away, grabbing her purse from the table. "Jer's waiting for me."

"Fine, go." Kate wasn't going to stop her. And she wasn't going to be the one to apologize first.

Not this time.

* * *

The moment the door clicked shut behind Rowan, Kate turned to the window, avoiding Ty. She didn't know what to say.

"I'm sorry," he said after a moment.

Kate snorted. "About the dead bodies or about your sister?" For some reason, she found it morbidly funny that he was apologizing for one of two things he wasn't responsible for.

"Ro will get over it. Her anger is dramatic but short-lived."

"Yeah." Rowan's hurt might fade quickly, but what about Kate's?

"I'm not sure what to say about the other thing."

The other *things*. "Ripley must have moved the bodies," Kate said, deflated. "Come back last night and taken them somewhere. Donald said he ran into her coming out of an elevator, so maybe that ruined her alibi and she had to go to plan B."

"Makes sense," Ty said gently. She couldn't tell if he was serious or placating her.

"I should have tried harder with the police," Kate said, pounding on the table in frustration. Her limbs felt heavy, leaden. "Made them listen. And I shouldn't have let fucking Donald intimidate me."

Ty sat on the table beside her. "I reported him."

"What?"

"Said I overheard him making derogatory comments about one of the tenants." He grinned, lopsided. "I mean, it wasn't a total lie."

Ty wasn't one to play fast and loose with the rules, and she'd never known him to tell even a half-truth, so this was a surprise. "I guess that's why he wasn't at his desk tonight."

"Serves him right."

Kate smiled and her eyes met Ty's for a heartbeat longer than was totally comfortable, before she turned back toward the window, sweeping her auburn hair over one shoulder. "Now what do we do?"

"I don't know." He pushed himself off the table and stood behind her, his breath tickling her neck. "I mean, it's difficult to erase all traces of a murder."

"Yeah?"

"The blood, for instance. She'd have to scrub or bleach it out of the carpet."

She glanced back at him. "Been watching *CSI* again?"

Ty chuckled. "My internship in Shanghai was with a law firm that defended criminal cases. Including murder."

"Oh." Kate probably should have known that. "Sorry. I forgot."

Ty's fingertips grazed hers. "You had other things going on, *Noelle*."

Kate felt her heart thunder in her chest as she continued to stare at the south tower, where the janitor circled Ripley's desk with a vacuum cleaner. Why was she so susceptible to Ty's touch? Why did she desperately want to turn around and gaze up into his dark brown eyes?

Holy crap, what is happening?

"Did you watch it?" she asked instead, desperate for conversation to fill the void of silence.

"Your show?"

"No, the moon landing."

"Do you care?"

"Very much."

"Yes, I watched. Day after I got back, Ro insisted I binge all ten episodes with her."

"Oh." That must have been unpleasant at best. Torture if Ty still had feelings for her.

"You were really wonderful, Kate. I mean that."

The words tickled her left ear. He was so close. A hairsbreadth between them.

Don't turn around. Don't turn around.

"Ty . . ." Kate couldn't help herself. She pivoted, lifting her eyes to meet his. Ty looked so lost. Lips parted, eyes half-closed. Kate felt as if he was letting his guard down with her, cracking himself open again along breaks that hadn't fully healed, hoping for a different result but unsure of what might happen.

Kate wasn't sure either. It was difficult to reconcile her current feelings with what they had been a year ago, as if she and Ty were two completely different people now. Which perhaps wasn't that far from the truth. They'd both expanded their worlds beyond the confines of Burbank. She had no idea what he'd seen and done while he was away, only that he'd come back so much more confident in who he was that it had made Kate question everything she thought she knew about her feelings for him.

Kate felt the heat radiating through his button-down shirt. She wanted to say something, but words wouldn't do. She needed his voltage. She placed a hand on his chest and wished for more.

Ty trembled beneath her touch, a body struggling to breathe. Had she overstepped? Misread the soft look in his eyes? Was the anger of the last time he'd opened himself to her preventing him from acting now?

She thought of that look Belle gave Dex, a glance of wordless need that somehow encompassed all of her innocent yearning and lustful urges, and she tried to soften her face to match the lines she'd seen in her former costar. A hint of a smile. Sad, searching eyes. An arched neck begging to be touched.

Ty sucked in a sharp breath, and the lungful of oxygen spurred him into action. His hands slid up Kate's bare arms, prickled now from excitement and anticipation rather than from the aggressive air-conditioning, and she was thankful that she'd tied her hoodie around her waist earlier as she was able to feel his skin against hers. Ty's hands lingered only a moment before he gripped her shoulders and slowly dipped his face toward her.

Kate couldn't believe it was happening. Her first real kiss with a boy who stirred feelings she didn't even know existed. And she had Belle Masterson to thank for it.

Belle.

Who'd visited Ripley's office just last week.

"Oh shit!" she gasped as Ty's lips were about to touch hers.

He reared back, eyes wide in alarm. "What is it? What's wrong?"

"Nothing." Her brain had the worst timing in human history. "It's not you. I just . . ." How was this not going to sound horrible? "I just remembered something."

"About me?"

Ugh. He was going to hate her all over again. "Belle Masterson met with Ripley in her office. Two nights ago."

The edges of Ty's mouth crinkled. "Why were you thinking of Belle Masterson while I was about to kiss you?"

"I . . ." How was this not going to make her sound like an asshole? *I'm so unconfident in my body that I was trying to channel someone who seduced a married man.* Yeah, pathetic. But she also didn't want Ty to think her changing the subject had anything to do with her feelings for him. "I was trying—"

"You know what?" Ty said, throwing up his hands as he backed away from her. "I don't want to know."

"Ty . . ."

"It's fine. Catching a killer is more important. I get it."

"I'm sorry."

"Some things just aren't meant to be."

Kate felt as if she'd been slapped. "I . . . I guess not."

"So," he said, clearing his throat. "What's your plan?" He was her supervisor again, cool and businesslike.

Maybe it was better that way. He was leaving for college in a couple of weeks anyway. Kate would be a high school friend in his rearview mirror by Christmas. She fought back the sob that was building in her throat and turned toward Ripley's darkened windows so he couldn't see the pain in her face.

"My plan is that I'm going on a friend date with Belle Masterson."

TWENTY-NINE

EVEN THOUGH AN ACADEMY AWARD NOMINATION DIDN'T FAC-
tor into Kate's five-year plan, she was about to give an Oscar-worthy
performance as Belle Masterson flounced through the main entrance of
the outdoor vegan café Kate had suggested for lunch.

She'd chosen that specific restaurant because the garden seating
offered quiet, secluded nooks, shielded from both the busy commercial street and from other diners by walls of shrubbery and strategically
placed canopies, in consideration of Belle's supposed harassment by the
paparazzi. But Belle arrived without the dramatic hoodie and sunglasses
that had been present the last two times Kate had seen her. She preened
at the empty hostess stand, one arm akimbo while she flipped her bouncy
blond waves with the other. Like she was inviting photographs.

So much for her persecution complex.

"Belle!" Kate called from the corner table, shrouded on two sides by thick foliage.

Belle turned and her face tightened when she saw Kate. Had she already forgotten who Kate was? And if so, who the hell was she expecting to meet for lunch?

"Hi!" Belle said with a flap of her hand that must have been a substitute for a wave. She threaded around some tables and pulled out the empty chair across from Kate. "This table is so far away. It's like we're hiding over here."

Kate wanted to ask "Far away from what?" but she sensed that would lead to an argument. She needed to play it cool while she manipulated Belle, like Iago working on Othello.

> *Though I do hate him as I do hell pains,*
> *Yet for necessity of present life*
> *I must show out a flag and sign of love.*

Except in this case, Iago was the good guy.

Bananas.

"I thought you might prefer it," Kate said, flashing what she hoped was a warm, kindly smile. "With the press and all."

"Hide from the press?" Belle laughed. "Why would I want to do that?"

Because you literally got our show canceled? "So how have you been?" Kate asked instead. Maneuvering through this lunch was going to be harder than she thought.

"Wonderful!" Belle cooed, settling into the chair. She placed her phone faceup on the table beside her. "You don't mind, do you?"

"Go right ahead."

"I just need to be available at all times in case wardrobe needs to do a last-minute fitting." She paused, sighing dramatically. "Preproduction is *so* much work."

She knew Belle wanted her to ask what the wardrobe was for, but she wasn't going to humor the ego. Besides, the circumstances behind Belle's new role in *Sunny's Side Up* still left a bitter taste in Kate's mouth. "I remember."

Belle waved her hand dismissively. "But *that* was just for a series. Features are *so* extra."

Don't roll your eyes. Don't roll your eyes. Kate needed to change the subject quickly, before she lost her temper. Thankfully, the waitress arrived to take their orders.

"Iced spirulina latte," Belle said, without looking at the menu.

"Got it." The waitress pressed the selection into her iPad. "And for your choice of milk, would you prefer coconut, oat, or our house-made almond?"

Belle arched an eyebrow. "Are they drought-sustainable almonds?"

"Of course."

"Then almond."

"And to eat?"

Belle shook her head. "I'm cleansing."

Kate wasn't entirely sure what Belle meant, but as the waitress turned to her, she suddenly wished she'd eaten something before leaving the house.

"And for you?"

"Um . . ." Kate quickly scanned the drinks menu, looking for something that might be more filling than espresso and almond milk. The smoothies looked promising but ingredients like chlorophyll and ashwaganda scared her off. "I'll have the Tropical Smoothie," she said at last, hoping that pineapple, mint, and avocado would mask the taste of cordyceps fungus, whatever the hell that was.

"Got it!" The waitress smiled, assuming that Kate was also not ordering food. "Be right back with those."

Kate's stomach growled in protest.

"A smoothie," Belle said, hand to her chest. "I miss them."

"Why can't you have a smoothie?"

"Too many calories, and all those carbs. It must be so nice not to care what you eat."

Kate gritted her teeth at the backhanded comment but managed to suppress her rising temper. "Pineapple and coconut water are perfectly healthy."

Belle's laugh managed to sound neither collegial nor lighthearted. "That's cute you think so."

As with every conversation she'd had with Belle, Kate was finding it difficult to control the narrative. She took a slow inhale and tried to curve things back around to why she was there in the first place.

"How are you doing with . . . things?" she began, leaning in like they were two girlfriends about to engage in a gossip session.

"What things?"

Kate shrugged. "Dex and the trial."

"Great!" Belle answered quickly. Then her voice sharpened. "Why wouldn't they be?"

Because your married boyfriend is going to spend the rest of his life in prison? Kate still felt horrible for Dex's wife and kids, getting dragged into the limelight while Belle actually basked in the notoriety, but she couldn't forget that Belle was a victim, too. "I can only imagine what a difficult time this has been."

Belle smiled. "I'm fine.

"It's okay not to be fine," Kate said, quoting something Ty had said to her last night.

"Dex . . ." Belle's bravado faltered. She grimaced as if in pain, and instantly she was the lovesick girl in the video. Then she swallowed and straightened her shoulders. "I know that Dex took advantage of me."

"Good." Kate seriously hoped this admission was the result of some decent therapy, and not just a memorized talking point from Clementine.

"He means nothing to me." Belle smiled coolly. "And I don't care what happens to him. I've even hired someone to make sure I don't have to testify in person."

Could a private investigator do that? It was worth a shot.

"Ms. Eldridge?"

Belle's smile vanished. Her eyes grew wide, and her jawline bulged from her clenched teeth. "What?"

Not who, but what. Kate was on the right track. "Ms. Eldridge. I heard she can help with things." She was grasping at straws, trying to make it sound like she knew what she was talking about instead of fishing for information.

"You heard that?"

Kate nodded, then decided to go for broke. "And I've heard that her assistant is smoking hot."

Belle might have been suspicious, but she couldn't pass up the opportunity to share a juicy piece of gossip. "He is," she said with a pump of her eyebrows. "But someone else is already barking up that tree, if you know what I mean."

You have no idea. "Really?"

Belle leaned in closer. "They are totally getting it on."

"Wow," Kate mouthed. She needed to get some names, the assistant, or the husband. If Belle even knew them. "What was his name? Brad? Todd?" Those sounded like typical white-guy names. But instead of taking the bait, or even questioning how Kate might know the name of

Ripley's assistant, Belle latched on to the one innocuous word in Kate's question.

"Was?" Belle straightened up. "She fired him?"

Shit. Kate was supposed to be the interrogator, not the informant. "I . . . I don't—"

Belle's jaw dropped. "She did. Oh my God. That's, like, a huge lawsuit."

Or a life sentence.

"Though she could totally afford it. The firm makes bank."

Kate was hoping Belle would elaborate a little bit as to what, exactly, Ripley did, but the waitress made an untimely arrival with their drinks. "One spirulina latte and one Tropical Smoothie. Enjoy, ladies!"

Kate eyed her glass. She wasn't sure she could drink the frothy green smoothie with a fuzzy mushroom-looking thing poking up from the foam. What, exactly, was tropical about that?

Belle didn't touch her latte either. She was staring hard at the ivy wall beside their table. "I wonder what he knows."

"Who?" Kate assumed she was still focused on Ripley's supposedly fired assistant, but she wanted to make sure.

Belle wasn't listening. "Like, if he knows where the bodies are buried, he could probably use that for leverage."

"Oh, he definitely knows where the bodies are buried," Kate mumbled.

"I mean, fuck a lawsuit. I bet he could blackmail her for, like, hundreds of thousands."

"Really?"

"With her A-list clients. I know a lot of people who would pay a shit ton of money for that information."

"I bet."

"Because, like, who cares about a stupid affair anyway?"

Dex's wife and kids? "Her husband."

Belle's eyes grew wide. "Who?"

Damn it. She was supposed to be coaxing information out of Belle, and instead, she'd let slip a detail that one of Ripley's clients probably wouldn't know. A suspicious Belle would tighten up like a dead clam, and Kate was so close to getting something useful, she could practically taste it.

She decided the best course of action was to pretend she hadn't made a slip at all. That this was common knowledge they were tossing about. "Yeah, tall guy, thinning hair."

"You saw him in the office?"

"Yep." And she didn't even have to lie.

Belle whistled, low and breathy, then said, more to herself than to Kate, "I wonder if Todd knows?"

Todd, ha. *Nailed it.*

Belle stared at her untouched spirulina latte, her mouth working as if she was reciting lines. Without warning, she pushed her chair away from the table, metal legs screeching in protest against the concrete. "I have to go."

"Um, okay."

"It's been lovely," Belle said, scooping her phone off the table before darting away. "Kisses, Noelle!"

As Kate watched her go, she wondered if Belle actually thought she and her character had the same name.

* * *

"His name was Todd," Kate said triumphantly as she arrived at Ty's cubicle. "Ripley's assistant." It felt awkward to pick up the conversation from the night before without referencing their almost kiss, but Kate still didn't have a handle on how she felt about Ty, and until this murder business was resolved, she didn't need complicated feelings muddying her mind.

Ty seemed to be of like mind. He nodded and jotted down the name. All business. "And you said her last name is Eldridge?"

"Yep. I looked up all the offices on the fourth floor of the south tower, and the only one that looks promising is called QED."

Ty added that to his notepad. "Give me an hour or two, and I'll see what I can find." Then he winked at her before turning to his computer screen. One gesture that made all of the weirdness between them melt away.

"Thank you." It felt good to have him on her team. On her side. Working on this together. Like if Ty believed her story, she clearly wasn't losing her mind.

Kate was still smiling when she slipped into the dungeon. Ripley wasn't around, her office dark and empty, but Kate didn't need to see her, didn't need to suss out any new clues by spying on her office activities. Ty was on the case, and if there was anything at all to figure out, he'd do it.

She didn't even mind the enormous pile of backlogged filing that awaited her. She attacked it happily, smiling the whole time, and the positive energy made her work faster, more efficiently. Like she was channeling Ty through the dungeon walls. By the time the sun began to set and the sky darkened, she'd cleared most of the clutter that had accumulated and only had a small stack of loose pages left to file away.

Ty would have been so proud.

She was so focused on her work that Kate almost didn't notice when someone entered Ripley's office.

If it had been twenty minutes earlier when the orange-red hues of sunset reflected sharply off the highly reflective south tower windows, Kate probably wouldn't have noticed. Ripley had just arrived, and judging by the violence with which she kicked the door closed behind her, she was pissed off. Again.

Ripley launched her purse and coat onto the sofa, not even bothering to hang them up. Then she began pacing behind her desk. Her steps were unhurried, as if the movements were less to alleviate anxiety and more to accommodate whatever thought processes were churning in her brain. After a few minutes, Ripley seemed to come to a decision. She sat calmly at her desk, pulled out a mirror to check her makeup, smoothing the line beneath her lower lip with her middle finger, then folded her hands one over the other and waited.

Kate continued filing, her eyes flitting up to the window every few seconds. Ripley sat still as a statue. Was she waiting for someone?

Finally, the door to Ripley's office opened and Kate got her answer.

Belle Masterson sauntered into the lobby.

THIRTY

IT WASN'T DIFFICULT TO INTERPRET THE SHORT BUT INTENSE conversation that took place between Belle and Ripley.

Lady Boss sat calmly at her desk while Belle put on a flamboyant show, taking her time as she approached Ripley's private office. She examined the furniture, the artwork, and the potted plant with feigned interest. An actress following her blocking. She spoke as she moved but avoided direct eye contact with the motionless Ripley until she sat down opposite her. At that point, Belle crossed one leg over the other, laced her fingers together over one knee, and leaned forward, delivering the final line in her monologue.

Whatever she said came as no surprise to Ripley, because she merely

smiled and said one line. Her words came out slowly, her diction so pre-
cise that Kate could lip-read every syllable.

"I have no idea what you're talking about."

Belle held her pose for a split second, then tossed her head back,
laughing. Kate had seen villains do that exact move in a dozen
action films.

Ripley remained unmoved, betraying no emotion on her poker face.
Her eyebrows were lifted in an unspoken question, and she kept her hands
still while looking Belle straight in the eyes. A challenge. Two alpha dogs
vying for supremacy.

Kate had a pretty good idea of who would win.

But Belle wouldn't be out-intimidated, even though she was clearly
out of her league. She was enjoying this role, relishing the power she felt,
and as Kate watched her speak again, this time meeting Ripley's unwavering gaze with her own, she realized it was probably her fault that Belle
was there in the first place.

The affair.

Ripley's husband.

Blackmail.

Had Belle guessed that Ripley had killed both men? No, that was
impossible. Belle merely thought Ripley had fired Todd, and she was
probably threatening to tell Ripley's husband about the affair.

Kate wanted to rush over and pull Belle from the office where she sat
so dangerously close to a murderer, but she couldn't. Her ID badge was
only good for her own floor in her own tower. She'd have to call security
again and pray that Donald didn't answer the phone. Maybe someone
else would be more inclined to believe her? Or maybe she could have Ty
call down?

She was trying to decide what to do when Belle pushed herself to her feet, planted both hands on Ripley's desk, and leaned toward the killer. One last threat.

Kate held her breath. If Ripley had that gun anywhere close, she could very quickly have a third death on her hands, but instead of a flash of movement toward her desk drawer, Ripley simply leaned back in her chair, one hand gesturing toward the door.

I think you should leave.

Belle shrugged, spun like a dancer on one toe, and pranced through the lobby, out of Ripley's office.

Kate exhaled. No gunshots. No dead body.

That was close.

She dropped her chin to her chest and took a deep inhale through her nose. Her heart was racing as if she'd been there in the room with Belle and Ripley. The invoice she'd been about to file when Ripley's office came alive was still in her hand, wrinkled from the ferocity of her grip, and as she smoothed it out on the table, her eyes caught a familiar name in the letterhead.

It was an invoice from QED.

Holy shit. QED was a vendor of Kleiner, Abato & Chen.

A smile spread across Kate's face, so wide it made her cheeks ache. This was it. This was their opening.

In an instant, Kate formulated a plan that might yield some proof that Ripley was a murderer. She glanced up, expecting to see her former idol still sitting at her desk, watching the door Belle had exited through.

But the office was empty.

* * *

Kate dropped into the chair beside Ty's desk and slid the crinkled invoice toward him. "I found this."

Ty's face was impassive except for an elevated brow. "Please tell me it's a photograph of our friend standing over two dead bodies while holding a smoking gun."

Kate snorted. "I wish."

"A boy can dream." Ty sighed, glancing down. His eyes widened as he realized what he was looking at. "She's a vendor?"

Kate nodded. "Yep."

"Good, we need a break," Ty said, running a hand through his hair. "Because I've come up empty. Todd is too common a name."

Kate tapped the invoice with her index finger. "I thought maybe this could be our in."

"In?"

"To her office. Literally."

"I don't follow."

Kate leaned forward, dropping her voice. "I wait for her, somewhere we know she'll show up, like the parking garage. She's got a reserved spot by the elevator bay, so I'll get here early tomorrow, park nearby, and wait. Then engineer a meeting."

Ty looked skeptical. "And say what, exactly? 'I'm a file clerk at Kleiner and I'd like to discuss your invoice'? Probably not going to get you invited up for a drink."

Kate didn't need a drink. She needed five minutes alone in Ripley's office with her cell phone camera to find some evidence of a double homicide. Like Ty said, there had to be something up there—a smudged thumb print, a batch of dried blood, a stray hair—that would link her to the crime. A few quick photos could be enough to convince the Burbank PD to at least investigate; then a forensics crew would do the rest.

"I'll tell her I'm a lawyer," she said, "and I need to discuss something about her case."

His left eyebrow crept upward again. "You realize that if she's a vendor, we're not working on a case for her, right?"

"Um . . ." Right, duh. "I can wing it."

Ty dropped his hands to the desk. "Wing it."

"Yep."

"This isn't an improv show, Kate. She's not going to play along with you."

"You don't think I can convince her that I'm an attorney?" Kate was pretty confident that the lingo she'd picked up over the last two weeks in the dungeon paired with her acting chops was enough to make this happen.

"Okay." Ty leaned back in his chair and drummed his fingertips against one another. "So, Ms. Williams, you said? Do you have a question about our linear and nonlinear document review methodologies, or would you prefer a technology-assisted review approach?"

Typical Ty. He went right for the nuclear option with some kind of legal stuff she didn't understand. She'd have been angry if he wasn't smiling as he said it. Not the superior, condescending smile that would make her want to slap him across the face, but a warm smile, indicating that his teasing was good-natured.

"Fine, you win. I am clearly not a lawyer." She slumped back in her chair, defeated. The plan had sounded good in her head.

"Not that you couldn't be," Ty said quickly. "You just haven't spent enough time around lawyers."

"Which isn't a bad thing."

"True. It can be a little . . ." He let his voice trail off as he sat straighter in his chair. "Stiff. You know, I've been working here on and off since I was thirteen."

"Really?" She knew he'd spent more time at the office than Rowan did, but she didn't realize he'd actually worked there so long. No wonder everyone knew him.

"Oh yeah." He shrugged like it was no big deal. "I enjoy helping out my dad. And the extra pocket money is a bonus."

Rich kids didn't typically need to work, and it had never occurred to Kate that Ty might actually *want* to.

"What was the rest of your plan?" Ty asked. "After conning your way into Ripley's office."

"Look around for evidence of two murders, snap pics, get the hell out, call the police."

Ty's grin grew mischievous. "In that order?"

"Hope so."

"Not much of a plan."

"You got a better one?"

"I could be your lawyer."

"Oh!" Kate was slow to catch on, but now she understood Ty's leading questions. "Do you think you could BS your way through a legal conversation with Ripley?"

"Easily."

She eyed his smooth chin with hardly a trace of stubble. "I'm not sure you look old enough to be an actual lawyer."

Ty laughed. "All Asian guys look twelve years old to white people. She'll buy what I'm selling."

"And you can get her to bring you back to her office?" Kate pictured Ripley and her last assistant getting busy on the boss's desk, and suddenly she wasn't so sure if she wanted Ty up there with a cougar.

"Sure." He paused, shaking his head. "But I can't exactly snoop around her office while she's sitting across the desk from me. How am I supposed to get her out of the room?"

This time, Kate had a plan she was positive would work. "Leave that one to me."

* * *

The next evening, Kate and Ty sat in the Chen family's Tesla on the first floor of the Burbank Garden Towers Business Park parking garage, trading yawns. The garage was warm, stuffier than the air outside, and paired with the muted light from the overhead fluorescents, it was making Kate sleepy. Ty was also fighting the urge to nap, and every few moments, Kate would watch his head droop down toward the steering wheel before it jerked up suddenly, his eyes semi-closed.

"How long have we been here?" he asked.

Kate stifled another yawn. "Two hours and twenty minutes."

"'Kay." Ty hooked a leg over the center console so it draped beside her, then closed his eyes. "Wake me up when it's showtime." Once again pushing aside the feelings she had no time to process, Kate shifted in the passenger seat, tucking her legs up beneath her. She angled the rearview mirror to catch any movement at the reserved parking spots near the elevator bay, and all she could do now was hope that Ripley came to the office. Every day that passed was one more opportunity for the evidence to disappear. It was now almost seventy-two hours since the murders. If there was anything to find in Ripley's office, they had to get up there immediately.

Dangerous, but a chance worth taking, and though her scheme was a rudimentary one, Ty had approved. Hell, he'd even volunteered to go into the lion's den. Rowan might not believe her, but Ty certainly did, and that had to count for something.

Does he believe you, or is he still in love with you?

The question made Kate's stomach clench. She looked over at Ty, resting serenely. What if she were using his feelings to put him in danger?

Maybe she should let him nap. If Ripley arrived, Kate could slip out of the car and approach, making the best of her limited knowledge of legal jargon to try to fool Ripley. The odds weren't that great, but at least Ty would be safe. That was better than—

Kate felt the reverberations through the reinforced concrete foundations of the parking garage before she even heard the rumbling engine. She looked up at the rearview mirror in time to see Ripley's vintage Porsche screech into one of the reserved spots.

Showtime.

"Showtime." Ty pulled his leg back from Kate's side of the car and quickly opened the door. She didn't even know he was awake. "Wish me luck."

"Wait!" Kate cried in a hushed tone. But it was too late. Ripley was already out of her car, tying a black silk trench coat around her waist. Ty never hesitated, he hurried toward the elevator bay with his head buried in his phone. He looked like a young associate lost in work correspondence, so Ripley was only annoyed, not suspicious, when he barged right into her.

"Sorry! I'm so sorry!" Ty's voice sounded sincere as it drifted in through Kate's cracked window.

Ripley dropped her keys on impact, then swiped them off the ground and dumped them into her coat pocket. "Watch where you're going," she said viciously, until she stood up and got a good look at him.

"Are you okay?" Ty asked.

Ripley pushed her brown curls out of her face, anger vanished. Instead, her smile was inviting. "Nothing a good massage can't fix."

Damn, she was smooth.

"I'm just buried in work email," he said, shoving his phone back into his pocket. "Fourth-year associate trying to make partner. You know how it is."

"What firm?"

The rest of the conversation was lost on Kate. A group of business-casual dudes exited the elevators, laughing boisterously. They obscured Ripley and Ty from her view as they spilled into the parking lot, and when they finally separated, the echoes of their frat-boy arrogance receding into the half-empty parking garage, Kate was just able to catch sight of Ty following Ripley into the elevator.

"Shit." She leaped out of the car, kicking the door closed with her foot as she raced to catch the next elevator. The door to the departing one had closed, and Kate pushed the call button frantically.

Three seconds of waiting felt like a lifetime as both elevators remained at the lobby level.

Five.

Ten.

Screw it. Kate pushed open the door to the stairwell and raced up a flight and a half. As she breathlessly rushed into the lobby, the phone in the pocket of her jeans vibrated with a text from Ty.

Invited up.

THIRTY-ONE

THOUGH SHE HATED THE IDEA OF TY ALONE WITH A MUR-derer, the plan was in motion. All Ty had to do was stay in Ripley's office long enough for Kate to cause a distraction, and in order to do that, she had to get upstairs to the dungeon.

Fast.

Donald was back at the security desk when Kate rushed by. She avoided looking at him but could feel his eyes on her and imagined the snarl curling his upper lip as he stared daggers at her back. But as she rounded the desk, he never said a word, and she wondered if Donald had been given a warning by building management after Ty's complaint.

Good. Fuck that guy.

But Kate was still glad to see him at his post.

Her plan depended on it.

One of the elevators in the north tower was stopped on the fourth floor, the other coming down, and Kate stabbed at the call button futilely, her anxiety mounting with every passing moment. She didn't want to leave Ty alone too long with that woman.

The Kleiner, Abato & Chen offices were deserted by the time Kate scanned her card and pushed open the front doors. Typical for a Friday. Her movement triggered the overhead lights in the lobby and again when she entered the second set of glass doors into the main office, which meant it had been at least fifteen minutes since anyone had been there.

Just as well. She didn't need witnesses.

By the time she reached the dungeon, the show across the courtyard was already in progress.

Ty stood in the reception area, hands shoved into his pockets as he pretended to admire the potted plant in the corner. Ripley dumped her purse on the assistant's desk before entering her office, half closing the door behind her. She peeled off her trench coat, revealing a sleeveless silk shirt underneath, then turned toward her closet and paused. Instead of opening the closet and hanging up her trench as she'd seen Ripley do before, she hung it on the hook outside the door.

Why had she decided not to open the closet?

Because there was something inside. Or had been.

Like a couple of dead bodies.

Kate's heart raced as Ripley walked to the credenza in front of the window. She had a perfect view as Ripley undid the top two buttons on her shirt, exposing enough cleavage to catch a peek of black bra.

Meanwhile, the instant Ripley's back was turned, Ty yanked both hands out of his pockets. He had his cell phone out and was typing frantically. Glancing down at her own phone, Kate saw the three blue dots indicating that he was writing to her. Had Ty already found the evidence they needed?

Kate's fleeting cell coverage vanished before she received Ty's message, but she didn't have time to run outside in order to see what he'd sent. Ripley emerged from her office, carrying a lowball glass in each hand. As soon as Ty saw her, his hands flew back into his pocket, removing the phone from her view.

Ripley handed one of the glasses to Ty, who awkwardly accepted it. Kate had never seen him drink before, but since he was pretending to be a fourth-year associate and presumably in his late twenties, he dutifully raised the glass to match Ripley's toast and then brought it to his lips. Kate could practically see the wince on his face as the liquid passed his lips.

Hard alcohol was *not* for beginners.

Ripley, clearly not a beginner, polished off her glass, then backed up through the doorway to her desk, easing herself onto it. Kate remembered this exact move from the night she watched Ripley seduce her assistant. Was she about to get sexy with Ty?

"Oh, hell no." Kate flew off the table and around the filing cabinets to the security phone mounted by the door. Time to set phase two of her plan in motion. She cleared her throat, picked up the receiver, and waited for Donald's voice.

"Security," he barked, just as friendly as last time. "Can I help you?"

"Donald!" Kate began, though even her own parents wouldn't have recognized her voice. She had raised it half an octave so it sounded more girlish, and rounded out the vowels to create a soft, Virginia drawl. Exactly like Ripley's. "I'm so glad you're here tonight."

"Ms. Eldridge!" Kate noted the familiarity in his voice with satisfaction.

He never doubted whose voice he heard on the line. "I—I didn't realize it was you. This call is coming from three-north and—"

"How very odd!"

"Ms. Eldridge?"

Kate winced at her own word choice. Was Ripley really the kind of person who would say "How very odd?" This wasn't *Downton Abbey,* for fuck's sake. She cleared her throat and started again.

"Donald, I've locked myself out of my car. Could you meet me at Parking Level One right away?"

"Um, yes, of course, Ms. Eldridge." Donald paused. "You said you're on P-One?"

He was suspicious. She'd have to bluff her way through.

"No, I'm in my office."

"Your office . . ."

Why would someone be prank-calling him from inside the building? Still, he hesitated, and Kate was worried that her lack of knowledge of Ripley's style combined with the location tracker would make Donald hang up and appear outside the dungeon again, threatening to call the police. She needed to act like a lady boss and regain control.

"Donald, I'm getting another call. Can you text me when you're heading down and I'll meet you?"

"Um . . ."

"You have my cell number, yes? Can you confirm it, Donald?"

She purred his name, which seemed to work.

"Eight-one-eight, six-two-two, sixty-one forty," he said quickly.

As if he had it memorized.

As if he'd been waiting for this moment his entire life.

"Perfect. Give me two minutes to take this call, then text me when you're ready."

"Two minutes." He paused, and Kate could hear his ragged breath. "You can count on me, Moira."

Kate grinned as she hung up the phone. Moira? So Donald was on a first-name basis with Ripley. She could only imagine how the actual Moira would have smacked him down in a heartbeat for getting too familiar.

But whatever. Her acting ruse had worked. Now for phase three.

Confidence flowing, Kate slipped out of the dungeon, into the deserted hallway. The lights flickered on again, and she almost felt as if she was onstage beneath a follow spot as she dialed Ripley's number into her cell. It rang, and Kate could visualize Ripley's attention being pulled away from seducing Ty in order to take the call, a look of irritation scrawled across her refined features.

One ring, two. Would Ripley pick up? Kate's parents had always warned her not to answer calls from numbers she didn't recognize, but surely a businesswoman—a private investigator, no less—would get lots of calls from numbers she didn't recognize. It was a chance Kate had to take. She couldn't figure out any other way to get Ripley out of her office long enough for Ty to snoop around.

Third ring and Kate was beginning to give up hope, and then—

"Who is this?" The same high-pitched lilt Kate had just imitated, laced with an edge of malice.

"Moira?" Kate barked. The name popped out of her mouth before she could stop herself.

"Only my mother calls me Moira."

Shit. She'd gotten sloppy in her cockiness, and one thing Kate knew for sure was that she couldn't slip up with Ripley. She was too smart.

"Er, building security gave your name as Moira Eldridge," Kate continued brusquely, then barreled forward before Ripley had time to reply.

"You drive a vintage Porsche Nine Eleven Carrera Two in candy-apple red, right?"

A pause. Like Donald, Ripley was suspicious. "I do."

"Sorry, but I accidentally backed my Suburban into one of your taillights."

"WHAT?"

Porsche drivers were so predictably obsessive about their cars, it was almost too easy.

"But since you were parked over the line anyhow, I thought maybe we'd report it to our insurance as mutual fault and move on."

"Mutual fault? Are you insane?" Kate could hear Ripley moving around her office, probably getting herself redressed. "Don't move. I'm coming down."

Then the call went dead.

Kate wasted no time gloating over the effectiveness of her plan. She quickly texted Ty to let him know he was in the clear.

You're good for five minutes. Check the closet.

His phone still showed the rippling dots to indicate he was typing a response, probably the one that Ripley had interrupted. She waited, hoping a text would come through, but every passing second felt like an hour. It would take Ripley two minutes to get down to P-One, another minute or two of confusion with Donald before she realized she'd been duped, then a max of two minutes to get back to her office. Which gave Ty less than five minutes before he needed to be out of there.

Now she had to hope Ty found something.

She set her own timer in case Ty got distracted and lost track of time, then practically skipped through the door to the dungeon and back around the file cabinets to the table in front of the window. She was just in time to see Ty typing on his phone.

Why was he still texting her back? He knew she didn't get reliable service in the dungeon.

Kate hesitated, debating what to do. Maybe he was confirming her message? Or finishing the one he started earlier? Either seemed like a total waste of thirty precious seconds of his time.

"What are you waiting for?" she said out loud.

Ty looked up, directly at her window, almost as if he could hear her. She waved, trying to get him to start his search.

"Check the closet!" she said, pointing to the corner of Ripley's office near the window. "Claw-set!"

But all Ty did was point down at the floor, then to Kate, then back to the floor.

Kate checked her phone, no service again, of course.

"What?" she said, opening her hands in a gesture that should have expressed her single word loud and clear, but Ty either didn't see her or didn't understand. He continued his pointing, alternating between Kate and the floor, though his movements were getting more frantic.

Kate had no clue what he was trying to tell her. She jumped off the table and was about to dash into the hallway to find out what was making Ty so agitated, when, suddenly, he stopped moving.

His eyes were on the ground over near Ripley's closet. Then Ty cocked his head to the side and approached the corner. He crouched, disappearing from Kate's view, and she held her breath. He'd found something, she was sure of it. Some tiny piece of evidence that would prove Kate wasn't out of her mind and had hallucinated a double homicide.

She glanced down at her phone. Only two minutes left on her timer. Ty needed to get out of there soon. What exactly was he doing on the floor, taking selfies? Conducting a full forensics investigation?

Her foot bounced on the ground, and she leaned across the table, as if doing so might allow her a viewing angle to find out what Ty was up to. She tried her phone again, desperate for a signal to call him, but no luck. Finally, she reached out and pounded on her window with her fist, a ridiculous move since there was no way Ty could have heard her through two sets of security glass at the distance of fifty yards.

"Please, Ty," she begged. Only sixty seconds left. "Get out of there."

He couldn't have heard her, but at that moment, Ty's head popped up into view, he was grinning in triumph as he turned for the door, phone in hand, typing furiously with his thumbs as he walked.

Ty only made it as far as the lobby when the door flew open, and Ripley stormed into her office.

He froze, a deer in headlights, and if Ripley hadn't been suspicious of him before, she sure as hell was now. Ty probably could have strong-armed his way past her, but Ripley's reaction time was quicker. Before he could even move, she'd dashed to her purse on the reception desk and pulled out a gun. The same one, Kate guessed, that she'd used to kill her husband.

She barked out questions while Ty backed away. She must have told him to drop the phone because he let the device fall to the ground. As he did so, his head turned toward the window for a split second.

A look. A glance. Kate saw him mouth a single word.

"Run."

Ripley stopped her advance on him, her mouth agape, frozen mid-rant. Her eyes traced a line from Ty to the window and back. Then again to the window, and this time she stared out through the glass, eyes squinted, searching.

Kate ducked down behind the table and scooted to the edge of the window where she could see Ripley's office without being as noticeable to the woman who currently held Kate's friend at gunpoint. Ripley scanned the courtyard from side to side, then lifted her head as she looked at the north tower. She must have realized Ty was signaling to someone and was trying to figure out where that someone was located.

Kate wasn't sure if she'd been spotted, but Ripley's eyes never lingered on the dungeon window. She waited, holding her breath as if Ripley was actually in the file room with her, stalking. She needed to do something, call for help, but she felt rooted in place.

All of a sudden, she saw Ripley back up toward the door.

Then her office went dark.

THIRTY-TWO

"NO!"

The cry was ripped from her body, taking with it her heart, her stomach, and most of her lower intestine. Had she sent Ty to his death?

This time, Kate didn't bother with Donald.

She sprinted out of the dungeon into the hallway, waving her phone in front of her as if the sheer velocity of movement might generate a spontaneous cell phone signal. She was halfway to the lobby when the bars finally appeared.

"Nine-one-one, please state your emergency," the female operator drawled after two breathlessly long rings. Kate hoped it wasn't the same person as last time.

"There is a woman holding my friend at gunpoint," Kate blurted out. "And she's already murdered two people!"

"Miss," the operator said, with the questioning tone of a teacher who'd just been told that the dog ate a student's homework. "Are you sure this isn't—"

Kate didn't have time for skepticism. "Burbank Garden Towers Business Park on West Olive. The QED offices in suite four-sixty on the fourth floor of the south tower. I work in the building across the courtyard, and I saw Ripley, I mean, the occupant, Moira Eldridge, pull a gun on my friend Tyson Chen."

"You witnessed the use of a firearm?"

"Yes," Kate said. "She's already killed two people. Can you please send help?"

Typing on the other end. That was a good sign. "Stay calm, miss. What did you say your name was?"

"Kate," she said, her breaths coming so quickly they threatened to choke her. No pseudonym this time. "Kate Williams."

"Kate, are you in a safe location?"

The cubicle bullpen at Kleiner, Abato & Chen wasn't exactly the most secure spot in the office, but since Ripley was in the other building and didn't have access to the north tower with her ID badge, Kate figured she wasn't in any immediate danger.

"Yes."

"Okay, units are on the way. Would you like me to stay on the line with you?"

It would have been nice to keep a voice on the other line, offering a sense of security that, though false, was at least another living, breathing human. The empty, deserted office around her wasn't exactly a comfort.

But she couldn't stay in the hallway while Ty was trapped with a killer. She needed to get back to the window. She needed to know what was going on.

"No. My signal is unstable."

"Okay, miss. Please stay in that secure location," she repeated, "until help arrives."

"Thank you."

The dungeon was now Kate's only connection to Ty, and as the deafening roar of the servers hit her, she prayed that he was still alive there in the darkness. The courtyard was only fifty yards across, but it might have been fifty miles since she had no way to cross it, and as the seconds ticked by, the darkness from Ripley's windows ignited a creeping panic.

Ty was dead. She'd lost him forever. And not only was it her fault, but when her stomach dropped out from under her at the thought that Ty was gone, Kate realized something else.

I love him.

She stared futilely at Ripley's window, unheeded tears streaming down her cheeks. She'd been so stupid, idiotic. Ty had always been there for her, would always be there for her. He made her smile when she felt like crap, he listened sympathetically when she needed a level-headed opinion, and he was way hotter than Kate had ever noticed. He loved her for who and what she was, body size and all. Why had it taken her so long to realize her own feelings? So much time had been wasted, feelings hurt, and now . . .

The waiting was hell. It felt like hours had passed, and every ticking second was a death knell. Her brow and neck were drenched in sweat despite the frigid temperature in the dungeon, and her chest trembled with each inhale while her eyes scanned the darkness like an owl hunting for prey at night, searching for any flickering light or shadowy movement in Ripley's office. Her only solace was the fact that she hadn't actually seen the flash of a gun.

It was her only indication that Ty might actually be alive.

And she clung to it with a desperation she'd never felt before.

Finally, a light in Ripley's office. The door swung open, flooding the dark interior with the bluish glow from the hallway, and then a hand reached into the room and flipped the switch. Kate recognized one of the janitors right away and wondered why the hell Donald hadn't been at his post.

Two police officers moved into Ripley's lobby, hands poised at their gun holsters. They examined the small room—under the assistant's desk, behind the large copy machine in the corner that Kate had never even noticed before, beneath the chairs—then opened the door to the private office and entered slowly. They checked the desk, the credenza, a potted plant behind the door that Kate thought had been in the lobby, even the closet.

And apparently found nothing. One officer spoke into the radio at his shoulder while the other retreated from the office. After a short conversation, the first officer followed, turning off the lights and closing the door behind him.

Kate felt her throat constrict in panic. Was she losing her mind? She didn't hallucinate Ty and Ripley. Where could they have gone?

New tears welled up in her eyes, blurring her vision so badly she almost didn't see the two police officers reemerge in the office on the third floor.

In her two weeks at Kleiner, Abato & Chen, Kate had never seen anyone on that empty floor. Even the cleaning crew skipped it, and it looked weirdly apocalyptic to see the two officers methodically move through the space, checking each cubicle and doorless closet carefully before moving on to the next.

Which was a complete waste of time because *the killer is upstairs.*

Or at least she was.

Wasn't she?

It took longer for the officers to thoroughly check this suite since it was significantly larger than Ripley's, but eventually, they let their guard down, reholstered their weapons, and retreated. As before, one officer lingered at the door, calling something in on his radio. When he left, he flicked off the lights, and shut the door behind him.

The south tower went completely dark.

No, not entirely dark. There was a dim light still emanating from the vacant third floor. With the bright overheads extinguished, there must have been a work light on somewhere, because there was glow in one of the windows. Except the space looked different now. Less empty. Like this phantom light was casting shadows that mimicked the appearance of furniture in the empty, unleased office.

Kate stared out of her window, trying to figure out what the hell she was seeing. She pushed herself up onto her knees so she was closer to the glass, then froze.

There was a figure staring out of the third-floor window across from her. A round pale face with auburn hair and a look of utter confusion on her face.

Kate was looking at her reflection.

She was still trying to process what that meant when a light popped on upstairs. Above her reflection, Kate saw Ripley standing at the window, staring down at her.

In her office.

Where there was no potted plant behind her by the door.

Kate's hands began to shake as reality dawned upon her. The gunshots she almost heard. Ty frantically pointing at her and then at the floor. The office that looked like Ripley's except for the giant copy machine and a potted plant in the wrong place. Searches that came up empty.

Ripley's office wasn't on the fourth floor of the *south* tower, it was on the fourth floor of the *north* tower.

Directly above the dungeon.

Kate had been watching a reflection.

THIRTY-THREE

HOW COULD I HAVE BEEN SO STUPID?

For two weeks she'd been watching events play out in Ripley's suite, trusting her eyes while her brain occasionally sent up a red flag that something wasn't quite right. From the get-go, she felt as if she was watching a movie, an effect, she now realized, of the highly reflective windows in the Burbank Garden Towers Business Park.

She'd known that from the first day, from the first moment she arrived at the office. The piercing rays of the setting sun, reflected off the windows, had momentarily blinded her as she pulled into the underground parking garage. That's why she never saw into Ripley's office until after the sunset—darkness enhanced the reflection, and whatever businesspeople actually occupied the fourth-floor suite in the south tower had gone home for the day, leaving their office dark, and their windows a perfect mirrored surface.

Only now did Kate realize that she'd never actually seen Ripley go into the south tower. Their shared elevator ride had ended at the security desk, and she'd lost track of her and Ty as they left the parking garage.

A host of other niggling details suddenly made sense as well. The way Ripley had never noticed Kate watching her. Same reason Kate never saw her own reflection in the south tower until the cops turned out the lights in the empty suite: The brightly lit floor counteracted the mirror effect. The gunshots she'd imagined she'd heard were not her imagination at all. The fact that the cleaning crew appeared in Ripley's suite a few minutes after they finished vacuuming the hallways of Kleiner, Abato & Chen was because they literally hopped on the elevator, got out on the fourth floor, and worked on the first suite by the elevators.

Such a simple mistake with such horrific consequences. The police had searched the wrong building while Ty was still trapped with a murderer.

Ripley continued to stare at Kate's reflection across the courtyard, and Kate realized that Ripley was probably doing her own set of calculations, not about the geometry of reflected light rays but about how much Kate might have seen from her vantage point, and whether or not Ty was involved. She appeared to come to some kind of conclusion, because a half smile crept up the side of her face.

Kate had seen that smile before.

Right before Ripley murdered her husband.

"No!" Kate yelled at the ceiling. She wasn't sure if Ripley could hear her or not, but the smile deepened, spreading across her entire face. Then she reached out her hand and pulled something out of Kate's view. Instantly, a set of blinds descended over the window.

Ripley and her office were gone.

Ty.

Kate had to get the cops back out there. They couldn't have gone far. Hell, maybe they were still in their squad car, making a report. She leaped off the table and sprinted for the door. Before she reached it, she heard a dull popping sound. Just one. It was a sound she'd heard before. Heard and ignored.

The sound of a gunshot.

"NO!" she screamed impotently at the ceiling. "Ty!"

Ripley might have fired the gun, but Kate had killed him. Ty loved her. Loved her so much that he put himself in danger to help her catch a murderer. His love had gotten him killed.

And Kate never even got to tell him that she loved him back.

She sank to her knees, the cold metal door stinging her cheek as she collapsed against it. She'd been so stupid for so long. She'd hurt him, downplayed his feelings, lorded her power over his heart, and yet he still loved her, still put up with all of her bullshit. And now he was gone and her body felt hollow inside. Drained of life.

Rowan would be devastated.

And Mr. and Mrs. Chen.

And basically everyone who'd ever known Ty because he was, like, the greatest guy. Kate had never deserved his love. Had never cherished it. And now it was gone.

She was hysterical, grief spilling out of her in croaking sobs as she sprawled on the floor of the dungeon. Ripley had won. She was going to get away with the murders of three people, and there was nothing Kate could do to stop her.

Or was there?

Kate stopped mid-sob, pushing up onto her haunches from a fetal position as her chest stilled. Was there really nothing she could do to stop Ripley?

Of course there was. She'd literally just been about to call the police. She needed to get them back, get them up to Ripley's office before she could dispose of more evidence.

Kate cringed at the thought that Ty's body was evidence, but if Kate wanted to see Ripley pay for her crimes, that's exactly what Ty had become.

Wiping tears out of her eyes with the back of her hand, Kate hauled herself to her feet with the other. Hell, maybe Ty wasn't even dead. Just wounded. She had to hold out hope, and if he was still alive, then he needed her help.

There was no time to lose.

Once out of the dungeon, Kate hit redial on her 911 call the moment a signal appeared on her phone. They'd have to believe her, right? She'd simply explain that they went to the wrong building and they'd come back.

"Nine-one-one, please state your emergen—"

"My name is Kate Williams, and I called in a report of a woman holding a hostage at gunpoint in the Burbank Garden Towers Business Park," Kate blurted out, not even waiting for the operator to finish her script. "The police came but the searched the wrong tower. She's in the north tower, fourth floor. Not the south!"

"You said you already called in this disturbance?" the operator replied. She was focusing on the wrong details.

"Yes, and it's a long story, but I thought Rip—I mean Moira Eldridge was in the south tower, but she's in the north one and she's just shot my . . . my . . ." Her voice shook, unable to say the words.

"Ma'am, are you saying that a firearm has been discharged at your location?"

"Y-yes," Kate stammered.

"At the Burbank Garden Towers Business Park on West Olive?"

"Yes." She took a deep breath. "Please send someone back immediately. The responding officers—"

"There have been no other reports of gunfire in the vicinity of twenty-five twelve West Olive," the operator said coolly.

"Well, there's no one else here."

"You called in the initial report?"

"Yes."

"Ma'am, we have received a complaint about someone calling in false alarms to the emergency operator from your location."

"It's not a false alarm!" Kate cried.

"Under section one-four-eight-point-three of the California Criminal Code," the operator droned as if reading from a script, "any individual who reports, or causes any report to be made, to any city, county, city and county, or state department, district, agency, division, commission, or board, that an 'emergency' exists, knowing that the report is false, is guilty of a misdemeanor."

"It's not false! If your patrol car is still here, they can run back inside and they'll see for themselves."

The operator ignored her. "Conviction would be punishable by imprisonment for a period not exceeding one year."

"She just shot someone!" Kate yelled. "I heard it!"

Tears again. She imagined Ty's body crumpling like Ripley's assistant.

"Please do not call this number again or you *will* be prosecuted," the operator continued in the same emotionless monotone.

The call went dead.

A call from this location. Ripley. She'd seen the police in the south tower, realized Kate had been the one to call them, and took a chance by getting ahead of Kate's follow-up.

Ripley was smart. Kate needed to remember that.

Because she wasn't going to let this go.

Kate scanned her card and marched back into the dungeon. Donald was a dick, and the odds of him believing her were basically zero, but he'd bought her Ripley accent once before—maybe he'd buy it again? Especially if Ms. Eldridge was calling to complain about, say, the horrible file clerk who worked downstairs. Kate would pretend to be Ripley calling because there was an intruder in her office. That should get him up to the fourth floor.

From there, well . . . Kate blinked back tears as she thought of Ty. If he was dead, there was no way Ripley could have gotten rid of the evidence of her third murder so quickly.

She cleared her throat, fixing Ripley's girlish southern lilt in her mind, and picked up the phone. It rang.

And rang.

And rang some more.

"Come on!" Kate said, surprised by the sound of the words, which might have come straight from Ripley's mouth. She was ready for Donald to pick up the damn phone already, but by ten rings, it wasn't happening. He was away from his desk doing God knows what at the one moment in his illustrious security guard career when he was actually needed for something important. Awesome.

Kate hung up the phone and slunk back into the hallway. 911, fail. Donald, useless. The determination she'd felt moments ago was faltering as she ran out of options. There was only one other person she could call who might be able to help.

Her hands shook as she dialed Rowan's number. What would she say? *Your brother's dead, it's my fault, I need your help?* That would be overwhelming. They hadn't spoken since the disastrous stakeout in the dungeon, and Kate wasn't even sure if Rowan would take her call. As the rings continued and the voice mail picked up, her fears came true. Rowan was either avoiding her or hooking up with Jeremiah. Or both.

She hung up and tried again. Five rings, voice mail. Again. Five rings, voice mail. Again.

It was pointless attempting to reach her. Rowan wasn't going to pick up. The fourth time she heard the voice mail recording kick in, she waited for the beep.

"Ro, hey. Something happened. An accident. I know you don't believe me, but I need your help. Ty is . . ." Her voice cracked. She couldn't say it out loud, not to Rowan. She swallowed hard and tried to steady her voice. "If you get this, I need you to get the police to come out to your dad's building. Fourth floor, north tower. I was wrong about which building, Ro. Wrong about everything."

Not trusting her ability to explain more without completely breaking down, she ended the call. Her hand dropped to her side, defeated.

Almost immediately, she felt her phone vibrate with an incoming call.

She answered without even looking at the screen. "Ro?"

The voice that replied was definitely not Rowan's.

"You're the girl from the elevator."

It was Ripley.

THIRTY-FOUR

DUH, OF COURSE IT WAS RIPLEY.

The call that had lured her out of the office had come from Kate's phone, and it wouldn't have taken a genius to put those pieces together.

"I'll assume your silence means I'm right," Ripley continued. She was used to being in control, asserting her dominance early in her personal interactions. Kate had witnessed that both in her encounters with her late husband and with Belle Masterson, and she realized the best approach was not to let Ripley feel as if she was in control.

"And you're the murderer upstairs," Kate replied, surprised by how steady her voice sounded.

"Is that what you think?"

"That's what I *know.*"

Ripley paused, waiting. Perhaps hoping Kate would fill in the silence with nervous chatter that might reveal what, exactly, she knew. She pinned her lips together, determined to remain silent. If Ripley wanted details, she could ask.

"We can ask your friend," she said at last, "if he thinks I'm a murderer."

Ask her friend? Kate inhaled so quickly she almost choked. Ty was still alive. "Where is he?"

"Here." Through the phone, Kate heard a faint click followed by a low groan. Possibly male. It could have been Ty's voice, but it was difficult to tell.

"That could be anyone."

"True." Another faint click. "But are you willing to take that chance?"

"Depends," Kate said, stalling. "If that was Donald, you can keep him."

"I guess we'll never know, then."

Silence, though Kate got the impression from Ripley's audible breaths that she was moving around. She strained her ears, desperate for another murmur from Ty, but the groaning voice had gone quiet.

"What do you want?" Kate asked at last.

"More like what I *don't* want." Ripley's voice echoed, as if she'd stepped into a large, tile-floored restroom. "I don't want you spreading lies about me."

"I know what I saw," Kate said, standing firm. Now more than ever, she was confident that Ripley was a killer.

"Which is?"

Might as well lay her cards on the table. Knocking Ripley's confidence down a peg might produce a mistake. And a mistake from Ripley was what Kate needed if she wanted to save Ty.

"I saw you getting it on with your assistant, Todd," Kate said. "I saw your husband show up and threaten you with a gun. Then I saw him drop the gun and start to leave, at which point you pulled on gloves, made him turn around, and shot him in the chest."

"Hmm, interesting."

"And then I saw you use his gun to kill Todd. Trying to make it look like they'd shot each other."

"They *did* shoot each other."

Kate wouldn't be gaslit. "Oh really? And how would you know that? Were you there?"

Now it was Ripley's turn to fall silent. Kate's goal of shaking her confidence was working. She needed to keep going.

"*I* think you planned to leave them in your office for the cleaning crew to find the next day. By which point you'd have an alibi."

"Then why didn't I?"

"Because Donald showed up," Kate said, omitting the reason why Donald had gone to Ripley's suite in the first place. "An eyewitness who put you at the office you'd been seen leaving hours earlier. Alibi blown. You were forced to move the bodies."

Ripley let out a low growl that reminded Kate of a feral dog. "I had absolutely no motive to kill either of them."

Kate had to admit she had a point. A clear motivation would make this a slam-dunk case, but it didn't discount what she'd witnessed.

"I'm sure when the police look into it," she said, calling Ripley's bluff, "they'll find one."

"You read too many mystery novels."

"You don't read enough."

"There's no proof. It's your word against mine." Ripley's voice had an ugly edge to it, the smugness of a narcissist.

Suddenly, Kate remembered her phone. "No proof, huh?" She opened the photo gallery. The photo she'd impulsively snapped of Ripley and her assistant during their second encounter was at the top of her gallery and she quickly texted it to her upstairs neighbor.

"So you're a pervert, is that it?" Ripley said, feigning disgust. The echo around her voice had vanished.

If Ripley thought Kate had photos of the actual murders, maybe she could use that fear as blackmail to keep Ty alive long enough for them both to escape. "One of many I took this week."

"I see."

"Never know when you'll be able to use a photo like this."

"I *see*."

"And the second I think my friend is no longer safe," Kate said, trying to mimic the edge she'd heard in Ripley's voice moments earlier, "I send these off to the police."

Ripley paused again, then hummed atonally. "I wonder why you haven't yet."

"Maybe I have." Ripley suspected Kate was full of shit, but she wasn't sure.

"Ah. Okay, since you're the expert on murder mysteries," Ripley said, speaking more quickly now. "What do I do next?" She wasn't sure if the shift in Ripley's mood was a sign she believed Kate's story or not.

"You . . ." Kate hadn't really thought about that. "You get rid of the witnesses."

"You're a smart one, sugarplum."

Sugarplum? That phrase was familiar, but before Kate could remember where she'd heard it, the handle on the emergency exit door at the end of the hallway rattled.

Kate backed away. Ripley was out there, trying to get in. How did she access the third floor? Her ID badge would only allow her to the fourth.

The hollow echo. It wasn't a restroom; it was a stairwell. Ripley had simply walked down the stairs to the third floor.

The rattle became more violent, and Kate had backed all the way down the hallway to the double glass doors that led into the lobby before the movement stopped abruptly.

Kate sighed. Thank God for all the security doors in the law office. Nobody was getting inside Kleiner, Abato & Chen without permission.

Then, out of the corner of her eyes, Kate saw movement.

At first, she thought it was a reflection. Maybe her brain, irritated at its own mistake with the mirror effect of the windows, was trying to overcompensate. It didn't help that the movement Kate detected corresponded almost exactly to her own. As she backed into view of the lobby, another figure emerged outside by the elevators.

But it kept moving after Kate had stopped. She turned and saw Ripley just outside the main doors of Kleiner, Abato & Chen.

She still wore her sleeveless shirt, which exposed her tanned, sinewy arms. Stilettos with high-waisted pants made her figure look even more imposing, especially with the gun she held in her hand.

Ripley tilted her head to the side as she stared at Kate, her eyebrows drawn together as if attempting to place her; then her eyes widened with recognition two seconds before she bolted for the main doors of the law firm, applying a ferocious yank to the handle. The glass doors banged against their electronic lock, giving an inch before snapping back into place.

She tried again, this time pushing and pulling the doors with both hands, as if that might be enough force to disengage the magnetic locking mechanism, and Kate smiled as Ripley's curly hair flew around her face in a frenzy. There was no way in hell she was getting the door open. After ten seconds of futile shaking, Ripley stepped back, blowing an errant curl out of her face.

Kate's breaths came more easily. She was as safe as a baby in the womb inside the Kleiner, Abato & Chen offices, and there was nothing Ripley could do about it.

Except she still had a gun, a fact Kate remembered when Ripley extended her arm and fired three shots into the glass.

For all the money her bosses had spent securing the dungeon, Kate had half expected the glass walls that enclosed the lobby to be made from bulletproof glass, but the three distinct holes that appeared below the firm's etched name proved otherwise. The plate glass didn't shatter, but the bullet holes were structurally fatal. Approaching the doors, Ripley pivoted her hips and struck the glass with a vicious side kick.

The door exploded on impact, raining pebbles of glass all over the lobby.

Kate didn't stick around long enough to watch Ripley do the same thing to the doors that separated the lobby from the main part of the office, and only heard the crunch of glass beneath stiletto heels behind her as she bolted down the hall to the dungeon.

Two more shots rang out as Kate fumbled with her card, practically dropping it with shaky hands as she pulled it from her pocket. The light turned green on the scanner pad, and she heard the lock retract at the same time the glass from the second set of glass doors blasted into the hallway behind her. She heaved open the door, ducking her head as she slipped inside, and as she pulled it closed behind her, three more shots rocketed down the hallway.

They weren't a warning.

Ripley was shooting to kill.

It seemed like an eternity before Kate felt the door rearm itself. Even then, sealed inside the most secure room in Burbank, Kate instinctively backed away from the door.

She felt rather than heard the pounding on the other side. The sound was obscured by the thickness of the security door and the roar of the servers, and Kate wasn't sure if Ripley was whaling away on the door with her fists or if she'd shot at it like she did every other door in the office. She wasn't going to get through this one, though. Bulletproof, fireproof, explosion proof. Ripley wasn't getting in unless Kate wanted her to.

But her sanctuary was also a prison. With no cell service and no way to contact the outside world, she was trapped, totally unable to help Ty, who was still a prisoner upstairs in Ripley's office. And in pain, if that groan had been any indication. A bullet wound might still prove fatal if he didn't get medical attention, so Kate couldn't sit there until someone came to rescue her. She needed to think.

Something Ripley had said had given her pause, before whizzing bullets made her brain stop working. What was it?

You're a smart one, sugarplum.

Sugarplum. Right. She'd heard that before. Just recently. Same cadence, same intonation, though the voice had sounded different. Kate ran through all the conversations she'd had in the last two weeks—Rowan, Ty, HR, the kids at theater camp, auditions, Clementine . . .

Clementine. Not her but in her office. The speakerphone call with Emmy.

Life ain't fair, sugarplum.

Emmy.

Moira Eldridge.

Only my mother calls me Moira.

The truth hit Kate so ferociously she staggered, bracing herself against the nearest file cabinet. It wasn't "Emmy" Clementine called her that day in her office, but "M.E." The reputation fixer.

That's why Ripley seemed to recognize her just now: She'd binged *Dirty Pretty Teens* before her conference call with Kate. And that's why Belle was in her office. Clementine had referred her to M.E. as well, but unlike Kate, Belle could afford five grand a month. Which was probably why Clementine had sent Belle on the *Sunny's Side Up* audition instead of Kate.

But M.E. was also familiar to Kate in an entirely different way. The huge triple file she'd found on her second day of work. Could it be the same company?

Ripley had gone quiet in the hallway outside the dungeon, and Kate wondered if she was trying to find a way to disable the security. *Good luck with that, lady.* While she sat impotently outside, Kate had plenty of time to put her theory to the test. She dashed around two rows of file cabinets to the last section in the corner. "M.E." was right at the front, all three file folders' worth, and Kate hoisted out the most recent one, opening it on top of the drawer.

The topmost pages, the most recent ones, were all dated from July. They were invoices from Kleiner, Abato & Chen to the company M.E. located at the Burbank Garden Towers Business Park, north tower, suite 410, all past due, probably printed for the file at the same time they were mailed last month. Six invoices in total, adding up to a mind-numbing two hundred and fifty thousand dollars in legal fees that M.E. owed the firm.

A quick flip through the rest of the file gave Kate a pretty good idea of the state of Ripley's business and her motive for murder. Kleiner, Abato & Chen had represented Ripley in a couple of major lawsuits. She'd been sued by two former clients, seeking damages for defamation of character. Both suits had been settled out of court.

Whether or not Ripley had paid out the undisclosed settlements was unclear, but she certainly hadn't paid any of her legal bills. The controller had handwritten "last notice" on the most recent invoices, which seemed ominous. Kate didn't know much about business, but she understood that debt could signal bankruptcy. Ripley's boast that she was a successful business owner who didn't need her husband's support had been a bold-faced lie. If for some reason Ripley got nothing in a divorce, she could be really screwed.

Screwed enough to kill for?

Maybe.

Kate pulled out her phone and quickly opened the camera, snapping photos of each page in M.E.'s file. She could show these to the police if she had to prove her point, and knowing Ripley's motivation gave her a sense of calm. One mystery solved; now she just had to figure out how to get upstairs and rescue Ty before—

She stopped mid-thought as a terrifying new sound pierced the rumbling white noise of the dungeon. It was a beep, faint yet definite, followed by the distinctive click of a bolt releasing a heavy door.

Someone had unlocked the door to the dungeon.

THIRTY-FIVE

KATE FROZE, CAMERA IN ONE HAND, FILE FOLDER IN THE other. Her eyes were trained on the opposite corner of the room, where a sliver of orange light emerged on the ceiling, spreading across the sound tiles as someone opened the door wider, before snapping shut and taking all the ambient light with it.

She wanted to believe that someone was working late in the office, or had come back to retrieve a file to use at home over the weekend, but her brain rejected that scenario. Once again, Ripley had outsmarted her, realizing long before Kate did that the guy bleeding out in her office would be carrying an ID access badge for Kleiner, Abato & Chen.

That's why it had gone so quiet in the hall while Kate was looking through the files. Ripley hadn't given up; she'd been retrieving Ty's badge from upstairs.

And now she and her gun were inside the dungeon with Kate.

There was only one way in or out, but Kate had two things in her favor. First, Ripley couldn't be 100 percent positive that Kate was still in the file room. Second, the dungeon wasn't an open space. Three rows of file cabinets broke the room up into short little corridors, which would allow Kate to reach the exit from two directions. If she could lure Ripley away from the door, she might be able to escape without a bullet ripping a hole through her chest.

It was her only chance.

The server fans would obscure her movements, but they also made it difficult to track Ripley's location. In this game of cat and mouse, Kate couldn't stand around waiting. She was an easy target in the corner. She needed to move.

As silently as possible, Kate ducked under the open file drawer and crouched low on the floor. The cabinets sat flush on the tile, so she couldn't see underneath them, but that meant Ripley couldn't either. She glanced from left to right, trying to anticipate which way Ripley might have gone, either straight ahead, down the wall of servers toward the window, or to her right, around the first of three rows of file cabinets. She listened for the sound of Ripley's stilettos clicking against the floor but heard nothing other than the server fans. Ripley might have been standing still, waiting for Kate to make the first move, or she might have taken off her shoes.

This is hopeless. Ripley was smarter, more ruthless, and armed. Kate was like a mouse in an open field with a falcon ready to swoop down and make a meal of her.

> *A falcon, towering in her pride of place,*
> *Was by a mousing owl hawk'd at and kill'd.*

The Old Man in *Macbeth* had a point. If the regal falcon could be caught by the lowly owl, maybe Kate had a chance? She had to think like a predator instead of prey.

Think like a killer.

If *she* entered the dungeon and walked down the long side of the wall toward the window, she'd be leaving an easier path for someone to escape. If Kate were in Ripley's shoes, figuratively, she'd move along the short wall, and check each of the rows for her victim, while still covering the exit if her prey made a break for it.

On hands and knees, Kate scurried around the corner of the file cabinet facing the window and pressed her back into the ice-cold metal. So far, so good. She was still alive, but she was at the farthest point from the exit. As long as Ripley had a sight line to the door, her bullets would travel faster than Kate's legs.

She needed Ripley to move.

As silent as a ghost, Kate pushed herself to her feet. She peeked around the corner of the cabinet to the row she'd just been in, praying she didn't come nose to muzzle with Ripley's gun. Thankfully, the coast was clear. With a quick jab at the M.E. folder still balanced on top of the open drawer, she sent the entire folder toppling to the ground.

Kate ducked back behind the cabinet in a heartbeat, ears straining for a noise from her stalker. She didn't have to wait long. A gunshot rang out, and Kate saw the bullet pierce the window to her right.

As soon as Kate knew Ripley was in the last row of cabinets, she dashed to her left, spanning the open row in two bounds before she took refuge again at the end of the stack. She didn't give herself time to second-guess herself. With a quick peek around the corner, she saw that the next row was clear and darted across it as well.

Her heart thundered in her chest, and Kate had to open her mouth wide and gulp down deep breaths of air to keep from panting like an overheated dog as a jittery mix of adrenaline and fear coursed through her body. She was one step closer to freedom. Just the narrow corridor between the first row of filing cabinets and the wall of servers stood between her and the door. She couldn't stay where she was for long. If Ripley had run down the far row toward the open drawer, she'd pop out by the window any second and Kate would be a sitting duck. If she made a run for it, she should be able to reach the door before Ripley could get off a clean shot.

Kate took one bracing breath and turned to make a break for it. But as she swung into the tight area next to the servers, she realized that her calculations had been way off. Halfway up the aisle between her and the door stood a barefoot Ripley.

The only thing that saved Kate's life was the fact that Ripley had lowered her gun. If she'd been ready, it all would have been over. They were eye to eye, bodies frozen—but Kate reacted faster. She threw herself back around the side of the cabinet as Ripley raised her gun.

The explosions from the muzzle were so loud, Kate's hands flew to her ears. She heard two bullets strike the window, a crunching sound like hard-soled boots on gravel, before the entire pane exploded. Tiny shards of tempered glass scattered across the table and onto the floor, bouncing like hail on the hard tile.

Bare feet and a floor covered in glass? Kate finally had an advantage.

She raced down the length of the room and ducked behind the final row of cabinets. She was two feet from the door, the handle tantalizingly close, but if Ripley hadn't moved, she was right there with an easy sight line to the door.

Stalemate.

Kate squatted low and chanced a quick look around the corner of the cabinet. As predicted, a barefoot Ripley still stood halfway down the row. Sparkling nuggets of glass were strewn around her feet, and her eyes darted back and forth, looking for a path through them.

Ripley's chin shot up in Kate's direction, and she whipped her head back to safety.

"I guess the question," Ripley shouted over the servers, "is whether my aim is better than your speed."

Kate didn't want to find out.

"Doesn't look like there's another way out," Ripley continued. "Unless you jump out the window. No stunt doubles in real life, Kate."

So Ripley *had* recognized her. That was going to complicate things.

"You can't hide forever, sugarplum. No one's going to show up to save you. Certainly not your friend upstairs."

Ty. She knew Ripley was baiting her, but she had to get to him. Kate was so close to the door. So close to an escape. If she could just figure a way out of that room. She thought of Ty, wounded, bleeding, in pain, while she was stuck in this stupid bomb shelter of a dungeon that he had been so proud of. She remembered the beaming smile on his face as he described the file cabinets.

Gypsum-insulated walls and drawers reinforced with fourteen-gauge welded steel wire . . . these are impact, explosion, and waterproof . . .

Walls *and* drawers. Did that mean, if she was able to open one of them, it would stop a bullet?

There was only one way to find out.

Kate stood up and smooshed her stomach against the side of the cabinet. The middle drawer would offer the most protection, and she should be able to reach the handle latch. As long as Ripley didn't shoot her hand. It was a risk she'd have to take.

In one lightning-fast motion, Kate thrust her arm around the corner, only exposing her head long enough to spot her target, the drawer handle. Her fingers found the lip and pulled just as Ripley let fly a volley. Two bullets struck the wall beside Kate, but the rest never made it. The drawer slid open, catching them.

That was all Kate needed to see. She threw herself at the exit door and wrenched the lever. It gave easily, and she tumbled into the hallway.

The freaking bulletproof filing cabinet had saved her life.

Ty would be delighted.

But Kate had no time to gloat over her escape. She slammed the dungeon door behind her, then sprinted for the emergency exit into the third-floor hallway.

Glass or no glass, Ripley would be close behind.

Kate ducked around the corner to the elevator bay and breathed a sigh of relief when the doors opened the instant she pushed the call button. She was about to dash inside when she had an idea.

If Ripley was with her on the third floor, then no one was upstairs with Ty. Maybe some old-fashioned misdirection would work this time?

Kate leaned in and pressed the lobby button, then leaped clear of the door. The stairwell was right beside her, and Kate slipped inside, watching the elevator through the cracked-open door.

Not a heartbeat later, Ripley rounded the corner. Her eyes were on the elevator, and Kate silently pulled the door to the stairwell shut. She ran up the concrete steps to the fourth-floor landing, freezing when she heard the door to the third floor fly open and bang heavily against the wall.

Kate instinctively ducked down and covered her head, as if her arm would be adequate protection against one of Ripley's bullets. She heard pounding footsteps echoing through the stairwell, and it took her a few seconds to realize that the sound was moving away from her.

Ripley was going down to the lobby. She must have seen the elevator doors close and the number on the floor indicator blip from three to two. She was trying to beat Kate down.

The stairs still shook with the force of Ripley's retreating footsteps as Kate backed slowly toward the door to the fourth floor. She kept her eyes fixed on the darkness below her, not entirely convinced she wouldn't see Ripley's face suddenly appear from nowhere, but when her foot bumped against something solid, she instinctively turned to look down.

The dim emergency lights created a disorienting play of angles and shadow that obfuscated the object lying across the concrete slab landing in front of the door to the fourth floor, so much so that Kate recognized the black security guard uniform first, before she even registered that the lumpy pile of clothes blocking her exit was a human body.

But as her eyes adjusted to the light, she could clearly see the man on his side, one arm out in front of him, the other thrown back, with both legs curled up behind him in a pose that would have been uncomfortable for even the most experienced yoga practitioner. His pale face seemed to glow in the blue lights of the stairwell, and though his eyes were open, the dark spot on his forehead with a trickle of shiny liquid oozing from it signaled that Donald's eyes wouldn't see anything ever again.

Kate clutched the railing as the muted interior of the staircase pitched and rolled around her. Ty might still be alive, but Donald sure the hell wasn't.

She squeezed her eyes shut, swallowing hard to keep from vomiting all over Donald's body. Even Donald didn't deserve to die like that—shot for no other reason than being in the wrong place at the wrong time, his body dumped in a staircase to be discovered God only knows when. Was this how she and Ty would end up? Two more of Ripley's victims, whose bodies might not be found for days or weeks, if at all. The thought made her hands go cold, icy fingers gripping the metal railing so fiercely she could feel the hard corners digging into her palms.

Kate couldn't let that happen. Not her, not Ty, not anyone else who might get in Ripley's way. Enough people had died because of this psychopath—Kate needed to end it.

Now.

Averting her eyes from Donald's unseeing ones, Kate stepped over his body. She eased the door open but had to push him out of the way to get enough of an opening to slip through.

The sound of Donald's corpse slumping back into place as the door swung closed made her gag.

Kate took a steadying breath and checked her surroundings. The fourth floor looked exactly like the third without Kleiner, Abato & Chen's custom glass doors that took up the wall beyond the elevators.

Well, *used* to take up. Ripley had seen to that.

The fourth floor had standard-issue office doors, each with a placard mounted beside it identifying the business. Kate's brain was fuzzy as she looked around, trying to envision the file room downstairs, and where it was in relation to the elevator bay. Ripley's office should be directly above it. She headed down the hall on the south side of the building, then turned sharply at the end. There, in front of her, was suite 410. M.E.

Kate gripped the handle, praying it wasn't locked, and twisted.

The door opened easily.

It felt weird walking into Ripley's office. Most of the locations they'd shot for *Dirty Pretty Teens* were real places: school exteriors, cafés, homes. The exception was one scene that was very specific to the book—the secret darkroom where Piper kept all the photos she'd taken of her high school's seedier side. It had to look part photographer's workroom and part cliché teen clubhouse, complete with a lofted bunk bed where her on-again, off-again boyfriend Asher hid out when he was wanted by the mob. In the end, production decided to build the set, and when Kate had to shoot in it, she'd had a tough time trying to keep her head in the scene.

It wasn't that it didn't look cool—the set designers had done an amazing job creating Piper's darkroom from the description in the books—but it was decidedly fake. The props weren't functional, the mattresses on the bunk were thin and hard as wood, and one whole side of the room was open to the studio where it had been built. Belle had rolled her eyes at Kate's naive wonder over the set, declaring that she'd worked on so many three-camera sitcoms that this set was positively homey, but Kate had never gotten over the weirdness she felt every time she shot a scene in that darkroom—it was the only time her Shakespeare crutch failed her and she felt as if she really had to "act."

Walking into Ripley's office felt a lot like walking into Piper's darkroom set—surreal, out of body, familiar yet wrong. Kate had been looking at the room as a flat projection for so long that she was almost surprised to feel the full three-dimensional nature of the suite. The lobby was wider than she'd thought, the assistant's desk was farther from the window, and the distance between the main door and Ripley's private office was substantially longer than she'd assumed.

And instead of the open fourth wall of the fake set, Kate had the office windows stretching down the exterior wall to her left. With the lights on, it was difficult to see the north tower closely, but as she stared out through the lobby window, she could sorta kinda discern the outline of three long rows of black file cabinets in a room across the courtyard, and the jagged edges of glass around the window that had been blown out by Ripley's gunfire.

Without thinking, Kate let her eyes drift to the floor in front of her.

Where Ripley's husband had died.

No obvious signs of bloodstains, but Kate noticed that the carpet appeared a shade lighter by the door than it did farther away by the wall. As if it had been recently cleaned.

So much for evidence. But maybe a forensics team could find something? *If* Kate could get the police to listen.

Big if.

Kate's eyes flitted toward the office door, still focused on the gray, flat woven carpet. Todd had fallen right there. Kate hadn't been able to see his face with his back to the window, but she could imagine the mix of horror, confusion, betrayal, and pain that must have been reflected in his handsome features. Kate didn't believe in ghosts, but it was difficult not to imagine that after such emotionally heightened deaths, Todd and Ripley's husband wouldn't be lingering somewhere nearby.

> *Thou know'st 'tis common; all that lives must die,*
> *Passing through nature to eternity.*

Yeah, Gertrude, but look what happened to Hamlet's father, lurking in the castle where he was murdered. And this wasn't even Denmark, just the Burbank Garden Towers Business Park.

What a sad fucking place to spend the afterlife.

Unlike Hamlet, Kate didn't have time to obsess over death. Pushing aside her memories of what had happened in that office, she sprinted through the suite, around Ripley's desk to the closet. If Ty were still alive, this is where he'd be.

She held her breath as she opened the door, terrified that she'd be staring into Ty's open but lifeless eyes. Instead, she found a prone body, covered in blood-soaked clothes.

Then Ty turned his head and blinked open his eyes. "Kate?"

THIRTY-SIX

"TY!" THE NAME EXPLODED OUT OF HER WITH SO MUCH JOY she thought the force of it might knock her over. Ty was alive. Hands zip-tied behind his back, pants and shirt literally soaked through with blood, but alive. Though judging by the sickly pallor of his skin, he might not be for much longer.

"I'm getting you out of here."

"Meh," he said with a minuscule shrug. "Thought I'd stick around and bleed all over her shit."

"Cute." She appreciated that Ty hadn't lost his sense of humor. "Don't move."

Kate scrambled over to Ripley's desk and found a pair of scissors for the zip tie. Ty's hands were a shade between magenta and violet by the time Kate released them, and he gasped in pain as the blood began to flow back into his fingers.

"Where are you shot?" Kate asked, eyeing the office door. She'd bought them a little bit of time with her elevator ruse, but not much.

Ty rolled over, gritting his teeth in pain as he exposed his right thigh. Through the wet, shiny chinos, she could see a jagged hole. "So I couldn't run."

"It's a miracle you're not dead."

"I think she wanted a hostage. Just in case."

Kate had taken one first-aid class through the Red Cross when she was fourteen, so to say she wasn't trained in the medical arts was somewhat of an understatement, but even she could see that moving Ty was going to be difficult. Plus, she needed to stop the bleeding, or at least slow it down, before he passed out.

She looked around the closet, desperate to find something she could use as a tourniquet. Then she remembered Ripley's black trench coat. She ducked her head out of the closet and found the coat hanging on the back of the closet door.

She whipped the belt through the loops, freeing it from the fabric, then carefully shimmied it up beneath Ty's leg, tying a loose knot about two inches above the gunshot wound. "On three," she said, wrapping the ends of the belt around each of her hands. "One. *TWO!*"

She didn't wait for three, but pulled the ends of the belt early, tightening the knot. Ty grunted but didn't scream, though as Kate tied off her makeshift tourniquet, his breaths came fast and jagged, and his body shivered uncontrollably from the shock. She yanked the rest of the trench coat off the back of the closet door and draped it around Ty's shoulders in a futile attempt to keep him warm.

"We've gotta get you to a hospital."

Ty shook his head. "She took my keys and my phone."

"We won't get far on foot."

"You'll have to call for help."

Except Kate had already tried that. More than once. "The cops were already here. Searched the wrong tower, and when I called back, they registered a prank caller from this address and threatened prosecution."

"Then we're trapped."

Kate's eyes trailed down to Ty's injured leg. The tourniquet would keep him from bleeding out for now, but it would do its own damage. It had already been fifteen minutes at least since he'd been shot, which meant time was not on their side. They were alone in the building, trapped with a killer, and Ripley had cut off their only means of escape. It was infuriating that the Tesla was sitting there in the garage, impotent without Ty's keys.

Keys.

Ty's Tesla wasn't the only car in the parking garage. Kate vividly recalled the moment when Ty had bumped into Ripley, right after she locked up her car and slipped the keys into the pocket of . . .

She reached over Ty's body and tugged on the hem of the trench coat. A jangle of metal in the pocket. Kate fished out the keys. Two of them, attached to a key chain with a Porsche insignia.

"Know how to drive a stick?" Ty asked.

Kate shook her head. "Can you?"

"Not with this leg, but I can walk you through it."

"Good enough." Kate looped Ty's left arm over her shoulders and hauled him to his feet. "Put your weight on me."

They just had to get to the elevator and then down to the car without running into Ripley or Ty losing consciousness. Kate wasn't sure they could accomplish either. Ty hopped on his good leg, jaw clenched and body rigid with pain. His injured limb dragged behind him, but though his face was an unhealthy ashen color, Kate noted the fierce determination in his eyes.

As they rounded the desk, Kate used her foot to kick the closet shut. That way, Ripley would have to walk all the way over to it in order to find out if Ty was still inside. Might buy them an extra thirty seconds in their bid to escape.

As she glanced back to make sure the door was closed, Kate's eyes caught something on the carpet. In the corner. With the door open, she couldn't have seen it, but with it closed, the three little brown spots stood out enough from the gray carpet to give her pause.

"Blood," Ty said, without even looking. "Dried and old. Just three drops, but that might be enough for forensics."

That's what Ty had seen in the office, the tiniest shred of potential evidence against Ripley. With any luck, those three drops would convict her of murder.

"'I'll prove this truth with my three drops of blood,'" she murmured, quoting *Troilus and Cressida* as she headed toward the door.

"What?"

"Never mind," Kate said, smiling cheerfully. "Let's get you out of here."

The digital readouts above the elevators indicated that both cars were in the lobby, and when Kate pushed the call button, both of them started up at almost the same time. The right elevator was moving slightly ahead of the other, passing the floors a second or two earlier.

"If they're both moving," Ty said, "someone must be in the other. The call button would only trigger one car."

"Shit!" Not just someone—Ripley.

"The first one that opens should be the empty one," Ty said. "If she had already pushed four, the system wouldn't have sent the second one up to us."

"You sure?"

Ty shrugged. "Not like we have a choice."

Which was true. Ty wouldn't make it down the stairs with that injured leg—he and Kate would probably collapse halfway, tumble down a flight or two, and break both of their necks—and if Ripley stepped out of the first elevator with her gun drawn and ready, they'd both be dead anyway.

The first elevator dinged, and the seconds that ticked by before the doors slid open felt like five lifetimes instead of five seconds. Kate held her breath as the interior slowly revealed itself to be empty. She hardly even registered the second bell as she hoisted Ty inside.

She pressed the lobby button, then flattened herself and Ty against the wall. Just in time. She heard the doors of the second elevator slide open.

They stood motionless, Kate hardly daring to breathe. She listened for Ripley's footsteps but didn't hear anything. Had she not been inside after all? She wanted to look, but didn't dare. Then as the doors began to close, she saw the back of Ripley's body as she walked into the hallway, scanning from side to side, searching.

By sheer dumb luck, Ripley didn't notice the other elevator until it was too late. She turned, gun leading her movement, right before the doors closed on her.

Kate didn't allow herself to breathe again until she felt the elevator move.

"She'll be right behind us," she said out loud as the elevator descended.

Ty shivered. Deep purple circles had developed beneath his eyes, and his cheeks looked hollowed out. "And she'll move faster."

He was right, but she wasn't about to leave him behind. "We'll make it."

"No, we won't."

The elevator passed through the second floor. They didn't have time to come up with a plan. "I'm not leaving you."

He looked up at her, eyes pleading. "I'll take the elevator back up. If she follows me, you can go for help."

"If she follows you, you're dead."

"'Kill me tomorrow . . .'" Ty took a halting breath, smiling wryly. "'Let me live tonight!'"

Kate shook her head. Was he seriously quoting Shakespeare right now? "Othello, act five, scene two." Her dad was going to love this. "But I still can't drive a stick shift."

"Through the front door to the courtyard," Ty suggested. "Down to the street. Gotta be someone out there on a Friday night."

Kate pictured the long courtyard between the buildings. She'd have to run all the way down it to reach the street. She'd be a sitting duck.

The garage was better, offered more hiding places, even if she couldn't figure out how to drive Ripley's car. Maybe she didn't have to. Kate pulled out her phone and pressed it into Ty's hand. "Find a way to get the police back here. I'll try to keep her occupied downstairs."

"Clutch is on the left," Ty said with a dry cough. Her chest tightened at the idea of leaving him in that elevator. "Hold it down to start the car and to shift gears, then give it some gas and release it."

"Okay."

"Don't be target practice."

"I'll try."

The bell dinged; they'd reached the lobby. "Get somewhere safe and stay there." Kate pushed the button for the third floor and stepped out.

He smiled. "*I'll* try."

Kate wanted to say a million things. To tell Ty how stupid she'd been, to apologize for her stupidity and her arrogance, and for almost getting him killed. But as she gazed at him, sprawled across the elevator floor, pale, trembling, drenched in his own blood, only three words came out of her mouth as the doors closed.

"I love you."

She wasn't even sure if he'd heard her.

THIRTY-SEVEN

KATE DIDN'T HAVE TIME TO WORRY ABOUT IT. THE INSTANT the elevator started to ascend, she turned and ran. Ripley would be right behind her, only slowed by the mechanics of the elevator doors. Which bought her ten or twenty seconds, max.

She needed to make them count.

Untying her hoodie as she ran past the security desk, Kate tossed it behind her, pushing aside the image of the dead security guard's body shoved into a north tower stairwell that would forever haunt her in dark places. Ripley should be able to see the hoodie as soon as she reached the lobby and would hopefully follow it, instead of the elevator currently lifting Ty out of harm's way. A faint electronic ding behind her meant that she'd soon find out.

Bait the hook well; this fish will bite.

She really hoped Claudio was right.

Kate didn't bother with the elevator to the garage. She slid to a stop in front of the staircase, cringing as she whipped the door open as if half expecting to find another dead body crumpled up and discarded there like so much used paper. Thankfully, the stairwell was clear, and Kate double-timed it down to the first floor of the garage.

And that was pretty much as far as her plan went. Get to the garage and stall.

She scanned the cavernous space, all but empty on a Friday night. Ripley's Porsche was parked in front of her, the Tesla around to the right. There was a pickup truck on the far side near some kind of equipment panel, and a nondescript gray sedan parked about halfway between Kate and the truck. Other than the concrete support columns that lined the garage, there wasn't anywhere else to hide.

How, exactly, was she supposed to stall Ripley without getting shot? They'd gotten lucky once when Ripley hadn't killed Ty immediately, the way she'd murdered Donald, and Kate was pretty sure that the next bullet Ripley let fly would not be a wounding shot.

Okay, think. Ripley would assume one of two things: either that Kate would hide in or near the Tesla, since that was Ty's car, or go for the gray sedan as the only other car in the lot. She needed to avoid those. The pickup truck made a good option, but as was the case with the courtyard, Kate wasn't sure she could get there in time and then she'd be a sitting duck.

Which made the Porsche the best choice. If by some miracle she could get the car moving, maybe she could get out of the garage alive.

Kate had never seen a car door you had to actually insert a key into like the front door to her house, but with a little bit of jiggling, she was able to get the door open. She'd just slipped into the driver's seat and heaved the heavy door closed when she heard another ding from the elevator bay.

Kate crouched behind the steering wheel as Ripley limped into the garage. Her head wasn't held as high as earlier, her body language not nearly as confident. Instead, she listed to one side as she stutter-stepped, her feet still bare, and her tanned face gleamed with a thick layer of sweat. As Kate had done moments earlier, Ripley scanned the garage, assessing Kate's options—the sedan, the pickup truck, the Tesla.

She never even looked at the Porsche.

Nodding silently to herself, Ripley was about to turn toward the Tesla when a loud bang emanated from the Porsche.

The car rocked back and forth seemingly of its own volition, and Kate scrunched lower in the driver's seat as Ripley's head whipped around in her direction.

What the actual fuck? Was this car alive? Were there rats in the trunk or something?

A muffled scream followed another set of thuds. It sounded as if it came from beneath the hood.

"Shut up, you little bitch," Ripley said. But she didn't approach the car. She wasn't talking to Kate.

Was someone else in the Porsche?

The screams turned to a stifled sob, and now Kate was positive she wasn't alone in the car. The vintage Porsche only sat four people in theory, and from Kate's vantage point, she could tell the rest of the interior was empty. But the cries were close by, as if they were coming through the dashboard.

Not that she could do anything about it now, but suddenly there were more than two lives on the line. Kate had the mystery sobber to protect as well as herself and Ty.

Ripley had limped over to the Tesla and was partially obscured by a support pillar. It was now or never. Kate inserted the key into the ignition, held her foot against the pedal on the far left, and turned the engine over.

The Porsche purred to life, rolled forward six inches, then died.

"Shit!"

The body in the trunk screamed, and Ripley's head popped around the cement pillar.

"Shit, shit, shit, shit, shit." Kate tried again. Clutch, key, ignition! Then she lifted up her foot to hit the accelerator, and the engine sputtered out once more.

"You're stealing my car?" Ripley roared. Her gun was aimed at the windshield as she limped toward Kate, but she hesitated. Kate knew the delay wasn't a sign Ripley didn't want to kill her, just that she wasn't willing to damage her precious Porsche.

Kate tried again. Clutch, key, ignition, but this time, she kept her foot on the clutch while she gave the car some gas.

The engine roared, fighting the low transmission gear and lurched forward. Kate heard the scraping of metal as she drove over the parking block at the front of Ripley's reserved space. The Porsche rocked heavily as the rear tire struggled to get over the concrete barrier, and Kate thought she might have snapped the axle when the car thudded to the ground again.

"No!" Ripley roared. For a moment, Kate still wasn't sure if she was screaming about the car or about Kate's potential escape, but when a bullet pierced the passenger door, she had a clearer idea. The Porsche was now collateral damage.

Kate cranked the steering wheel and revved the engine. It strained against the gear, and she could hear the roar of machinery coming from behind her.

Oh right. Porsche engines were in the back of the damn car. Which meant the trunk was in the front.

With someone trapped inside.

Another shot shattered the rear window, and Kate ducked her head as glass flew through the interior. Ripley was moving as fast as her injured feet would allow, a lopsided job that, though not exactly lightning speed, was fast enough to gain on the slow-rolling Porsche. Kate needed to move faster before Ripley was literally walking alongside.

Clutch, shift, accelerator. Okay. She could do this.

She held the clutch down and tried to move the gear shifter, but the stick would hardly budge.

"You've fucked up enough of my life already, sugarplum," Ripley yelled. Another bullet hit the frame of the car above Kate's head as she frantically tried to get the car in gear.

"You fucked up your own life!" she yelled back. She pulled her foot off the gas, and the engine stalled again. Why would anyone design a car like this? Bananas.

"I had everything under control."

Kate glanced in the mirror. Ripley was only a few paces behind the car now. She fired again, and a bullet embedded in the dashboard. What if she hit the person in the trunk?

Come on, you stupid fucking Porsche.

"You killed three people," Kate said through clenched teeth as she tried to muscle the transmission into whatever gear she could.

"I'm about to make it four."

Ripley's voice was too calm and too close, but Kate didn't dare look. She felt the shifter give, then eased off the clutch and floored the gas.

Instead of forward, the Porsche lurched backward. Kate had somehow shifted into reverse and was racing toward the cinder-block garage wall. Before she could stop, she felt something bounce off the back of the car.

Kate slammed on the brakes, screeching to a halt a few inches short of the wall. She expected to hear a gunshot ring out at point-blank range, but Ripley and her weapon had gone quiet.

The car idled in reverse for a few seconds, then stalled again with a violent shudder. Kate tentatively opened the door and peeked around the side of the car. She saw a pair of bare feet sticking out from behind the Porsche; one sole was caked in blood.

Ripley might have been playing possum, but something about the angle of her legs reminded Kate of Donald's unnatural position in the stairwell. She rounded the back of the car and found Ripley facedown on the concrete, pinned between the tires and the wall. The gun was six feet away.

Kate kicked the gun farther into the garage. She'd watched too many horror movies to believe that Ripley might actually be dead. Content that the weapon was too far out of reach, she was about to run upstairs to check on Ty when she heard another pair of thumps from the trunk of the Porsche.

Right! That poor person.

Kate hardly registered the distant sound of police sirens getting louder by the second as she reached into the car and pulled the release, then raced around and lifted the trunk.

Staring up at her, with a red face and terrified eyes, was Belle Masterson.

EPILOGUE

SLEEP WAS STUBBORN.

Kate had been fending it off for a while, sitting stock straight in the hospital waiting room chair, feet planted on the hard tile floor, spine rigid, as if the uncomfortableness of her stance would keep her awake.

Minutes crawled by and the abject boredom of Kate's situation made sleep even more alluring, but the idea of missing something—some word, some update—terrified her, so she remained upright, eyes open, despite her exhaustion.

Rowan hadn't been able to resist, not that Kate blamed her. After a prolonged jag of hysterical crying, she'd collapsed into a fitful sleep in the waiting room, head resting on Jeremiah's leg with his jacket draped over her shoulders.

Rowan's parents, if surprised by Jeremiah's presence and intimacy with their daughter, didn't show it. They had bigger concerns than their daughter's boyfriend, but once or twice Kate saw Mrs. Chen's concerned eyes flit over to Jeremiah, who had stroked Rowan's hair until he, too, had drifted off to sleep with his head against the wall.

It had been a tense meeting when the Chens arrived at the hospital. Kate, smeared in Ty's blood, met them in the OR lobby after Ty had been wheeled away for emergency surgery. She'd tried to explain what happened, but it all sounded so fantastical. "I witnessed two murders in your building, and Ty tried to help me prove it" was like a plot from a shitty mystery novel, the kind that got made into Lifetime movies that played in reruns on Sunday mornings.

Rowan had stepped in, and as usual, she had all the words.

"Your upstairs neighbor is a psychopath who murdered her husband and assistant, and Kate was the only witness except no one believed her but Ty, and then Ripley almost killed them both, and oh my God, I am so sorry, Kate."

She'd thrown her arms around Kate's neck and sobbed nonstop until the doctor had arrived with his first update on Ty's condition.

Kate didn't understand most of what he said; phrases like *acute ischemia* and *popliteal artery* were a word salad. All she could process were two facts: Ty was still alive, and surgery would reveal the extent of the damage.

She wanted to stay there and wait for the next update with Ty's family, which was why she was desperately trying to stay awake, but the Burbank PD had other plans.

"Kate Williams?" one of two officers asked as they strode into the lobby. Kate recognized him and his partner right away: They were the two officers who had searched the south tower hours ago.

"Yes."

"Will you please come with us? We need to ask you some questions."

Kate didn't want to leave, but she sensed she didn't really have a choice, and as she followed the two officers down a hallway, she half expected to end up cuffed in the back of a squad car. Instead, they escorted her into a conference room where a cup of watery coffee and a vending-machine Danish sat on the table.

"Your parents should be here soon," the first cop said. He was a middle-aged Latino with a pair of aviator sunglasses perched on top of his shaved head. "We thought you might be hungry."

Before Kate could answer, Mack and Andrea stormed into the conference room.

"What is my daughter being charged with?" her mom demanded. She had arrived prepared for battle, while Kate's dad, as usual, was all touchy-feely.

"Katie-Bear!" He rushed to her side and wrapped his arms around her as if protecting her from the elements. "Have you said anything? Don't say anything until our lawyer gets here."

Her family had a lawyer?

The young Black officer with the cheerful smile approached Kate's mom, palms forward as he tried to defuse her energy.

"Mr. and Mrs. Williams, your daughter is not being charged with anything."

"Uh-huh," her mom said. "Sure she isn't."

"Kate witnessed a crime," he continued, "and we want to get her statement now while the suspect is still in custody."

Suspect. Ripley was still alive.

"Does it have to be now?" her mom pressed. "Our daughter is clearly traumatized and exhausted. And . . . Kate, is that blood on your shirt?"

"What happened, Katie-Bear?" Her dad squeezed her shoulders, and if she hadn't been so desperate to share her story about Ripley, she'd have sunk into his arms and let her parents take her home. But she wasn't leaving that hospital until Ty was out of surgery, and besides, even with Belle alive to give her own testimony, Kate needed to share her version of events now before Belle or Ripley tried to distort the truth.

"Mom, Dad. It's okay. I want to explain what happened."

"You sure?" her dad asked.

"Positive."

Her mom narrowed her eyes. "Fine. But we're not leaving this room."

"Nor would I ask you to," the Latino officer said. He gestured to the chairs on either side of Kate while he sat across from her with a small recording device. "What can you tell me about the murder of Donald Proffit?"

"That he was the *third* victim of Moira Eldridge," Kate said without hesitation.

His eyebrows shot up, almost reaching his aviators. "Third?"

Kate started at the beginning, with the first night she'd witnessed the encounter between Todd and Ripley, and shared every detail she could remember—Ripley's husband, Belle's visit, Ripley's staging of the murders, Kate's encounter with Donald and her attempts to report the crime to the authorities, and finally, with some embarrassment, the plan she and Ty had concocted. The officers exchanged a look at the last part, an indication of just how stupid they thought she and Ty had been, but she barreled undaunted through to the end, where she'd accidentally run Ripley down with the Porsche in the parking garage as the police arrived.

Her mom gasped, her dad sniffled, and the lead officer nodded his head as she finished.

"Tyson Chen was able to corroborate most of this in the ambulance," he said. "As I'm sure Belle Masterson will once her lawyers allow her to give a statement."

Typical Belle. She and Clementine were probably trying to figure out a way to spin this to Belle's advantage, conveniently leaving out Belle's attempted blackmail.

"And we'll have cadaver dogs search Ms. Eldridge's home and property for the other bodies."

Bodies. She and Ty had almost become two more.

"Is there anything else you can add?" the officer continued. "Any details you can remember would be helpful."

"In her office," Kate said, looking him in the eyes. "On the carpet by the closet. We saw three drops of blood. She'd scrubbed the rest of the rug pretty thoroughly, but missed those. They might belong to one of the victims."

"Good." He smiled again, then turned to Kate's mom. "Your daughter makes an excellent witness. She remembered every detail and was able to recount them in a calm, coolheaded manner. You should be proud."

"Oh, we're very proud," her mom said, choking down a sob. "We always have been."

* * *

Kate's parents wanted to take her home after the interview, but Kate wasn't leaving. Her dad was about to insist, but it was Kate's mom, oddly, who took her daughter's side.

"We'll go home and get you a change of clothes," her mom said, running her fingers softly through Kate's tangled hair. "Maybe a toothbrush?"

"But we can't leave her here alone!" her dad pleaded.

Kate's mom rolled her eyes. "The Chens aren't going anywhere. They'll look after her."

"But our baby needs us."

"I'm okay, Dad. I promise."

"But—"

"Mack . . ." her mom started with a warning glance. Then she took Kate by the shoulders. "Kate's a grown-up now. If she wants to stay, she can stay."

"Thanks, Mom."

"If you talk to Ty," she continued, her smile deepening, "be sure to tell him *everything*."

How did she know? "I will."

"Good." Kate's mom planted a kiss on her forehead and dropped her voice. "I'm so proud of you, Katie-Bear."

Despite the horror of the day, the fatigue, the trauma, the violence that would take years of therapy for her to get over, Kate was smiling as she returned to the OR. Until she saw the entire Chen family on their feet, surrounding a doctor. Then her heart stopped for a moment as she tried to figure out if Mrs. Chen's tears were from joy or pain as the doctor led Ty's parents away.

"Kate!" It was Rowan, wide-awake. She raced over, and the moment Kate saw her smile, her blood began to pump again. *Ty's going to be okay.*

"Ty's going to be okay!" Rowan cried, grabbing Kate's hand.

Kate didn't trust her voice. She swallowed, her tongue heavy and thick in her mouth, and tried to smile despite quivering lips.

Rowan squeezed her hand. "I'm sorry," she said, brows pulled together. Kate realized she wasn't talking about Ty anymore. "For everything."

"It doesn't matter," Kate said.

"It *does*. I was an asshole that night at the wrap party. If the roles had been reversed, you never would have left my side."

Not that she needed Rowan to apologize—Kate and her creep of a showrunner bore the responsibility for what had happened that night—but it was nice to know that Rowan cared enough to do so.

"And I'm sorry that I abandoned you," Kate said. "I was so wrapped up in my career plans I never even thought about how you'd feel."

"Whatever. I'm a big girl." Rowan laughed. "I can be jealous of your auditions and gigs and still love you."

Kate shook her head. "You won't have to be jealous of either. I'm not dropping out of school."

Rowan's eyes widened. "What?"

Kate hadn't even realized she'd made the decision once and for all until the words came out of her mouth, but the events of the last few hours had reminded her of what was really important to her: her friends, her support system, and enjoying them both until college changed things for good.

"I'm going to have to fire Clementine anyway," she said with a shrug. "Might as well wait a few years before I try this adulting thing again."

"College will be more fun, anyway."

"Definitely." She smirked. "Day jobs suck."

"Kate?"

Mrs. Chen had returned to the lobby. Her eyes were still pink and puffy, but the strain had vanished from her face as she smiled.

"Yes?"

"Ty would like to see you."

"Me?" Another heart stoppage, but this time for a very different reason.

Now it was Rowan's turn to smirk as she dragged Kate forward. "Go on."

"But—"

"Shush." Rowan kissed her index and middle fingers, then turned her palm to face Kate. "Just spare me the gross details."

Kate's head swirled as she followed Mrs. Chen down the hall, around a corner, through two sets of double doors, around yet another corner, and finally into a small room with a single hospital bed surrounded by machines.

Ty's eyes were closed, but the color had returned to his face and she could tell by the rhythmic rise and fall of his chest that he was resting calmly. His left leg was bandaged from his groin to mid-calf, and a heart rate machine silently recorded his heartbeats.

"I'll let you two talk," Mrs. Chen said, backing away. "For a few minutes; then he needs to rest."

"Okay," Kate said softly. The moment she spoke, Ty's eyes fluttered open and he turned his head toward her, smiling weakly.

"Kate," he breathed. "Are you okay?"

"You're the one in the hospital." She approached his bed with timid steps. "How did the surgery go?"

"I can keep my leg," he said with a pained grin. "But I'll need some physical therapy for the next year or two."

"Shit."

"I'm alive. That's what matters."

"That's what matters."

His eyes searched her face. "Besides, I needed an excuse to defer Stanford until the spring."

"Can you do that?"

"Probably."

"So you'd stay here . . ." She smiled, stepping closer to him.

"Is that okay?"

She didn't know what to say, didn't know if he'd even heard her words as she left him in that elevator. She reached out and slipped her hand into his, squeezing gently.

Ty pushed himself up to his elbows, wincing as he scooted to a sitting position. "Back at the elevator, emotions were heightened, and if you were just saying that because you thought I was going to die, I understand. But I need to know . . . if you feel the same way you did last summer."

The same way. Kate could have explained that her heart had changed, though she didn't entirely understand why or how or when, only that it had. And she could have apologized for being so awful last year, or her combative attitude since he'd been back, or almost accidentally getting him killed.

But it all sounded hollow, even in her head, and as the seconds of her silence accumulated, she saw Ty's smile droop to a frown, which reminded her of her first day at Kleiner, Abato & Chen when Ty had quoted *The Taming of the Shrew.* The very character she'd been named after. At the time, his quote had pissed her off, but suddenly, Kate knew exactly what to say to him.

Her fingers laced in his, she pulled his hand to her chest. "'My hand is ready,'" she said, quoting the end of Katherine's controversial final speech, "'may it do him ease.'"

It took a second for Ty to realize what she meant, but only a second. His smile returned, all traces of pain vanished, and as he pulled her in, he added Petrucchio's response.

"'Come on and kiss me, Kate.'"

And she did.

THE END

ACKNOWLEDGMENTS

I'VE WRITTEN MANY ACKNOWLEDGMENTS OVER THE YEARS, but not since my debut novel have I been this excited to do one. Why? Because this is the first time I get to start by thanking . . .

Ginger Clark of Ginger Clark Literary! I'm so honored to be on the esteemed roster of authors at her new agency, and equally honored to have Nicole Eisenbraun and Mary Pender working on behalf of GCL. An author is only as good as her team, and mine is spectacular.

And I have another new thank-you—my editor Kelsey Sullivan! This is our first book together, and from the get-go, Kelsey understood me and my aesthetic, and her insights were vital to shaping this novel. I know my books are in excellent hands.

The entire team at Hyperion is stellar, and I would be remiss if I didn't thank them all individually: my favorite-ever designer, Marci Senders; copy editor Jody Corbett; copy chief Guy Cunningham; Holly Nagel, Dina Sherman, and Matt Schweitzer in marketing; Marybeth Tregarthen in production; managing editor Sara Liebling; the hardworking publicity team of Christine Saunders and Ann Day; and the wonderful Kieran Viola. As always, your hard work is appreciated.

This novel required some insider knowledge, and I could not have figured out the twists and turns of the entertainment industry without the help of Mary Schmitberger Samuels, Lisa Lynch, Loretta Fox, and my nearest and dearest Josh Sabarra. Their willingness to share and their insightful answers to all of my silly questions truly helped shape some of the major plot points of this novel.

Being an author-mom is challenging, especially with two toddlers at home, and there is literally no way I could get any work done without the support of Cecilia Ortiz and Veronica Rodriguez. We are truly lucky to have them in our family.

And lastly, to John, John Flynn, Katie, and my mom. Another book filled with murder. Thanks for the help and inspiration. HA-HA-HA-HA-HA.

Discover More Thrilling Books from
GRETCHEN MCNEIL

The #MurderTrending Series

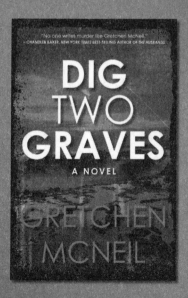

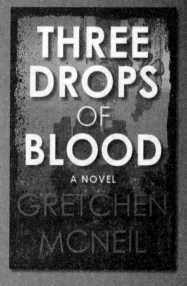